FORCE OF
NATURE

Praise for Kim Baldwin's *Hunter's Pursuit*

"Her...crisply written action scenes, juxtaposition of plotlines, and smart dialogue make this a story the reader will absolutely enjoy and long remember."—**Arlene Germain**, book reviewer for the *Lambda Book Report* and the *Midwest Book Review*

❧

Hunter's Pursuit is a "...fierce first novel, an action-packed thriller pitting deadly professional killers against each other. Baldwin's fast-paced plot comes...leavened, as every intelligent adventure novel's excesses ought to be, with some lovin'. Even as she fends off her killers,...the heroine...finds the woman she wants by her side — and in her bed."—**Richard Labonte**, Book Marks, *Q Syndicate*, May 2005

❧

"'A riveting novel of suspense' seems to be a very overworked phrase. However, it is extremely apt when discussing Kim Baldwin's... exciting page turner [about] Katarzyna Demetrious, a bounty hunter... with a million dollar price on her head. Look for this excellent novel of suspense..."—**R. Lynne Watson**, reviewer for *Mega-space*

❧

"Clever surprises and suspenseful drama resonate on each page, setting the wheels in motion for an exciting ride. Action sequences fire rapidly in succession, leaving the reader breathless. Once you pick up *Hunter's Pursuit*, there is no putting it down. *Hunter's Pursuit*...has been nominated for a Golden Crown Literary Society Award for 2005 and deservedly so."—**Cheri Rosenberg**, reviewer for *Independent Gay Writer* and *JustAboutWrite*

❧

"The writing is crisp, especially as the tension mounts in the second half of the book. A terrific action/thriller from a promising new writer..."
—**Lori Lake**, the *Midwest Book Review*

FORCE OF NATURE

NATURE

by

KIM BALDWIN

2005

FORCE OF NATURE

ISBN 1-933110-23-6

This Trade Paperback Original Is Published By
Bold Strokes Books, Inc.,
Pennsylvania, USA

First Printing September 2005

Credits
Editors: Jennifer Knight and Stacia Seaman
Production Design: Stacia Seaman
Cover Design By Sheri (GRAPHICARTIST2020@HOTMAIL.COM)

By the Author

Hunter's Pursuit

Acknowledgments

First and foremost, I must thank the cherished circle of friends who provide me with unflagging encouragement and support for everything I write. Linda and Vicki, Kat and Ed, Marsha and Ellen, Cousin Tim, and Felicity, the Queen of All Things.

Thanks also to my wonderfully insightful and meticulous beta readers, Sharon Lloyd, co-owner of Epilogue Books, and Connie Ward. I look forward to your help on many future projects.

I am deeply indebted to Lieutenant Sue Erickson, a professional firefighter and emergency medical technician for over twenty years, and to Scott Lakin, RN and former volunteer firefighter, for their invaluable help in lending authenticity to the fire and medical scenes.

Many thanks to Sheri, whose artistic wizardry once again produced a cover that truly reflects the spirit of the story inside.

My heartfelt appreciation to my editors, Jennifer Knight and Stacia Seaman, for such a rich and rewarding learning experience and for the expert technical advice. Your contribution to this book cannot be measured.

And most especially, my profound gratitude goes to Radclyffe and Lee, the forces behind Bold Strokes Books. I cannot imagine a more nurturing environment for an author to be blessed with.

Force of Nature was written with deep respect and appreciation for the women and men who daily put their lives on the line to protect and serve their communities as firefighters.

It is dedicated with all my love to my partner, M., my inspiration for Gable and the kindest, most giving individual I've ever had the privilege to know. You have taught me the importance of living a life of character and purpose. And by your example, you encourage all those around you to be the very best individuals they can possibly be. Every word I write, I write for you. Now and always.

Dedication

For M.
Grádh geal mo chridh'

CHAPTER ONE

G able McCoy slowed the Jeep and craned forward to look out the windshield. Branches large and small littered the roadway. No other cars were about. Above her, the sky was a color she'd never seen before, a sickly greenish yellow. Directly ahead, a low wall of clouds churned and boiled with furious intent. She tried to shake off a feeling of unease that threatened to overwhelm her.

The emergency radio at her side was crowded with voices, overlapping each other and fighting to be heard above the relentless static. Many were harried and anxious, reflecting the unusual strain on the emergency dispatchers, firefighters, and police. None of them had ever experienced a storm like this.

It was a freak weather phenomenon, a convergence of hot and cold fronts coinciding with a change in the jet stream. An unusually muggy April morning had spawned a violent afternoon. Tornadoes were touching down all over Michigan. Two had already been spotted in her county and three more in the surrounding areas.

Gable had come through torrential rain and a brief burst of walnut-sized hail that left two small cracks in her windshield. But it had stopped all at once, and that was somehow more unsettling, as if the storm was gathering its strength to launch an all-out assault. She took another look at the dark, foreboding sky and increased her speed slightly—there were several more houses she wanted to check before nightfall.

She was still in her one-year probation period as a volunteer with the Plainfield Township Fire Department, one of only three women on the squad. The demanding physical training had not been a problem for her, though at forty-six she was older than many of the other volunteers.

She had been athletic all her life, and the taut musculature on her tall, lean frame reflected many hours spent kayaking and mountain biking.

So far, all the callouts she'd attended had been for relatively minor things—fender-bender auto accidents and small brush fires started by discarded cigarettes or careless campers. Today was different. This time she was responding to a full-out mobilization of SAR—the county's search and rescue squad, which involved fire departments, law enforcement, 911, and other local emergency personnel.

Right after she'd finished her initial training, SAR had paired her up with a veteran firefighter, Tim Scott, and assigned them a five-square-mile area west of the village of Pine River, three miles south of where Gable lived. The entire region was mostly state forest, but there were a number of cottages and year-round homes scattered here and there, tucked back off the road and hidden by trees.

Tim had taken her up and down the mostly dirt roads in his pickup until she was familiar with the area. She was now especially grateful he'd been so thorough. When she'd gotten the callout two hours earlier, the dispatcher told her Tim was out of town. No replacement was available, so she was on her own.

She felt the full weight of that responsibility as a ferocious wind gust tried to wrestle the steering wheel from her hands. Butterflies crowded her stomach as she struggled to keep the Jeep on the road. *Lives might depend on you today.* She had to bury her fear and try to remain focused.

Most of the places she'd checked so far were summer cottages, still locked up and vacant. Power was out in a few of the year-round homes, and wind had caused minor damage to roofs, but no one had been injured.

Gable slowed to turn onto Cedar Trail and rolled down the window. Something was very wrong. Suddenly there was no wind at all, where a moment ago it was buffeting the Jeep. She braked to a stop and got out. Stared up at the sky. Sniffed the air. It was eerily quiet, a kind of quiet she didn't think she'd ever heard in the forest. Where were the birds?

The hair on the back of her neck stood up and her pulse began beating double time. The air seemed charged by electricity. The ozone crackled around her. It just felt...*wrong*. Like there was too much air pressure.

That was when she heard it. Just like it was always described. A distant, muffled roaring, like an oncoming train. Dense forest surrounded her. The trees blocked her view except where the road cut through. She couldn't see the twister.

The unearthly roar got steadily louder. A series of sharp reports, like rifle shots, sounded in the near distance. *Those are trees! Shit!*

To her left was a lone, boarded-up convenience store on the corner where she'd stopped. A simple wood-framed building, locked up tight. It didn't look like potential shelter.

Gable ran to the opposite corner of the intersection, where the edge of the road sloped away into a drainage ditch. Beneath the roadway was a concrete drainpipe that looked about three feet across. A tight squeeze, but her only chance.

In a whirling hail of sticks and stones and leaves, she scrambled down the bank, her hands shielding her face. The wind tried to blow her off her feet, and the noise of the tornado was deafening, like a jet aircraft parked directly overhead. Squinting between her fingers, she saw the twister cut out of the woods and onto the highway a quarter of a mile away. It looked like a mammoth V-shaped plume of black smoke.

Frozen with horror, she stared at the debris rotating within. Huge limbs whirled around the funnel with astounding velocity, crashing into each other in the air. The tornado was fifty yards wide, and headed straight for her.

Adrenaline jolted her from her inertia and she dove into the pipe, ignoring the stench of rotted matter and the cold slimy water that soaked her to the skin. It was upon her in an instant, trying to suck her from the pipe, tugging at her with fierce determination. She fought back, bracing herself against the sides, but they were slippery with algae. *PleaseGodpleaseGodpleaseGod.*

It was hard to breathe, caught in this incredible vacuum. The whole drainpipe seemed to be vibrating. She began to lose ground, slipping by inches, her fingers clawing at the slick surface. Her feet protruded from the pipe, then her calves. Sticks, dirt, and stones pelted her. *Can't hang on much longer!* Her arms began to tremble, braced against the pipe. *Please God, don't let me die like this!*

It lasted no more than thirty or forty seconds, but it seemed an eternity. While her life didn't exactly pass before her eyes, she had time enough to think about family and friends, and to feel a pang of regret that she hadn't seized upon every experience she'd wanted to try. Then, all at once, the world was calm again.

Gable wriggled out of the drainpipe, gasping for air. Her heart pounded in her chest like a runaway jackhammer, and her body shook all over. The adrenaline rush was so intense she thought she might faint.

It registered that one of her tennis shoes was gone, ripped from her foot and nowhere in sight. All the stuff that had been flying around had pelted her legs pretty good, and she'd have some impressive bruises to show for it. But she was otherwise uninjured. She could hardly believe she was alive. *Thank you, Lord.*

The convenience store on the opposite corner was now only concrete foundation and scattered wood, plaster, bricks, and assorted wreckage. The store's large metal Dumpster was lodged in a tree, twenty feet off the ground. Pieces of lumber and store shelving and dozens of cans of food littered the road. *Any one of those could have killed me.* Right where she'd stood only minutes ago, the tornado had driven a huge two-by-four several feet into the ground. A few feet away, an enormous white pine had been pulled up by its roots, leaving a gaping hole seven feet wide.

Stunned, she climbed up onto the roadway and surveyed the area around her. Her Jeep was still right side up, but the front windshield was shattered and the vehicle was sitting half on and half off the road, a dozen yards from where she'd parked it.

The rain started anew as she reached for her radio and headed to the Jeep. "Dispatch from McCoy. Reporting tornado touchdown, Cedar Trail at Wolf Run Road. Debris in the area. No injuries. Over."

Though she tried to keep her voice even, she could not completely disguise how much the twister had scared her. She had grown up in Tennessee, and though she retained the soft-spoken slower cadence of a Southerner, she had mostly lost her accent. It surfaced in the occasional word, and was more apparent when she was stressed. Tornado came out *tornayduh.*

Gable had thrown a pair of knee-high Wellies in the back of the Jeep in case she hit some flooding. After the dispatcher responded, she pulled the black rubber boots on and got behind the wheel. As she reached up to adjust the rearview mirror, she caught a glimpse of herself. *Holy shit.* Her short brunette hair was standing up at odd angles, as if she'd stuck her finger in an electrical socket. A pungent slime from the drainpipe covered her face and neck, turning her normally bronzed complexion an eerie greenish gray, and her eyes were so dilated that the black pupils had nearly overtaken the hazel irises.

Her soaked clothing was filthy too—her T-shirt and jeans were the color of mud, and they clung to her uncomfortably. She looked like an extra in a grade B horror flick, a member of the undead, rising from the grave. Somewhat apropos, she thought.

The pavement had disappeared where the tornado traversed it, and branches and downed trees lay scattered all about the roadway. She put the Jeep into four-wheel-drive and maneuvered over and around what she could, but she had to get out several times to haul some obstruction out of her way so she could proceed.

The road curved up and over a hill. At the top, Gable braked to a stop and sat gawking at the devastation below her. *Dear God!*

The twister had carved out a path of destruction a quarter mile wide through the forest. Trees were snapped like matchsticks, jagged edges uniformly cut five feet off the ground. There were two homes within the area, and from a distance, both looked like they'd been hit by bomb blasts.

She headed toward the nearest one and keyed her radio. "Dispatch from McCoy. Two homes leveled on Cedar Trail. Stand by."

The two-track driveway to the first of the flattened homes was overgrown with high weeds and blocked by a padlocked gate. The place was obviously another seasonal cottage still closed from winter. *Thank God.* She reported it to dispatch as she sped toward the other house.

This driveway was open. And despite the rain, Gable could tell from the tire impressions in the dirt two-track that it had been recently used. *Shit.* She gripped the steering wheel harder and headed up the drive toward the house, which was set well off the road in a small clearing cut into the forest.

The first thing she came to was a red pickup truck lying on its side, partially blocking the driveway. She was able to squeeze the Jeep around it, but a few yards farther on, the home's five-hundred-gallon propane tank prevented further progress.

The smell hit her at once. *Gas! Holy shit!*

Her heart pounding, she cut the engine and eased out of the Jeep. The tank was intact but on its side, gas hissing from a broken pipe that stuck out of the top. When she turned the valve beneath it, the hissing stopped. She grabbed her helmet and a thick pair of leather work gloves from the Jeep and went the rest of the way to the house on foot.

A portion of one wall still stood—the area around the fieldstone fireplace. A massive section of the roof was propped against it, forming a nine-foot-high lean-to. An intact bookcase rested beneath it, empty of all its books. Everything else around her was debris—insulation, lumber, electrical wiring, shingles, bits of furniture—all precariously jumbled together in towering heaps. It was impossible to negotiate through it. Jagged pieces of glass and metal were everywhere, the footing uncertain. Here and there lay various clues about the homeowner. Sheet music. A computer keyboard.

"Hello? Anybody here?" Gable listened for a response, but could hear nothing but the howl of the wind and the drumming of the rain. Picking her way around the perimeter, she tried again on the other side of the house. "Hello?"

She thought she might have heard something human. Or maybe it was the wind playing with her imagination.

"Hello!" she yelled as loud as she could.

This time it was unmistakable. Through the pounding rain, she heard a muffled female voice. "Down here! In the basement!"

"I hear you!" Gable shouted. "I'm with search and rescue. Keep talking. How many of you are there? Are you hurt?"

"No, I'm not hurt. And it's just me, but I'm trapped. Get me out of here!" The voice had a panicky sound.

"Hang on. I'm coming. How do I get to you?"

"There's a storm door right outside the house in back."

Gable stared around. She was already behind the house. Finding the door beneath the mountain of rubble in front of her would be a daunting task. "I'm calling for more help. Sit tight and try to relax."

"Hurry! Please hurry!"

Gable reached for her radio and turned it up. The bedlam of voices was even worse than before. While waiting for a break in the radio traffic, she pulled her work gloves from her back pocket and started picking through the debris, searching for the door. "How are you doing?" she shouted. "Can you move around?"

"I'm in the basement shower! Part of the ceiling came down. I can move around but I can't get out of here."

As soon as there was a lull in the cacophony on the radio, Gable reported in and requested assistance, but was told that all available resources were tied up on other calls at the moment.

Knowing she was on her own, she resumed her search with a heightened sense of urgency. The debris of the house didn't appear to be shifting, so the trapped woman was probably not in any immediate danger. But it was going to be dark very soon.

"I'm Gable McCoy, a volunteer firefighter," she hollered. "What's your name?"

"Erin. Erin Richards," came the muted reply. "Have you seen my cat? He's charcoal with a white mustache."

The devastation was so complete, Gable had trouble imagining anything as small and defenseless as a cat living through it. "No, I'm sorry, Erin," she shouted. "I don't see a cat."

"Maybe he'll come out if you call his name," Erin begged. "It's Earl Grey. Maybe he's hurt or scared, and just hiding."

Gable wanted to get the woman out of there. It went against her better judgment to spend time worrying over a cat, but something about Erin's plea touched her deeply. So she hollered Earl's name and kept an eye out for him as she dug through the wreckage, searching for the entrance to the basement. She came across a snowshoe. A green and white Michigan State University baseball cap. A diving mask and snorkel. Lots of mementos of Erin Richards's life, but no door.

"Erin, we need to concentrate on getting you out, then we can both look for your cat, okay?"

"All right. I understand."

"It will help me if you can direct me to exactly where the door is," Gable shouted. "It's covered up."

"It's outside the bathroom window."

Gable frowned. "That doesn't help. Erin, I'm afraid your house is pretty much gone. It took a direct hit. There are no windows and no bathroom left."

There was a lengthy silence.

"Erin? You still with me?"

"The house is gone? Everything's gone?"

"Yes, I'm sorry. Try not to think about that now. Help me find you."

"Isn't there anything at all I can save?"

Gable looked around. "Maybe. It's hard to tell—everything is all piled up. Erin, you can't worry about that now. You gotta concentrate on helping me find you."

After another brief silence Erin hollered back. "The door is a couple of feet outside the house. About a third of the way down from the corner nearest the driveway."

"That's great. Hang in there."

The area Erin described was covered by a large pile of wreckage, topped off by the stove. Gable cleared what she could, then put her back to the appliance to shove it out of the way.

"Is more help coming?" Erin shouted.

"As soon as they can." Gable gave the stove another push, putting her long legs into it. A jagged edge tore her jeans, cutting into the flesh of her thigh. It wasn't deep. She ignored it.

The stove toppled off to one side. She dug through the rubble beneath it, spotted the edge of the big metal storm door, and cleared a space around it. The door was dented in and wouldn't budge, despite her best efforts. She had to run back to the Jeep for her tire iron to get the job done.

Several steps led downward, out of the rain. Following them, Gable found herself in a concrete basement about fifteen feet wide and thirty feet long. One wall was lined with shelves containing home-canned goods—peaches and pears and tomatoes in jars, undisturbed. Cardboard boxes and large plastic storage containers were stacked high along the opposite wall, each one carefully labeled—"Old dishes," "Winter clothes," "Christmas ornaments," and the like.

Two-thirds of the room was untouched by the tornado. Farther in, much of the ceiling had given way, toppling onto a desk and file cabinet. It caved in right over the only door. It had to be the bathroom. She knew she couldn't move the enormous beam that blocked her way, and even if she could, doing so might bring the rest of the house down on top of both of them. It would take more than human hands to get the woman out of there.

Picking her way through the rubble, she got as close to the door as possible. Creaks and groans from over her head were frequent, as though the remaining wreckage would collapse upon her at any moment. It was a scary, precarious situation. Her mouth was dry.

"Can you hear me, Erin?"

"Thank God." A muffled response filtered from the other side of the wall. "I'm here. In here."

"How you doing?" Gable glanced upward. A bit of sky was visible through a three-foot-wide hole above her, and she felt a mist of rain against her face.

"All right, I guess. I'll be fine as soon as I'm out of here."

"The door is blocked on this side," Gable said. "It'll take heavy equipment to move everything out of the way safely, so you'll have to be patient. It may be a while before anybody can get to you."

There was another long silence.

"Erin? Keep talking to me. How you holding up?"

"How much longer do you think it'll be?"

"I'll see what I can find out."

Gable stepped back into the untouched half of the basement. She had turned her radio down, but she'd heard no letup in the turmoil of voices and static. Unclipping it from her belt, she increased the volume to listen to what was happening.

Another tornado had touched down. Three homes were destroyed and six people were injured. Resources were stretched thin. When there was a break in the voices, she radioed in with an update.

The dispatcher told her it would likely be morning before the required manpower and equipment could be spared to her location. But she wasn't needed elsewhere at the moment, so she was free to stay and do what she could for Erin, at least for the time being.

Amid more groans and creaks from overhead, she made her way back to the bathroom door and called, "Erin? You're gonna have to be patient. We probably won't be able to get to you until morning."

"Morning? You have to get me out of here! I can't wait until morning!" There was a manic desperation to Erin's voice.

"Look, I know you're scared. But you should try to stay calm."

"You don't understand! I have claustrophobia! Really *bad* claustrophobia, know what I mean? I *have* to get out of here!"

Oh great. What do I do now? Gable thought for a moment. Oddly enough, having Erin's discomfort to focus on dispelled some of her own unease.

"And there's another problem," Erin said, in a much more subdued voice.

A chill ran over Gable and her arms puckered with goose bumps. Something about Erin's tone told her this would not be good.

"I'm terrified of the dark. It's worse even than my claustrophobia."

Oh crap. "Well, that's just a bit more of a challenge, that's all." Gable tried to keep her voice even and reassuring. She angled her head to see through the hole above her. Rain pelted her in the face. It was already early twilight. It would be dark in less than half an hour. "So... you still have some light to see by over there? Can you see the sky?"

"There's a hole in the ceiling near me. It's been letting light in," Erin said.

"How big a hole?"

"Couple of feet across, I guess."

Gable tried to picture where they were in the house in relation to the wreckage above. "Got anything you can stick up through the hole? A towel bar, a piece of wood or something?"

She could hear sounds coming from the other side of the wall as Erin shifted things around. Before she could open her mouth to warn Erin, there was a loud crash as a piece of ceiling gave way above the bathroom.

Hearing a sharp cry, Gable put her ear to the wall. "Erin? You okay?"

"Damn! I pulled on the wrong piece of wood and the ceiling caved in. Well, part of it did, anyway. I have even less room to move around now, and I cut my arm."

"How bad is it? Do you have first aid supplies in there?"

"It's a pretty deep cut," Erin said. "It's not very big, but it's bleeding quite a bit. I have a towel wrapped around it. I can't get to my medicine cabinet."

"Is the hole in the ceiling above you big enough that I could maybe get some supplies through it to you?"

"Yes, I think so."

"I'm going upstairs. See if you can find something to stick up through the hole to help me find you. But be careful!"

"I've got a piece of wood that will reach," Erin said.

"Good." Gable started toward the storm door, but Erin's voice stopped her.

"Gable?"

"Yeah, Erin?"

"Would you have another look around for Earl Grey while you're up there? Please?"

"Sure."

On her way back through the basement, Gable glanced again at the boxes. It was getting decidedly cooler out, and she felt a bit chilled in her soaked clothing. She imagined Erin might be feeling the same.

"I see you have a box marked *winter clothes* out here," she called. "Are you warm enough, or do you want me to try to get something to you?"

"Yes! Some sweats would be great. Thanks."

Emerging through the storm door with the clothes, Gable discovered the wind had picked up considerably, but the rain had diminished to a steady patter. The sky was getting darker by the second.

She opened the back of the Jeep and reached for the daypack SAR had issued her. She emptied it out and sorted through the contents, selecting a flashlight and extra batteries, three candles and matches, a bottle of water and two power bars. These went back into the pack along with the sweats and several items from her first aid kit. Antibiotic ointment. Gauze. Tape. An Ace bandage. The flashlight she kept in the glove compartment of the Jeep went into her back pocket. After tying one end of a twenty-five-foot length of thin nylon rope to the pack, she returned with it to the house.

"Erin!" Her voice was getting hoarse from yelling. "Show me where you are!"

Near the middle of the wreckage, a long strip of wood waved back and forth. The hole it came out of was a bit larger than a basketball hoop. Gable couldn't get nearer than ten or fifteen feet. Too much debris was in the way, and the flooring around the hole was too uncertain. She didn't want to bring more of it down on Erin's head.

Standing as close as she dared, she instructed, "Okay. Back away from the hole."

"Go ahead!"

It took two tries to get the pack to Erin. After another quick look around for the cat, Gable headed back to the basement. The light was fading fast, and she had to use her flashlight to find the bathroom door.

"Erin? How you doing?"

"Better. Warmer. I got a candle going and took care of my arm. It's stopped bleeding."

"Good. Hey, you mind if I borrow some sweats? I got soaked through."

"Of course. Help yourself."

Gable found a lone large sweatshirt amid the preponderance of mediums, and managed to get on a pair of Erin's sweatpants. They were tight and several inches too short, but she felt worlds better. As she changed, she listened to the radio traffic. It sounded as though things were finally beginning to quiet down. She returned to the door.

"I'm back."

"Gable, I'll never be able to thank you enough for everything you're doing," Erin said. "Especially for staying with me."

"I'm just sorry you're stuck there till morning." As soon as she'd spoken, Gable immediately regretted it. *Why remind her she's trapped, idiot? You need to be taking her mind off it.*

She found a spot near the door where she could sit comfortably out of the rain. Though she'd rather have been in the undamaged portion of the basement, the rain was really coming down again, and if she got farther away she and Erin would have to shout so loud to hear each other they'd be hoarse in no time. Even sitting just a few feet from the door, Gable had to raise her voice to be heard over the frequent downbursts.

"I'd rather be anywhere else, that's for sure," Erin said. "I want to be out looking for Earl Grey. I keep hoping he's just scared and holed up somewhere."

"Well, if I'm not called away, I'll go up at first light and have another look-see," Gable promised.

"Do you think you *might* be called away?"

"Ya never know. It's been a really wild, busy day. But I checked in not long ago and it sounds like things are quieting down. There haven't been any tornados in a while. Not since it's cooled off."

"I hope you *can* stay," Erin said. "But I certainly will understand if you have to go help someone else who needs you worse than I do. You know, I was amazed at how fast you got here, by the way. I couldn't believe it when I heard your voice. The tornado had just hit the house. Did you see it?"

"I sure did. It was coming right at me. I had to dive into a storm pipe."

"Were you scared?"

"Terrified. Absolutely terrified. You?"

"I didn't have time to be," Erin answered. "I turned on the TV and saw we were under a tornado warning, but I couldn't find Earl Grey. I was down here looking for him when the house blew apart. It happened so fast I hardly had a chance to register what was happening. Not until it was over did it really hit me. I still don't think it's really sunk in fully yet. Probably won't until I get out of here and see what's left of my house."

"This half of the basement wasn't badly hit. Everything in your bins down here is okay. And you might be able to salvage some things from upstairs. I saw a bookcase and some clothing."

There was a loud groan as debris above them shifted. Gable ducked just as a portion of the ceiling near her fell a foot and then inexplicably stopped. She held her breath, waiting for it to fall farther. Her heartbeat pounded in her ears. *You shouldn't be sitting here. It's too dangerous.* But she felt compelled to stay within earshot of Erin. "How you doing over there?"

"Could be better." Erin's voice seemed to get a bit higher whenever the ceiling shifted.

"Let's try to take your mind off where you are," Gable suggested. "First, get as comfortable as you can. How much room you got? Can you lie down?"

"More or less."

"Got a towel or something you can use as a pillow?"

"Yeah."

"Good. Now I want you to close your eyes and try to relax. Concentrate on your breathing. Nice deep breaths. In and out. Pretend you're someplace nice and peaceful."

"Okay."

"Good. Now describe where you are to me. Really *be* there. What do you see? Smell? Hear?" Gable cleared a path in the debris around her so she could stretch out her legs.

"Hmm, let's see…I'm lying on a beach. And that isn't rain I'm hearing, it's…the sound of the surf. The air smells like salt."

"Very good. Now I want you to try to relax. Why don't you tell me about yourself?"

"What do you want to know?"

"Start anywhere. Whatever you want to share."

CHAPTER TWO

W ell, let's see. I'm thirty-nine. Single. I teach music at the elementary and middle schools in Pine River. This is my first house—I bought it last summer after I moved here."

"So you're new to the area?"

"Yeah, you?"

"I've been here just over a year. I live probably seven or eight miles north, about halfway between Pine River and Meriwether. Where did you move from?" Gable asked.

"I was born in Petoskey and lived there until I went to Kalamazoo to go to Western. After I got my teaching certificate, I wanted to move back up here somewhere, but there were no jobs at all. I've been downstate—first in Mason for a couple of years, then in Grand Rapids, and most recently in Saint Joe. My job there was axed by budget cuts. Fortunately, I found this opening right after that. I love it up here." Erin paused. "I also give piano lessons. Or at least I did. Any sign of my piano?"

"Nope. Sorry." Gable turned her flashlight off, conserving the battery. She could see a dim glow of light above her and through a tiny crack in the wall that separated her from Erin.

"Oh well. I can get a new one." Erin sighed. "It's not like I had an emotional attachment to it." There was another brief silence. "I sure hope Earl Grey shows up."

"I wish I could do more to find him." Gable had never had a cat, believing them to be generally unsociable creatures that clawed the furniture. But it was obvious that Erin loved her pet, so she was genuinely sorry that Earl Grey had gone missing and was probably dead.

"He's a sweetheart." Erin's voice was husky with emotion. "He sleeps tucked up against my neck every night."

Gable didn't know what to say. "Erin, do you have a place to stay after this?"

It was strange, she felt oddly protective of this woman, though she barely knew her. She felt as though she had a personal stake in Erin's future, and that realization surprised her. *Is it because we're surviving this together? Because we've had this shared, life-altering experience?* She'd heard of that happening. Bonding from sharing adversity. *That's what makes friends for life.*

"I hadn't thought of that. I'm homeless! Jesus. That's a reality check. I don't know what I'm going to do."

"The Red Cross will be sending people in," Gable said. "I can put you in touch with them. Or if there's anything I can do…" *What were you just about to volunteer? You were going to invite her to stay with you, weren't you? You don't even know her.* The impulse disconcerted her. A very private person, Gable rarely welcomed overnight guests who weren't members of her immediate family.

"Thanks, but that's not necessary. I'll figure something out. I could go stay with my mother," Erin considered aloud. "But I'll want to be nearby while I go through everything—see what I can salvage. And figure out what I'm going to do. Maybe I'll stay at the Blue Moose for a while."

Gable was familiar with the place. It was a motel on the outskirts of Pine River that consisted of neat log cabin units, set off by themselves in the woods. "Erin, I don't mean to get too personal. If you don't want to answer this I'll certainly understand. But…are you insured? You going to be okay?"

"I do have insurance, and it'll cover everything, I hope. I should be able to rebuild."

Gable found herself unexpectedly pleased to hear that Erin would remain in the area. "I'm glad you're not going to let this chase you away."

"Oh, it couldn't do that. I have a great job, and I love it up here with all the trees and animals."

"Me too."

"Besides, what are the chances that tornadoes would hit the same place twice?"

Gable found herself smiling. "That's a good way to look it at."

"Well, my mother always told me...when things look bad, take a deep breath and count your blessings. Try to look on the bright side. Then forge ahead! I guess the bright side of this is that I can design my new house to be exactly the way I want it. No more ratty carpet. No more drafty patio door. And I can finally get a bathtub and some storage space."

Gable was impressed that Erin was dealing so well with what had happened. She could tell that Erin seemed not quite as stressed as she'd been earlier. Her voice, once she relaxed, had an interesting timbre to it. Low and rich, it resonated warmth and humor.

"What about you?" Erin asked. "Forgive me if you've told me this already—are you a cop?"

"I'm a volunteer firefighter. Still a rookie. I've never experienced anything like this before."

"I doubt anybody has. Are you just out of college?"

Gable smiled broadly. "Not hardly. I'm forty-six."

"Oh! When you said you were a rookie, I pictured you in your twenties."

"No, only that I've been on the squad less than a year. Right after I moved here, I went to pay my property taxes at the township hall and saw a flyer saying they needed volunteer firefighters. So I signed up and went through the training."

"Have you fought a lot of fires?"

"A few. Brush fires, mostly. And we respond a lot to car accidents."

"Where did you move here from, if you don't mind my asking? Do I detect a trace of a Southern accent?"

"I grew up in Chattanooga, and most of my family is still there."

"What brought you to Michigan?" Erin asked.

"I came up here a lot over the last several years to visit my brother Stewart, who lives in Kalamazoo," Gable explained. "We'd drive up to Pine River to go canoeing or camping, and I fell in love with the area. In the south, you don't really get the changes in the seasons the way you do here. And I like small-town life a lot better than the noisy sprawl of a big city."

"I feel the same way."

Gable shifted position to get more comfortable. She wanted to lie down, but there was not enough room. She turned on her flashlight and began clearing a wider space. Amid the pieces of wood and flooring, she found a framed photograph, the glass shattered. She picked it up and shone her flashlight beam on it.

It was an eight-by-ten of a bride and groom, circa early 1940s, she guessed, by the man's World War Two U.S. Army uniform. He looked a bit like Van Johnson, with blond hair combed back and a movie-star smile. The bride, petite and delicate, was recognizable as such only by her veil; she was otherwise clad in a nice, but everyday dress. She looked very young, and she was carrying what appeared to be a checkerboard. *Kind of odd.*

"I found a picture out here in a frame. A wedding couple. Are these your parents?"

"Yup, that's them. Dad passed away a couple of years ago. Mom's still going strong—nearly eighty but going on twenty, and a real pip. I can't keep up with her."

"They both look so young."

"They were. Mom was only seventeen, Dad was eighteen. They were high school sweethearts, and he was going off to war."

"Can I ask why she's carrying a checkerboard?"

Gable heard the sound of laughter through the wall. It made her smile.

"That's her purse. It was the height of style then, she keeps insisting. But we—my sister and I—we kidded her and Dad for years about how exciting their honeymoon must have been."

That got Gable laughing too. There was another long, sustained creak, as if the house were groaning, from directly overhead. It startled them both into silence.

Gable shone her flashlight around. It didn't look like anything had moved. But she knew Erin had to be as nervous as she was, probably much more so. *Keep talking. Keep her mind off it.* "So what did your dad do?"

"He was a high school teacher," Erin said. "Calculus and trigonometry."

"My worst subjects."

"Mine too, unfortunately. Apparently a talent for advanced mathematics is not genetic."

Gable smiled.

"But he did pass down his love of education. I always wanted to be a teacher. So you're a volunteer firefighter, you said? Do you have another job?"

"Yeah. I'm a pharmacist at Lakin's drugstore in Meriwether. I've always done some kind of volunteering, though, wherever I lived. In Chattanooga I helped out with the Red Cross."

"Is volunteering something you get from your parents?"

"Not really," Gable said. "My folks were wonderful people. But they both worked long hours. My dad usually held down two jobs. They didn't have a lot of spare time for anything. I'd have to say it was Camp Fire that got me into volunteering."

"Camp Fire? You mean, like in Camp Fire Girls?"

"Yup. I was involved in it for a long time. Heard of the Boy Scout oath?"

"Sure. Do your duty, be honest, and all that?"

"Exactly. Well, we had the Camp Fire Law. And even as an adult, I always thought it was a pretty good thing to live by. One of the 'laws' is 'Give Service.' You know—do what you can to make the world a better place."

"Well, I admire that," Erin said. "I can't say I've done my share. I'd like to argue I never seem to have the time, but I guess that's just an excuse. Other people make the time."

"It's never too late to make a difference," Gable said.

"That's true."

"So you teach piano, you said. Do you play anything else?" Gable asked.

"Well, as a music teacher I have to know something about most every instrument. But the only other ones I've actually played a lot are flute and trombone."

"That's an odd combination."

"Well, my parents started me on piano lessons when I was seven," Erin said. "I took up flute to play in my junior high school band, back at a time when girls were discouraged from playing what I really wanted to play—trombone. I finally got myself one a few years ago on eBay."

"I wanted to play drums. But they made me play clarinet."

"Didn't you hate that? That was just so unfair."

"Sure was."

"Do you still play?" Erin asked.

"No, not in years," Gable answered. "What's your favorite kind of music?"

"Well, you're probably not going to believe this, but I like the old standards best. You know—Cole Porter, George Gershwin, Irving Berlin."

"Me too. I love that stuff. My current favorites are the new Rod Stewart American songbook CDs. I was never really a fan of his growing up, but I love what he's done with those great old songs."

"I have all three of those! Well, I *had* all three, anyway," Erin amended. "Guess my music collection is gone. Damn. It was a good one too. I think I had every Ella Fitzgerald album available on CD."

It tugged at Gable's heart to think about all that Erin had lost. "I'm sorry this happened to you, Erin. I wish there was more I could do to help."

"I appreciate your concern, Gable. I'll be fine. I really will. And I look forward to meeting you, when I get out of here. I really feel like I've made a new friend."

"I do too. I admire the way you're keeping your chin up through this."

"I'm trying to be positive. I know I'm lucky to be alive, and I'm a firm believer of counting your blessings. So I'm just going to concentrate on the good things right now. I've got my health. A job I like. Great family and friends. And I'm still hoping Earl Grey will turn up."

"That's the spirit," Gable said.

"I just wish I could get out of here. What time is it, do you know?"

Gable clicked on her flashlight and shone it on her watch. "Nine thirty."

"Only nine thirty? Oh man, this is going to be a long night."

"It'll pass before you know it. We just have to keep your mind occupied. So…we've covered music. How about movies? What are some of your favorites?"

"Hmm. Well, *Gone With the Wind* is a classic. And I love all the old Hepburn-Tracy movies. Oh! And Carmen Miranda! And those Judy Garland, Mickey Rooney 'Let's put on a show!' films. And most of the great old musicals. *My Fair Lady. South Pacific. King and I. Music*

Man. Oklahoma."

"I love those too!" Gable broke into a boisterous chorus of "76 Trombones" and Erin joined in, with a lilting soprano that complimented Gable's rich alto perfectly. By the end of the song, they were both laughing.

"You have a lovely singing voice," Erin said.

Gable could feel herself blushing. "Nice job on the harmony," she replied.

"How about…" Erin broke into "I'm Just a Girl Who Can't Say No" from *Oklahoma*.

Gable countered with "Tonight" from *West Side Story,* and thus began nearly two hours of shared show tunes. They sang until they could sing no more.

"Okay, we've covered music and old movies. How about more recent films?" Gable asked. She had to nearly shout to be heard through the wall. The rain was really coming down again.

"Well, let's see…I really liked *The American President. Sleepless in Seattle* and *You've Got Mail*. I love just about anything Tom Hanks is in."

"Yeah. I like him a lot too. And Annette Benning is wonderful in *American President."*

"What are your favorite flicks?"

"Oh, I'm a big man-against-nature fan," Gable said. *"Vertical Limit, The Perfect Storm, Castaway. The Edge, Touching the Void, Titanic*. And old war movies: *In Harm's Way* and *The Longest Day,* and *Tora! Tora! Tora!"*

They moved on to TV shows. Both never missed *Survivor, Alias, Medium,* and *Joan of Arcadia*, but Gable was alone in her devotion to the History Channel and college football, and Erin had a fondness for old *Little House on the Prairie* reruns that Gable didn't share.

Around midnight they drifted to literature and found they both liked mysteries and shared many of the same favorite authors: Nevada Barr and Sue Henry, Steve Hamilton and Dana Stabenow.

They covered food for the next hour, discovering a mutual fondness for Asian and Mexican cuisine. Cappuccino. Crème brûlée. Tiramisu. And chocolate, especially dark chocolate. And both were fervent devotees of a medium-rare Victoria's filet from Outback Steakhouse, with garlic mashed potatoes on the side.

Two to three a.m. was devoted to funny stories about past vacations each had been on.

Hobbies took up another half hour. So did religion—both were lapsed Roman Catholics.

Politics and social issues were next. Both were decidedly Democratic and they shared a deep concern for the environment and other issues.

Gable kept Erin talking while keeping an ear tuned to her radio.

About the time that dawn was breaking, the questions and answers began getting more and more personal. Gable was nearly hoarse from having to raise her voice half the night. But the rain had stopped, finally.

"How did you get your name, Gable? I don't think I've ever heard of anyone named that before."

"My mom really liked old movies, and she named all of us after actors she liked."

"Oh! Clark Gable! I get it! It's unusual, but I like it very much," Erin said. "You said 'all of us'? I take it you have brothers and sisters?"

"Eight brothers, no sisters. I'm the baby of the family."

"You have eight older brothers? Oh my. That must have been fun when you were young! Tell me about them. What are their names?"

"Well, there's Grant, Stewart, Kelly…" Gable counted them out on her fingers to make sure she got them all. "Flynn, Mason, Wayne, Fitzgerald and Tracy. And we're all very close. Dad died when I was ten, so they all kind of stepped up. Grant taught me self-defense. Flynn took me fishing and showed me how to shoot a gun. Kelly turned me into a pretty good poker player, and Fitz taught me how to shoot hoops. With Mason it was whittling and carpentry, and with Wayne it was fixing cars. Stewart's really good with computers. I've learned a lot from them and they've all really been there for me. But they are awful overprotective."

Erin laughed. "Well it was quite different for me growing up. My sister Sue was so much older—twenty years—that she was out of the house before I was born."

"Did you say twenty *years*?"

"Yeah, I was a major surprise—Mom was forty when she got pregnant with me. It was like being an only child, really. I was spoiled rotten. Got anything I asked for."

"Okay. Favorite Christmas presents, then," Gable prompted.

"Hmm. Well, my first two-wheeled bicycle, when I was seven. It was pink. I got a phone in my room, when I was fourteen. And a Mustang convertible—used—after I turned sixteen. *That* was a memorable one, as you can imagine. And two weeks in Paris, the year I turned eighteen."

"Pretty cool presents," Gable agreed. "I never got anything near that good, but then I did do well in the sheer volume category."

Erin laughed.

"Course, back when we were growing up, a lot of the presents were homemade," Gable said. "I'd get all sorts of things whittled out of wood or molded out of clay. Homemade kites. Vases that couldn't hold water. Wallets made at summer camp. But the boys have all done pretty well for themselves since they got out into the working world, so I've been really raking it in the last several years."

"Part of me, especially as an adult, misses having a lot of siblings," Erin said. "Sue is married, with four kids, and lives in Seattle. We hardly ever see each other, and don't often talk on the phone."

"That's a shame. I can't imagine not being close to my brothers, especially Stewart—he's only a year older than I am. And Grant, because he took me in and became kind of a second father to me."

"Grant took you in?" Erin repeated.

"Six years after Dad died of a heart attack, Mom got killed in a car accident," Gable said, her voice thick with emotion. "Being the only girl, my parents both really doted on me. It was real hard." She took a deep breath. "Anyway, I was just sixteen. Grant—he's the oldest—he was married by then and had a house. He took care of me until I went away to college, and he and the rest of my brothers all chipped in to pay for my tuition and dorm. I don't know how I'd have come through it without 'em."

"It's wonderful to have people in your life who you know will be there when you need them."

"Sure is," Gable agreed.

"I certainly needed *you* tonight," Erin said. "And I won't forget all you've done, Gable."

Gable smiled at the words. She knew that she and Erin were building a very special friendship tonight. And the thought warmed her from within.

Growing up a tomboy in a house full of brothers, she'd always found it much easier to talk to men than women. She fit right in at the firehouse and was accepted as one of the guys, but they were mostly superficial relationships. Apart from the occasional poker game, she rarely socialized and never had anyone over to her house. She was an intensely private person, and her innate shyness had so far kept her from developing the kind of close friendships in Michigan that she'd had in Tennessee.

But there was something different about Erin. It was easy to talk to her—like they'd been friends a long time. Why was that?

Gable hadn't considered her life lacking. She was comfortable with the status quo. But the thought of having Erin to hang out with…*catch a movie, try a new restaurant. Maybe catch a play in Traverse City. We sure have a lot in common.* The prospect sent a ripple of excitement up her spine. *And won't it be great to have someone close by that you can really be yourself with?*

That brought up a whole new question. *How will she react to that bit of news?*

Gable had not a clue about Erin's sexual orientation. Their love lives had not really come up—Erin had only said that she was single. *She's thirty-nine and she lives alone. She's either divorced, or widowed, or homely as hell, or…or maybe she's just like me and hasn't met the right person yet. What kind of person is the right person for you, Erin?* Her curiosity suddenly shifted into overdrive.

"Erin? What do you look like?" *Are you cute? Are you gay?* She wanted to ask, but of course she couldn't. *You're supposed to be professional here. You're acting as a representative of the fire department.*

"Well, I'm five-five. A hundred twenty pounds. Red hair. Strawberry-blond, really. Down to my shoulders. And I wear glasses. You?"

"I'm five-ten," Gable said. "Short hair, dark brown. And I wore glasses too, until a couple years ago. I had radial keratotomy."

"Ew. I considered that, but the thought of someone coming at my eyes with a sharp instrument or a laser or something gives me the willies."

"It wasn't so bad." Gable couldn't help smiling. *How do I find out what your story is, Erin?* "Do you have any kids?"

"Nope. Just cats. Earl Grey was number nine."

"*Nine* cats?"

"Yeah. My first was Mamma Cat." At Gable's small chuckle, she said, "Yeah, I know, real original. My mother's choice. I was six at the time. This cat showed up at our door during a snowstorm and gave birth a few days later."

"Hence the name. I get it. And after Mamma Cat?"

"There was Whiskers and Buford. Then...let's see...Cookie and Crumb—they were brother and sister. Then Freeway, and Jake. And Festus—he was a Siamese. Then Earl Grey."

"That's a lot of cats."

"I usually have at least two at a time. Strays just seem to find me. I never actually go out looking for one," Erin said. "Do you have any pets?"

"Nope," Gable said. "We had a golden retriever when I was growing up. Her name was Sally. But nothing after that."

"Oh, that's a shame. I love having pets to come home to. What about you? Do you have any kids? Are you married?"

"Nope, no kids. Never married. You?" Gable held her breath.

There was a lengthy silence. "I was married once." Erin's voice suddenly sounded a bit funny. Strained. "It didn't last very long. He was a real asshole."

Gable felt her heart sink. "I'm sorry. That's a shame." *Of course she's straight. They're always straight.*

The radio at her side blared to life. "McCoy from dispatch. Respond accident involving two trucks, intersection Lincoln Road and M-42."

Gable keyed the mike as she got to her feet. "Dispatch from McCoy. Responding."

"You have to leave, don't you?" Erin asked.

"'Fraid so. But hang tight. Help should be here soon."

"I'll be all right. You go," Erin urged. "But I want to take you to dinner or something soon. I owe you, big-time."

"I'd like that. And I'm glad I could help. Take care, Erin."

Gable jogged to the Jeep and started to back down the driveway, but paused when she heard the approaching rumble of heavy equipment. She pulled off onto the lawn as two cars and a construction crane appeared in the rearview mirror. The lead car contained two of the veterans on her firefighting squad—Radley Stokes and Oscar Knapp. She quickly briefed them and asked them to keep an eye out for Erin's cat.

Maybe if this is a quick callout I can make it back by the time they get her out, she thought as she turned on her emergency flasher and sped down the road. *I really want a face to put with that voice.*

CHAPTER THREE

Eight days later, Gable still had no better idea of what Erin looked like.

The accident that had called her away that night had taken hours to clear—a lumber truck collided with a Road Commission truck, pinning one of the drivers in his cab and spilling gravel and logs all over the highway. It was midafternoon the next day before Gable arrived back home, exhausted, to find a message waiting on her answering machine. Her brother Stewart, telling her he'd lost half his roof to the high winds.

After quickly arranging to take some time off, she drove to Kalamazoo to help with the repairs. The damage was much worse than she'd expected and she found herself stuck at her brother's for a week, working ten or more hours a day. Although she was constantly occupied, her mind wandered on and off to Erin throughout each day.

Gable missed her.

It was weird missing her without having a face to put the voice to. She hoped that when they finally met, she'd be able to get past this maddening *fascination* she'd developed over what Erin looked like. It seemed to be all she could think about.

You're being silly. You know she's straight. It's just that you really haven't had a close woman friend in ages. That's all. And you met under extraordinary circumstances, and had nothing to do all night but get to know each other. Naturally you want to see her face.

When the repairs were finally completed, Gable was happy to escape the congestion of the college town and return to her remote woodland home. Her ten acres were off a dirt road, surrounded by hundreds of acres of state forest but within easy reach of the two small villages she frequented. Pine River, five miles southeast, had the nearest grocery store, and Meriwether, seven miles west, had the nearest pharmacy, where she worked.

Erin's place wasn't *exactly* on her way home. It was a good ten-minute detour off her fastest route back from Kalamazoo. But she took the back roads there anyway, as if seeing what was left of the place would somehow preserve her connection with its owner.

Although the lot had been cleared and leveled, Gable was disappointed to discover that no construction was underway. She nearly stopped at the Blue Moose motel next, convinced suddenly that seeing Erin would put an end to her irrational fixation. But she needed to shower and change before coming face-to-face with the woman she longed to see, so she swung home instead, prolonging the torture.

She tried on various outfits, eventually settling on jeans, a white shirt, and her leather jacket. She was so nervous her palms were sweating. She brushed her hair until it shone, feeling every bit like she was on a very important first date, though she knew that wasn't the truth.

Stomach churning, she headed to the Blue Moose. Once she'd parked in the lot, she took a moment to control her breathing, then wiped her palms on her pant legs before she went into the office.

"Hi, I'm here to see Erin Richards," she told the bespectacled older gentleman behind the counter. "Can I have her room number or can you ring her for me?"

"Erin Richards, you say?"

The man typed the name into his computer using only two fingers. Who knew what could happen if he hit the wrong key? Clearly, he was terrified. He would look at the keyboard, searching for the letter. Strike it with painful deliberation, then peer at the monitor over his reading glasses to make sure it was there.

Gable bit her tongue to keep from telling him to hurry. Finally, he announced, "I'm sorry, we have no one here by that name."

She stopped breathing for an instant. "Not here?" she repeated. "*Was* she here? Can you tell me that?"

He looked back at the computer screen, then called over his shoulder, "Martha! Can you come out here a minute?"

There was an open door behind him that led into an inner office. After a moment a diminutive woman with gray hair and a ready smile emerged.

"Hi." She greeted Gable. "What's up?" she asked the man behind the desk.

"Erin Richards. Does that name ring a bell with you?"

"Yeah, that's the teacher that was in fourteen for a couple of days. Lost her house in the tornado?" She directed the last sentence to Gable.

"She was only here a couple of days? Did she say where she was going?"

"Don't think so." The woman cocked her head slightly. "I remember her because her pickup was all caved in on one side, and I asked her about it. She told me what happened. Hey!" Her face lit up with recognition. "I bet you're Gable, aren't you?"

Gable couldn't help the faint flush of embarrassment that warmed her cheeks. *She talked about me!* The realization made her a little giddy with happiness. Apparently she'd made an impression on Erin. "Yes, I'm Gable," she said.

The woman held out her hand. "Martha Edwards. Nice to meet you, Gable." They shook. "She'll be sorry she missed you. She told me how you sat up all night keeping her sane."

"I'm sorry too," Gable said. "Thanks. It's been nice meeting you."

She sat in her Jeep for a moment, drumming her hands on the steering wheel. She didn't want to go home. She was too keyed up. She decided to drop in on Carl Buckman, a poker buddy who ran a bait and tackle shop when there were no emergencies demanding his attention. Carl was a volunteer firefighter too, as well as the local 911 director.

The store was only a few minutes away and Gable spent the drive time practicing normal-sounding conversation.

"Gable! You're back!" Carl waved as she walked in the door. "Missed a good game last night. I won twenty bucks off ol' Don Baum."

She chuckled. "And did he pay up?"

"He promised to bring it in today."

She laughed harder. "Keep dreaming. You'll be lucky to get a free haircut out of him."

Carl shrugged. "Say—I know what I was supposed to tell you. You know that woman you sat up with the night of the tornadoes?"

Her heartbeat picked up. "Erin Richards?"

"That's her. She called the firehouse a couple of times looking for you. Right after you left, and then again a few days ago. She said she'd keep trying until you got back."

She wants to find me too! "Did she say where she was staying?"

Carl ran a hand through his hair. "Don't think so. Oh—there's something else too. After she called the last time, Dick came in with news about that cat of hers you were asking about."

"Has somebody seen him?"

"Sounds like it. Dick was having breakfast the other day at the café in town, and he overheard some woman talking. Apparently her son found a hungry-looking cat in the woods a couple of days after the tornado. Turns out it's gray with a white mustache, just like you said!"

"Where's the cat now?"

Carl pulled a slip of paper out of his wallet. "Here's the number of the people taking care of it. The woman told Dick she'd give it back when we found the owner."

Gable called the family and arranged to pick up Earl Grey. She'd look after the cat while she searched for Erin, she decided. She didn't want him settling in too comfortably with a new family. She stopped at the grocery store on her way there and got a bag of dried food and several cans of moist, along with a litter pan and litter and a variety of toys.

Gable had to admit that Earl Grey was truly adorable; a Groucho negative, all dark gray but for his perfect white mustache. The cat had viewed her with suspicion at the start—and hid under the car seat all the way home. She lured him out with a handful of treats, and he clung to her shoulder crying pitiful mewling sounds when she carried him inside.

Within a week, he had charmed her in a way she'd thought impossible, sleeping curled beside her every night and wailing loudly how much he'd missed her when she returned home from work.

Gable did everything she could think of to find Erin. The school where Erin taught was no help. The principal had given her a month off and said only that she'd be back in touch once she got things settled.

Why didn't you give her your number, idiot?

She hung out a lot at the fire station when she wasn't working, hoping Erin would call. But when another week passed with no word from her, she began to worry that maybe Erin had reconsidered her decision to rebuild. Maybe there was a problem with her insurance.

She drove by Erin's place again, and her heart skipped a beat when she spotted the Oakleaf Log Homes truck parked in the driveway. A crew of workers was busy putting up log walls.

After that, Gable went by regularly to check the progress. The house looked like one of those prefab kits. It sure was going up fast. Sometimes she rode her bike out there—the fourteen-mile round trip was a satisfying evening ride after work. Other times she drove and took Earl Grey with her, riding on her lap. Soon the way to Erin's became as familiar to her as her route to work. Off her dirt road, she headed south along a paved two-lane until she came to the farm with the twin silver silos, glinting in the sun. Left onto a gravel road for a half mile, then right onto another paved road and over the bridge to Pine River.

This time of year, the bridge was usually lined with cars belonging to the fishermen who were trying to catch rainbow trout in the sparkling water below. A mile or so beyond was the intersection where she'd encountered the tornado. Gable always slowed and said a prayer of thanks as she passed the concrete slab that marked where the convenience store had stood. When she reached the final quarter mile, her heartbeat would begin to pick up. She always hoped to get a glimpse of Erin, but was disappointed each time.

Finally, after a month or so, the new cabin looked done from the outside. After that, she'd see the occasional electrical company truck or plumber's van in the driveway, but still no Erin.

One Friday evening, two months after the tornadoes hit, Gable got off work early to attend the bimonthly supper meeting of the volunteer fire department.

Carl greeted her as she stepped into the Plainfield Township fire garage. "Hey, girl, you playing with us later? Going to have a game over at Billy's."

"Maybe," Gable replied. "Let's see how late this goes."

"You hear the news? Chief Thornton says we have a new volunteer. You won't be the rookie anymore."

"Oh, it hasn't been so bad. Y'all have been pretty easy on me."

"I'd know that voice anywhere," came a warm, familiar tone from behind her.

Erin! Gable whipped around.

Her stomach turned cartwheels and her breath caught in her throat. The sweet and caring music teacher she'd gotten to know just happened to be a damn fine-looking woman with a body to die for. Petite and fit, her arms and legs softly muscled. Round breasts beneath a snug-fitting yellow cotton blouse, and a firm backside accentuated nicely by her denim shorts.

And that face. Gable thought Erin surely must be Irish, with her green eyes and reddish-blond hair and faint hint of freckles beneath the small wire-rimmed glasses that rested on her nose. She had delicate features, and a ready smile Gable found irresistible. There was an excited rosy blush on her high cheeks and, more than that, a vivaciousness about her—a spark of life and vitality—that was immensely compelling.

They stood frozen, grinning at each other, for a very long moment.

Then Erin threw herself at Gable and embraced her tightly. "Thank you," she whispered into her shoulder, in a way that sent shivers up and down Gable's spine.

She could feel Erin's warm, moist breath on the skin at the base of her neck, a particularly sensitive spot. "You're welcome," she managed, her throat tight. Her body was acutely aware of Erin's, pressed up against her, thigh to thigh, breast to breast.

Erin broke the embrace and looked her up and down. "You're just like I pictured you! I'm sorry I haven't been in touch sooner. My mother came and abducted me from the motel. Have you been out to my place?"

Gable blushed. She couldn't admit she'd been there almost every day since she got back from Kalamazoo. "Yeah, it looks very nice! I can't *believe* how incredibly *fast* it went up."

Erin nodded. "Wasn't that amazing? It's one of the reasons I went with that company. They promised it would be finished in six to seven weeks. It was one of those kit deals where they build the walls and roof elsewhere, and just have to assemble it on site."

"Have you moved in?"

"I just now got back in town. Tonight will be my first night."

"Oh, that's exciting!" Gable felt her grin get bigger. "And I have the perfect housewarming gift."

Erin smiled back. "Let me guess. A weather radio? Fire extinguisher?"

"Good choices, but mine's better."

"Do I get a hint?"

"Do I get an introduction?" Carl interjected.

Gable had completely forgotten he was there. "Sorry, Carl. This is Erin Richards. The woman I sat up with, the night of the tornado."

"I gathered that. Pleased to meet you, Erin." He extended a hand.

"Carl Buckman here is our 911 director, and my closest rival in our Saturday night poker games. All-around great guy, and fortunately an extremely bad bluffer."

"Do all rookies get to play?" Erin asked. "I'm a force to be reckoned with when it comes to five-card stud."

"You're the new recruit?" *Someone pinch me. She's joining the squad?*

Erin rested a hand on her shoulder. "Don't look so surprised! I got to thinking a lot about what you said, about giving service…and it never being too late to make a difference. And what *you* do, as a volunteer firefighter, can mean the difference between life and death. I sure know *that* firsthand." She winked at Gable, whose heart fluttered in her chest.

She joined up because of me. Gable felt a surge of pride at the realization. *And that means I'm going to be seeing her a lot!*

"Hey, Gable, who's your friend?" The voice belonged to a ruggedly cute thirtysomething fireman with honey blond hair and a matching mustache.

"Hey, Tim!" Gable greeted the newcomer with a hug. "Tim Scott, meet Erin Richards. It was her place that got hit the night of the tornadoes."

"And you're the Tim who's assigned to my zone with Gable, right?" Erin asked.

"That's me. Very pleased to meet you, Erin." They shook hands. "Sorry I wasn't around to help you out that night. Did I hear you say you're joining the squad?"

"Yes, you did," Erin replied. "I start training next week."

"Well, welcome aboard. We're happy to have you." Tim was grinning at Erin in a way that Gable recognized. *He likes her.* The thought made her kind of queasy.

"Thanks, Tim. I look forward to meeting everyone else." Erin smiled back at him, and Gable wished she knew her well enough to be able to read her expressions as easily as she could read Tim's.

"Hey, we better get in there or there won't be any food left!" Carl gestured impatiently for the women to go on ahead.

"Food? I didn't know we were eating dinner," Erin said as she and Gable headed inside. Tim and Carl fell in line behind them.

"Well, having everybody in the firehouse share a meal is kind of a time-honored tradition in the firefighting community," Gable said.

"Particularly in big cities, where you live at the firehouse," Tim added from behind them. "Even though we're all volunteers here, we honor the tradition by centering our meetings around a community meal. Kind of acknowledges that we're family, that we watch out for each other."

"Everybody takes turns cooking," Carl said. "You'll get your turn, probably sooner rather than later."

"Sounds like a good tradition," Erin said.

They went through a set of swinging double doors and found themselves in the large rectangular room normally used for training. Six-foot-long folding tables stood end to end in the middle of the room, surrounded by enough folding chairs to seat at least two dozen people. Just about as many as were currently milling about and chatting. An elderly man and woman were covering the tables with large plastic tablecloths in ubiquitous red and white checks, while two more men stood by with a pile of china plates and a bucket filled with silverware.

It took a good thirty seconds for everyone to notice there was a new face in the crowd, but once they did the room fell silent.

"Hey, everybody," Gable said. "Come say hi to the newest addition to our group, Erin Richards."

Erin was immediately surrounded and introductions made, too fast for her to remember. It had taken Gable a while to get all the names when she joined up too, but everyone was friendly and welcoming. The volunteers were a diverse group, ranging in age from twenty-one to seventy, and included farmers, shopkeepers, bankers, and even a couple of college students.

In short order the tables were set, and Erin was directed to a seat at one end, with the chief occupying the other.

Gable flanked Erin on her right, Carl her left.

"Who's cookin' today?" Gable asked.

"Larry," someone farther down the table replied.

"That means beef stew," Tim told Erin. "One of the rules for the meal is that everything has to be made from scratch. Larry makes a mean stew, but that's the extent of his cooking abilities."

A middle-aged man wearing a large apron dotted with stains appeared with a huge pot of beef stew and set it down next to the chief, who ladled it into big deep bowls that got passed all the way down the line. Erin was the first person served. As that was being done, the cook made several more trips to the kitchen to distribute pitchers of lemonade and plates of corn muffins and Parker House rolls.

No one ate until everyone had a bowl in front of them and Larry had removed his apron and joined them at the table.

"I'd like to welcome Erin, our new rookie." The chief lifted his glass of lemonade.

"To Erin!" the assembly chorused, raising their glasses.

"Okay, everybody, dig in!" the chief said, and all eyes looked expectantly at Erin as she picked up her spoon and tasted the first bite.

"This is really good stew," Erin said, and a woman a few seats away snickered. So did the man sitting next to her.

"Glad you like it," Larry said loudly from three tables away. "It's my own special recipe with a secret ingredient."

More snickers.

Erin showed no sign of wilting under the scrutiny. "Secret, eh? I'm pretty good at guessing ingredients." She dipped another spoonful and tasted it, and set off another round of sniggering. Erin acted as if she hadn't heard it. "Tarragon? Thyme?"

More laughter.

Erin was clearly determined to rise to the challenge. She took another spoonful. "Worchester sauce? Beer?" Half the group was laughing now, full-out laughter, bowls of stew forgotten.

Erin's expression grew more determined. Her spoon went into her stew again, stirred it up…and the light suddenly dawned. She scooped out the hard, alien object she discovered at the bottom of her bowl and found it to be a partial dental plate, with four false teeth attached.

Loud roars of laughter shook the room.

"Ah. I see." Not chagrined, Erin held the teeth up for inspection. "I thought the stew had a bit of a bite to it."

They howled. Gable laughed so hard she had tears streaming down her face. Carl snorted lemonade out of his nose.

It took several seconds for the chief to regain enough composure to tell Erin, "Well done, lass. And by the way, it *was* sterilized. We're not totally cruel."

"I must admit I kind of freaked when they did it to me," Gable told Erin as the rest of the crowd resumed eating. "We were having soup, and I didn't find it until I was about half done. Thought I was gonna heave."

"Me too," one of the guys near them chimed in.

"Ah, but you forget I work at an elementary school," Erin said. "You develop a pretty strong stomach when you take care of kindergarteners during flu season. And no one can touch a fifth grader when it comes to practical jokes."

Gable had a hard time not staring at Erin throughout the meal. The woman was not only great looking, she was charming, and funny, and totally at ease in the room full of strangers. And Gable wasn't the only one enchanted. Tim and several of the other single young men—and a couple of the married ones too—kept glancing in the newcomer's direction.

When they were nearly done eating, Chief Thornton thanked everyone for coming and made a few announcements. "The duty roster is posted. In addition to the two regular training gigs we've got set up this month, I'd like to schedule several training sessions for Erin, if I can get some volunteers."

The words were barely out of his mouth before a dozen hands shot up, Tim's a fraction ahead of Gable's.

"Great," the chief said. "Let me know when you're free and I'll be in touch. Erin, you mentioned you're pretty flexible until school starts back up, right?"

"Sure, Chief. I'm eager to get started. You can schedule me most any time. Whatever's best for you and whomever I'm working with."

"Excellent," he answered. "You'll do some of your training here, and next month you'll get the classroom courses in Charlevoix that we talked about. Okay then, for the rest of you, a reminder that we've got the big Fourth of July picnic coming up, and we need all the help we can get. Pass the word. Any questions?"

There were a few more announcements and a recap of recent callouts. As the meeting finally wound to a close, Carl turned to Gable and Erin. "Cards, ladies?"

"Can't tonight," Erin glanced at her watch. "I'd like to hit the grocery store before it closes."

"I think I'll pass too," Gable said. "I have an important errand to run."

"Aw, can't it wait?" Carl whined, waving a deck of cards at her.

"Nope, sorry, Carl," Gable replied.

"If you change your mind, we'll be at Billy's." He scanned the room for other possibilities. "Good to meet you, Erin," he said, moving away.

"You too, Carl." Erin got to her feet and turned to Gable. "I wish we had more time to catch up, but I need to take a rain check. My cupboard is truly bare and I at least need to pick up coffee and cream or I'll never survive tomorrow morning."

Gable fell into step beside her as they joined the departing firefighters. "Do you mind if I stop by after you get home?"

Erin looked her way. "Tonight?"

"I'll only stay a couple minutes."

"Sure, all right," Erin said. "Give me a half hour?"

"See you then."

Chapter Four

Earl Grey greeted Gable at the door with his raspy mewl. It was the cry he made to remind her that his stomach was indeed empty and would she please remedy that straightaway?

She picked him up and set to work scratching the spot under his chin that always made him lean into her touch. He began purring immediately—a tiny engine on low idle. "I got a surprise for you, Earl. I'm gonna take you to see your mama in a bit. I bet you can't wait to see her." She carried him to the kitchen for a snack.

When he finished, she carried him into the living room and set him on her lap, petting him and talking to him until it was nearly time to go. She cleaned out his litter box and packed it up, along with a half-full bag of litter. Then she put the cat food into a shopping bag, along with the toys and treats she'd bought. In a separate bag, she put the sweatshirt and sweatpants she'd borrowed the night of the tornado.

"Guess that's everything," she announced to the cat, which had followed her from room to room, intently watching her every move.

She glanced at her watch. It was after nine. Erin would be home by now and she knew she really should get going. But she found it much harder than she thought it would be to say good-bye to Earl. *I never dreamed I could get so attached to an animal.* She stooped down to pet him.

"Are all kitty-cats sweet as you?"

Earl purred his response and stood up on his hind legs, his front paws propped against her pant leg. He was demanding to be picked up, and she complied, hugging him and kissing him behind the ears and trying very hard not to cry. "C'mon, you. Time to go. Just ten more minutes till you see her! I can't wait to see her face."

She carried him out to the Jeep and set him on her lap as she always did. But the cat sensed that this excursion was different than the rest, and he remained alert and awake, as restless with anticipation as she was.

"Why didn't you tell me your mama was such a looker, Earl?" Gable asked as she pulled out onto the two-lane and headed south. "All those trips out to her place, and it turns out she ends up finding *me*."

Earl meowed loudly as if in answer, and got up and began to pace about on the passenger seat.

"Was she looking for me, do you think? Or did she just get the volunteering bug, like she said?"

Gable wanted to believe that Erin had been every bit as intent on finding *her* as she'd been in her efforts to track down Erin. She felt a flush of happiness when she recalled how Erin had virtually flown into her arms and held her tight. *That sure was awful nice.*

She glanced at Earl Grey. "I know, I know. I shouldn't be thinking like that. Your mama and I don't apparently have *that* in common." She sighed and scratched his head. "But you gotta give me a break. It's been a while, okay? I kinda forgot what it felt like to get all stirred up."

Her own dating relationships had been mostly brief and largely forgettable. The women had all been nice enough, but she hadn't fallen head over heels like she'd always dreamed she would. She hadn't met *the one*—the one person who could make her heart stop—the one person who would complete her. And she pretty much gave up hope she would when she hit forty-five and moved to the boonies. She suspected that her dating days were probably behind her.

And she hadn't been at all unhappy with the way things had turned out. She loved her job and her home, and she had some good buddies among the guys on the squad.

But Erin had made her suddenly aware that something was missing in her life here. Being close to someone—having someone to share things with—she needed that. It enriched every life experience. Maybe she couldn't have the kind of relationship with Erin that she might have liked—her hormones apparently hadn't gotten the news yet that Erin was straight. *But I can have something very special with her, I think, even without that part. I sure hope she wants that too.*

Gable braked to a stop at the intersection where she'd encountered the tornado. She remembered thinking that day that she should have seized more opportunities in her life. And she vowed that things would be different from now on.

Erin's new cabin was ablaze with light, a welcoming beacon in the darkness. But Gable walked slowly up to the front door, savoring her last bit of time with Earl Grey. She hid him under her jacket, a maneuver only partially successful. It concealed his identity, but she could not disguise the fact that something very *alive* was protesting its confinement against her chest.

Erin's smile when she opened the door and spotted Gable turned to a look of bewilderment when her eyes focused in on the squirming bundle of energy beneath her coat.

"Your housewarming present," Gable explained. "Anxious to be opened, as you can see." She smiled mischievously.

Erin stepped aside. "Well, do come in."

The cat let out a loud *rowl* as Gable stepped over the threshold. She hadn't heard this particular cry before, but she thought it sounded clearly like *get me the hell out of here right now!*

"A cat?" Erin guessed. She had a big grin on her face. "You brought me a cat?"

"Not just any ol' cat," Gable said as she unzipped her jacket.

"Earl! Oh my *God*! Earl Grey!" Erin scooped him up from Gable's outstretched hands and held him close against her. "I can't believe you're here!"

Earl was momentarily startled by the abrupt change but when he recognized Erin's familiar scent he mewed a soft, sweet sigh and rubbed his chin and whiskers against her cheek.

Gable thought it was one of the nicest reunions she'd ever witnessed, and said a prayer of thanks for the family that had found Earl and taken him in. Sad as she was to lose him, she was nonetheless gratified by Erin's joy at getting her cat back.

"Where...how?" Tears of happiness streamed down Erin's face as she reached over to embrace Gable with one arm, the other cradling

Earl. "Oh, thank you, Gable. Thank you so much."

Gable was near enough to inhale Erin's cologne, a subtle aroma she found very appealing. The proximity of their bodies unnerved and excited her. Her heartbeat accelerated. She reached out to scratch Earl under the chin, and he leaned into it as usual, his eyes closed and his purr kicking into high volume.

"He's really taken to you," Erin observed. "He's usually pretty stand-offish. How long have you had him? How did you find him?"

"Well, I'd asked a few of the guys to keep an eye out for him. A family found him, and word got around. I've had him a few weeks," Gable said.

"I just can't believe you found him," Erin repeated, shaking her head. "I'd given up all hope."

"I thought you were the eternal optimist!" Gable chided.

"Well, I am now!" Erin said, and they both laughed. "Seriously, though, I won't ever be able to repay you for all you've done for me."

"Not a problem, really." A faint blush warmed Gable's cheeks. "I was happy to do it. Oh, I've got a bunch of stuff for Earl in the car—litter box, food, toys. And I brought you back the clothes I borrowed. I'll get 'em."

She retrieved the bags and handed them to Erin, who was watching Earl Grey scout out his new surroundings.

"Make yourself at home," Erin said. "Excuse the lack of furniture! I'm going to put the litter box upstairs and set out food and water for Earl. I'll be right back." She headed up a short set of stairs at one end of the room that led to a narrow hallway with doors leading off it.

Gable took in her surroundings. She was in the cabin's great room. Though it was still mostly unfurnished, it had a warm and homey feel—constructed entirely of wood and stone and natural materials. The walls were rough-hewn pine and the ceiling was supported by a framework of massive logs; the spicy scent of new wood lingered subtly in the air. The floor was wood too, except for the entryway, which had been given over to terra-cotta tiles the color of Georgia clay.

The soft track lighting was expertly aimed, spotlighting the log rafters, high ceiling and fieldstone fireplace with dramatic emphasis, bringing out the warm amber glow of the wood.

Erin came back down the stairs and headed to the kitchen in the corner, giving Gable a big grin as she passed by.

The lighting does some really nice things for you too, Gable thought as she watched her fill one bowl with water and another with cat food. When Erin bent over to set them on the floor next to the refrigerator, Gable found her eyes lingering on her sculpted ass.

She quickly averted her gaze as the neatly built woman straightened, and resumed her study of the great room. The only furniture thus far was a brand-new dining table and chairs, set up near the corner kitchen, and a sofa and TV. The TV rested on a large wooden crate. Off to one side, against the wall, were several stacks of boxes and plastic storage containers, some of which she recognized from Erin's basement.

Erin came to stand beside her and followed her eyes. "That's what I was able to salvage. Still have a lot of things to get, as you can see." She turned slowly, surveying the room. "I'm really happy with everything, though. It's set up very much like the old place, but I made some improvements. The porch is bigger, the basement has a reinforced ceiling, and I've replaced my tiny shower with a brand-new whirlpool tub!"

Keeping her eyes off Erin was a hopeless task. Gable had never dreamed she would have such tiny, delicate hands, soft lips, and lustrous, silky hair. *Stop staring. Stop it. Stop it. Stop it.*

She pried her eyes away and said, "Well, I'd better get going. It's late."

"Can I treat you to dinner tomorrow to say thanks?" Erin asked. "I'd cook for you, but I don't have pots and pans and dishes yet. I have a lot of shopping to do."

"Tell you what," Gable said. "I've got the weekend off. Why don't I come shopping with you? I can help lug packages and we can grab dinner while we're out. I'll let you pay—as long as it's nothing too extravagant. A burger's fine with me."

"That would be wonderful!" Erin seemed delighted. "I'd love the company. I'm actually kind of looking forward to picking things out for the place and restocking my closets. And we sure seem to have the same tastes about a lot of things!"

"We certainly do." Gable wore her own silly grin from ear to ear. It didn't seem to matter at the moment that she absolutely abhorred shopping. Ranked it right up there with getting a cavity filled. All that mattered was spending more time with Erin. Standing so close to her, she swore she could feel heat coming off their bodies.

"Do you mind getting an early start?" Erin asked. "I was going to leave about nine and get to Grand Traverse Mall about the time it opened."

"Sure. And I'll drive, if you like," Gable offered.

"That's awful sweet. You sure you don't mind?"

"Nope. Not a bit. Well then, I'll see you tomorrow." Gable turned to leave, and Erin followed and opened the door for her. But her voice stopped her before she could cross the threshold.

"Gable?"

Gable turned and faced her.

"I...well, I just wanted to say thanks again for taking care of Earl Grey. And for getting me through the longest night of my life. You made it not only tolerable, but actually...very memorable...in a good way." She had a shy grin on her face when she said this, and an expression that looked almost...*expectant.*

Gable was struck by how extraordinarily *breathtaking* Erin was at that moment. Suddenly the room was much too warm. "I'm really glad you're back, Erin. I'm looking forward to spending some time with you." Her palms were sweating. Her heart hammered in her chest. She needed air. She took a reluctant step through the doorway.

"Me too, Gable. Me too," Erin said, letting her go. "Tomorrow, then?"

"Tomorrow."

CHAPTER FIVE

"Come on, Gable, help me out here. Get on this bed!"

It had finally come to this. Gable should never have volunteered to go shopping with Erin. The entire day had been one long exercise in temptation and restraint. Everywhere they went, she was taunted by provocative thoughts and images, and everything Erin said seemed like a double entendre.

Things had started out innocently enough. She picked Erin up at nine a.m. and they got to the mall in Traverse City just as it was opening. Erin had salvaged several items of clothing from her ruined home, but she was tired of living in the same half dozen T-shirts and jeans.

First stop: Marshall Field's. Erin went through the aisles with purpose, pulling a sweater off an aisle display, then two blouses from a rack, pausing only to check for the right sizes.

"Hold these, please," she said, shoving the items at Gable before reaching for a gray-green tank top that matched the color of her eyes. "What do you think?"

She held it in front of her, and Gable could easily picture the provocative top accentuating the curves of Erin's nicely rounded breasts. She realized her mouth was hanging open and shut it abruptly. A faint flush crept up her cheeks and she prayed Erin wouldn't notice.

"Well?" Erin said. "Think it would look good on me?"

Gable nodded, not trusting her voice. *Oh, this is so not going to be easy.*

Erin tossed the top to her, adding to the pile of prospective purchases, and continued on through the racks. Another shirt, three pairs of dress slacks. A blazer. Then, a leather skirt.

Dear God. Gable groaned. *That will barely cover her ass.*

"You know, I usually hate to shop," Erin said, sending a pair of khakis in Gable's direction. "But this is kinda fun." She surveyed the bundle of clothes in Gable's arms. "That'll do for now." She headed off in the direction of the fitting rooms, crooking a beckoning finger over her shoulder.

Gable hesitated at the dressing room door, but Erin pulled her inside.

"Sit over there," she commanded, pushing her toward the small bench off to one side and closing the door. "I want to know what you think. Be honest, now."

It was a spacious corner stall, and the bench Gable sat on faced a trifold, full-length mirror guaranteed to capture every possible angle of the body standing in front of it. Gable almost whimpered aloud as Erin took the clothes from her and hung them up. *Uh-oh. I'm in serious trouble here.*

Erin considered her selections aloud as she absentmindedly kicked off her shoes and stepped out of her jeans. "Those charcoal pants will go with everything. And I really like this." She peeled off her top and reached for a nicely tailored white button-down shirt.

Gable tried to pry her eyes from the soft expanse of flesh between Erin's cream satin bra and matching panties. *I can't do this, I can't do this.* Her heartbeat pounded in her ears. Her mouth felt stuffed with cotton.

Erin pulled the shirt on, leaving three buttons unbuttoned to expose entirely too much cleavage, and stepped into the khakis. Checking out the outfit in the mirror, she glanced at Gable. "Whatcha think? I like these."

Gable nodded mutely and forced her eyes away so she wouldn't be caught staring. But her gaze fell instead on the short leather skirt hanging on the wall, and she worried she would hyperventilate.

Before she knew it, Erin was nearly naked again in that damn lingerie, giving her yet another chance to study some fascinating body part. Her eyes were drawn to lightly freckled shoulders and upper arms, the muscles bunching and expanding as Erin reached for another ensemble.

This time it was a burgundy blouse with a high round collar and subtle pattern, over the charcoal dress slacks.

"Teacher clothes." Erin shrugged as she stepped in front of the mirror. "I'd love to have a job where I could go to work in jeans. That's one of the perks of teaching piano at home. Speaking of which..." She whirled to face Gable, who tried her damndest not to blush under the scrutiny. "I think you should take up an instrument again. Wouldn't it be fun to play together?"

Fun? Play together? Instrument? Gable's mind was not her own. It refused to think coherently, filling instead with all sorts of images that were not at all remotely connected to music. She felt herself blushing. What the hell was happening to her? *You've been celibate way too long.*

"Gable? You all right?"

"Uh, sure, sorry. Drifted off there for a minute."

"You tired of shopping already?"

"No! Not at all." *If shopping was always like this, I might just live at the mall.*

"Good. So what do you think?"

"You...uh...you look very nice." *Brilliant. Very original. Nice vocabulary you got there, Gable.*

"I mean about taking up an instrument. Wouldn't that be fun?"

"I don't think I can remember much," Gable protested halfheartedly. "I doubt I could even read music anymore."

"I can fix that. Put yourself in my very capable hands and we'll be playing beautiful music together before you know it."

"Whatever you say." Gable tried not to read anything into the choice of words.

Once again, Erin was stripping before the full-length mirror. This time she reached for the leather skirt. Slipping it on, she turned slowly to see herself in the mirror. "Does it show too much?"

Not if you wear it around me. Gable kept that compliment to herself. *No one should have those legs,* she thought, admiring Erin's firm calves and toned thighs. She could only imagine how the boys at the fire station would react. The skirt definitely showed too much, she decided. But that was being selfish.

"You have the body to wear it," she said, trying to keep her voice even.

"Thanks. You're not so bad yourself," Erin said offhandedly. Stripping off the skirt, she reached for a pair of navy dress slacks.

She looked at Gable's reflection in the mirror as she zipped up the fly and adjusted the belt. "So...maybe this is too personal, but...you and Tim...any...uh, did you ever go out or anything?"

The question caught Gable off guard. *Why are you interested?* "Nope. Good friends, that's all. Why?"

Erin shrugged. "Just curious."

Why are you curious? Has to be Tim. She likes Tim. Gable felt queasy again all of a sudden. It didn't help that Erin was stripping down to her bra and panties yet again.

She got to her feet and headed for the door of the fitting room. "It's pretty warm in here, I'm going to stretch my legs. Take your time. I'll meet you at the entrance to the mall."

She escaped without waiting for a response and found a bench outside the store entrance. While Erin finished trying on clothes, she took the time to compose herself. Her self-therapy included a pep talk. *You have to get over this. You're being ridiculous. She's the best prospect for a friend you've had in ages, and you're going to screw that up if you keep mooning over her like this. She's straight. Get over it already.*

She wasn't ready to tell Erin she was gay. With her hormones so out of control at the moment, she would feel far too *exposed* if Erin knew. No. It took her no time at all to decide. She wouldn't tell Erin until she got over this...this crush. That's all it was. A crush on a straight woman. *You've had them before. It'll pass.*

It had been a while since she'd come out to anyone. No one, in fact, since she'd moved to Michigan, not even the guys at the station. She hadn't felt close enough to any of them to volunteer something that personal. And she hated the idea of getting kidded about it mercilessly over their weekly poker games.

Besides, these days you're hardly even a lesbian. You're more asexual than anything. You haven't been out on a date in, what... She did the math in her head. *Let's see. I was seeing Jane back when...Oh my God. I haven't been on a date in four years? Oh, you really are pathetic, Gable. No wonder you're panting after this woman.*

The object of her musings appeared at that moment, exiting the store with large shopping bags in each hand and a concerned look on her face.

"You all right?" She settled on the bench beside Gable and put a hand on her back.

Gable swore she could feel the heat of Erin's palm through her clothing. Her throat felt tight. "I'm fine. Just seemed awful warm in there."

"Want to quit?"

"Nope. I'm okay. Where to next?"

"Well, we can kind of work our way down the mall. Let me know when you get tired and we'll stop for lunch. My treat."

"Sounds good. Let's go."

Gable suffered through another dressing-room strip show at JC Penney, where Erin loaded up on another armful of clothes. They dropped off their purchases at the Jeep and then spent nearly three hours in Target, filling two carts with essential odds and ends: cleaning supplies and kitchen ware, garden hose and tools. Bandages. A flashlight. Clocks and rugs. Curtains, towels, sheets, and blankets. A boom box and several CDs. Telephones and an answering machine.

After a stop for lunch at China Wok, they made brief forays to several other mall stores. She thought she'd come through the worst of it, temptation-wise, until Erin paused in front of Victoria's Secret.

"Let's go in here. I need some new bras and panties, and they have a good selection."

Oh Lord. Give me strength, Gable thought as they headed inside. She tried not to look at the provocative lingerie displayed all around her. Lacy camisoles. Push-up bras. Sheer negligees. Teddies. Thongs. She tried not to imagine how they would look on Erin. She really did. But her mind and body conspired against her. She could feel the wetness begin to pool between her legs.

"What do you think of these?" Erin held up a sexy black demi-cup bra and matching panties, made of silk.

"I think...I think..." Gable's ability to form a coherent sentence left her and she felt light-headed. "Fine. Just fine. I'm going to sit over here."

She found an easy chair outside the fitting rooms and plunked down into it as Erin shrugged and continued shopping. Closing her eyes, she tried to dispel the naughty images cascading through her brain. But she was not at all successful. So she was both relieved and mildly disappointed when Erin appeared a short while later with another large bag, ready to go.

"Furniture next. Let's head to Art Van," she announced as they departed the store for Gable's Jeep.

Oh good. This part won't be so bad.

She was wrong.

It was in the bedroom display area at Art Van's that Gable realized her libido was now controlling her life. There was Erin, stretched out on a queen-sized mattress, looking tantalizingly kissable, beckoning and smiling, wanting an opinion on the firmness.

"Come on, Gable, help me out here. Get on this bed!"

That night, she called her brother Stewart. Just thirteen months older, he had looked out for her since they were in grade school, and he was the one person in the world she confided in. He knew her whole pathetic dating history and had seen her through more than a couple of crushes. And through it all, he was always a sound and reassuring voice of reason.

"How's the roof doing? Any leaks?" she asked after their hellos.

"Works like a charm. We had a downpour last week. Oh, Steven wants to say hi."

Her six-year-old nephew got on the phone. "I miss you, Aunt Gable. I play with the fire truck you gave me all the time."

"Are you saving lots of people?"

"Yes, today I saved the Lego people in Pirateland."

"I see. Well, that sounds very brave of you."

"Daddy wants to talk now. Bye, Aunt Gable."

"Bye, Steven."

"Can't thank you enough again for all you did," Stewart said. "I owe you. So…what's up? It's not like you to call without a reason."

"What's that supposed to mean?" Gable asked indignantly. "I call you just to say hello."

"No, you never do."

"I do too."

"Name the last time."

"I called you right after I got home," she reminded him.

"To ask whether we'd seen your sunglasses."

"Oh, yeah. Well, I…I called you a couple weeks before the tornado, didn't I? You told me about Steven's karate classes."

"After you asked me what you should get Tracy for his birthday."

"Oh." There was a pause. "I really never call you unless I want something?" Gable asked. She felt awful if that was true.

"No. But that's okay. Because you want something often enough that I get to keep up with what you're doing."

"Well, jeez, then I should apologize, Stewart. That's kind of lame, to only call you when I want something."

"Not a problem, sis. Your heart's in the right place, I know. So spill. What is it this time?"

"Well, I…I need some brotherly advice. Or maybe I just need to tell someone, I don't know. I seem to have developed this…" She stammered and bit at her lip. It had been a while since she'd talked to Stewart about her love life, and even with her brother it wasn't exactly *easy* to pour out all her innermost feelings.

"Gable, are you all right?" Her brother's voice was suddenly serious. "Are you ill?"

"No, no," she hastened to reassure him. "I just…well, I seem to have developed this rather maddening crush on this woman…"

"Crush?" The mirth was back in his voice. "Crush?" he repeated. "You've got the hots for someone? Oh this *is* news! This is why you called me?" He started to chuckle, and Gable's embarrassment turned to irritation.

"Well, you're a big help. I'm so glad I called and confided in you."

"Oh, honey, don't be pissed. I'm just teasing. You gave me a scare, there. So, for real? You've got the hots for somebody? It's been a long time. Who is it?"

"You remember that woman I told you about? Erin?"

"Trapped-all-night so-much-in-common Erin?"

"That's the one."

"Didn't you say she was straight?"

"She is. She's also drop-dead gorgeous *and* my new best friend. We went shopping together today, and she bought lingerie and a bed."

"Oh, I see. Very tough."

"Yeah."

"Well, you said you two really hit it off. Any chance she might be open-minded enough to consider some new possibilities?"

"You mean switching sides? Stewart! I'm surprised at you!"

"Why? I want you to be happy. You've been alone too long."

"Well, that may be true, but…"

"So do you think she's interested?" he asked.

"No, she's definitely straight. Besides, she has no idea I'm so smitten with her. I haven't even told her I'm gay yet."

"You haven't? Why not?"

"I don't know. I don't want to do anything to muck up our friendship. It's just getting started."

"But that's kind of an important piece of information to keep from someone you want to be close to, isn't it?"

"I know. And I will tell her. But today was really only the first full day we spent together, face-to-face anyway, and it was torture most of the time. I mean, I gotta tell ya, bro…I got it bad. I can't stop thinking about her. And I'm afraid if I come out to her, then she'll be able to see how I feel about her." She sighed. "I keep hoping it will get easier. Maybe I just want you to tell me I'll get over this."

"I wish I could, hon. But I doubt you'd be calling me about this if she was just a passing fancy."

"Big help you are."

"Sorry. Best I can do is to tell you to follow your heart."

"I'll try to remember that," Gable said. "Thanks for listening."

"Any time, sis. Good luck."

Gable fell asleep that night repeating her resolve to get a grip on her hormones. She was *not* going to let her emotions get the better of her, damn it! Her friendship with Erin was too important to screw up.

"Come on, Gable, help me out here. Get in this bed!" Erin lounged on her side on the queen-sized sleigh bed, one leg straight, the other slightly bent, a provocative pose, especially considering her apparel. She had on a black silk demi bra and matching panties, and Gable could see her erect nipples through the lingerie, small dark circles straining against the sheer fabric. A few wisps of reddish-blond hair escaped the edge of the panties, a tiny triangle that left very little to the imagination.

Erin's hand gently patted the silky cotton sheet beside her. "I'm waiting for you." She moistened her lips with the tip of her tongue and stared at Gable with a piercing look of desire. The bedroom was lit by candles, and soft soothing music played low in the background.

"Waiting for me?" Gable asked, drawn to the bedside.

"Mmm-hmm." Erin reached for her hand and pulled her down onto the bed.

Gable went willingly and lay on her side, drinking in every detail of the reclining woman—the fair skin, lightly freckled on her face, shoulders, arms. The inviting cleavage between her breasts. The flat plane of her stomach, with tiny blond hairs trailing down to disappear beneath the sheer material of the panties.

"Are you…do you…" she stammered, unable to believe what was happening even as she reached out her hand to caress the side of Erin's face. So soft. So incredibly soft. She knew it would be.

"Mmm-hmm," Erin purred again, leaning in to the touch. "I do want you, Gable. Just as much as you want me. I don't want to wait anymore."

"I don't either." Gable slid her hand around the back of Erin's neck to pull her closer.

Erin's hand slipped around her as their mouths came together, lips slightly open. Soft at first. Tentative.

Then, pressing harder, her tongue caressed Gable's lower lip, and the kiss deepened as their bodies closed the distance and heated flesh met heated flesh. Breasts pressed against each other. Erin's leg insinuated itself between Gable's. The lingerie was suddenly gone somehow, and Gable was mildly surprised to discover that she was naked too.

Her arousal went from simmer to boil in an instant when Erin moaned and climbed on top of her, not breaking the kiss until she had to draw breath. Erin's leg pressed harder against her aching center, and Gable's body began moving of its own accord, rocking against Erin, creating a delicious friction that cried out for release.

"Touch me, Erin," she pleaded in a whisper. "*Please.* I ache for your touch."

"Of course, love," Erin whispered back. "Close your eyes."

Gable obeyed, and she could feel Erin's body shift, the leg between hers replaced by a hand. Fingers toyed at the edge of her wet folds, as

Erin's lips found a nipple and began to suck, bite, lick.

The pounding of her heart rang in her ears. She spread her legs wider and lifted her hips to meet the caressing hand. Erin knew just how to stroke her. Harder. Faster.

Gable was poised on the edge of ecstasy when reality came crashing down and she awoke sweating in her own bed, her own hand between her legs. She was so disappointed to find it all a dream that she was unable to continue, unable to find relief.

In the damp tangle of her sheets, it took hours for her to fall back asleep.

The dream kept resurfacing in Gable's mind as she accompanied Erin to Cadillac the next day. She supposed it should have bothered her to spend her entire weekend off work trailing around stores—not exactly a habit of hers. But she found she didn't mind it one bit. She couldn't keep her eyes off Erin, stealing frequent, surreptitious glances at her, her mind's eye dressing Erin in the lingerie of the dream.

She felt vaguely aroused all day, and so was grateful Erin's shopping for the more risqué items on her list was already complete. This time, they spent hours in Home Depot and Meijer, selecting innocuous items like shelving and bird feeders, clocks, a vacuum cleaner, a ladder. Two full carts of groceries to fill Erin's empty pantry.

Erin insisted on cooking dinner for them that night, since their meal plans the previous evening had been thwarted by Gable's sudden loss of appetite while they were furniture shopping.

"After we eat, would you mind helping me put up some curtains?" Erin asked as she chopped salad vegetables on her new cutting board.

"Whatever you need." Gable watched Erin from a seat at the dining table, Earl Grey curled in her lap, purring contentedly. "Sure I can't help with dinner?"

"Everything's under control. Why don't you just relax. I've worked you pretty hard the last couple of days."

"I enjoyed it." *Perhaps a little too much.*

"You know, when I think back on the tornado, it's just not quite as traumatic as it probably should be. I mean…it was awful, sure. But it brought me the best friend I've had in a long time. I really feel like I've known you for ages."

"I know what you mean. I haven't had a lot of women friends," Gable admitted. "Growing up in a houseful of guys, I guess. But it's nice. You're easy to talk to."

"Same back atcha. I'd have really been a basket case that night without you."

"I think you're stronger than you give yourself credit for. I really admire the way you've come through all this."

"Well, I admire the fact you were there in the first place," Erin said. "Putting yourself at risk in order to make a difference. To help a stranger in trouble."

"Well, you'll be doing the same in no time."

Erin set the salad on the table and lit two candles she had bought that day at Meijer. Gable tried not to think about how romantic the setting seemed.

"I'm looking forward to the training," Erin said as she added a bowl of mashed potatoes to the table, and two New York strip steaks she had seared in a cast-iron skillet. "I'm a bit nervous about it, though, I'll admit. I'm certainly the smallest person on the squad. Okay, we're ready to eat. Help yourself."

"Everything looks great! And don't worry about the training, I know you'll do fine." Gable assured her. "Some of the drills do require a certain amount of brawn—pulling hoses and putting up the big ladders. But we always put a lot of people on that stuff. The hardest part for me was the classroom tests. Learning fire science and how fires spread. Building construction. Michigan fire laws. What precautions you gotta take around hazardous materials."

"That reminds me, I need to stop off at the station tomorrow," Erin said. "The chief said he'd have my training schedule worked out."

"You'll be able to start going out on callouts after a couple weeks of training, though you'll have limits to what you can do," Gable said. "No going into burning buildings right away."

She cut several small pieces of steak and fed them to Earl Grey, still curled contentedly in her lap. "During your training, you'll work one-on-one with some of the guys to learn things like ropes, portable extinguishers, how to ventilate buildings. Communications and equipment on the trucks. How to use an SCBA—that's your self-contained breathing apparatus. Some of the other stuff takes several people—rescue operations, working the hoses and ladders. And you learn a lot on the job itself."

"So when we get a callout, we go right to the station?"

"Well, if you're really close to it, yeah. We're so spread out here that most of us keep our gear in our car, so we can go directly to the scene."

"How often do you get called out?"

"Hard to say. There's always way more in the summer because the tourists are up here. The population triples. So you get more car accidents, more brush fires from cigarettes getting tossed out windows."

"Well, I'm glad you're on the squad. Makes me feel less nervous about everything, knowing I can ask you for help if I need to."

"You bet. Any time."

After dinner, Gable washed dishes and Erin dried and put away. As she soaped up the last plate, she allowed herself a momentary wistfulness over how great it would feel to share such domestic chores with Erin on a regular basis. Then they retired to the living room to tackle putting up Erin's curtains.

"I measured and marked everything last night," Erin said, setting the ladder in place by the large patio doors. "But it was too awkward to try to put the rod and curtains up myself. Hope you don't mind." She handed Gable a screwdriver and three screws.

"Not a bit. Happy to help. I know you've got a lot of stuff to do yet around the place. Anytime you need a hand, just give me a holler." Gable got a small stepstool and set it at the other end of the sliding doors.

Erin stood on top of the ladder with one end of the curtain rod and Gable took the other end. Getting that part installed was no problem.

Next, Gable got the heavy floor-length curtains and handed one end up to Erin before she mounted the stool to hang her end. Just as she was about to hook it, the rod slipped out of Erin's hands. Erin leaned over to grab it, too far, and the ladder started to tip.

Gable dropped the curtains and lunged forward, catching Erin as she fell, wrapping one arm around her waist. She should have let go of Erin right away. But for some reason her body insisted that she hang on for a few seconds longer than was necessary.

"Hey thanks. But you can let go any time now, Gable. I'm fine," Erin said, amusement in her voice.

Gable could feel the rush of heat to her face.

"You're cute when you blush, you know." Erin smiled up at her with a twinkle in her gray-green eyes. But then she climbed back up the ladder and reached down for the curtains without further ado.

Was she flirting with me? crossed Gable's mind, but she quickly discarded the notion. *Nah. Wishful thinking.*

Chapter Six

The latter half of June was Gable's favorite time of the summer. It was still mild out, with temperatures in the sixties in the morning and never reaching eighty during the day. And it was when animals from the woods surrounding her house brought their young ones by to forage for the scattered seed that escaped her many bird feeders. There were clownish raccoon babies, as intent on play as on food, and strings of downy-feathered turkey chicks, clustered protectively around their mothers.

Thirteen months ago, when she had driven up to the house for the first time, she had spotted a fawn, curled motionless in the tall grass not forty feet from the screened-in front porch. It had made the decision for her—she had found her perfect refuge in the woods. The two-bedroom home sat on ten acres of rolling mixed hardwoods, with a creek running by just off the porch. And best of all, it was surrounded by hundreds of acres of state forest, so it was home to abundant wildlife: deer and black bear and bobcats. Coyotes, fox, and otter.

She slept with the windows open, and the chorus of birdcalls at first light always woke her well before she had to get up to get ready for work. Ordinarily, Gable relished that quiet time on the porch with her coffee, seeing what animals were out and about. This particular morning, however, she failed to appreciate the snapping turtle crossing her creek, or the pileated woodpecker working on the half-dead oak tree twenty feet away. After spending the whole weekend with Erin, she could think of nothing but seeing her again.

As she showered and got ready to leave, she replayed those moments in the dressing room over and over in her mind and wondered how she'd make it through a day at work. She wished she'd made definite plans with Erin on when they would get together again. *That reminds me. I should stop at the firehouse on the way to work and pick up a copy of her training schedule.*

The detour to the station only took a few minutes. A copy of Erin's schedule was waiting for her in her mail slot. The chief had some kind of training or drills scheduled for Erin nearly every day for the next three weeks, taking maximum advantage of her summer off from school. Gable saw her own name among those assigned to a trio of evening first aid classes this week, beginning in a couple of days. She was also among two large groups that would participate in Erin's search-and-rescue training drills later in the month.

Tim Scott, she saw, was in the same groups, and he also had several one-on-one sessions with Erin. That was no surprise. Tim was one of the most senior firefighters on the squad, and he'd been instrumental in some of Gable's training. But though she expected this, she felt a twinge inside her gut when she saw his name linked with Erin's on the page that way.

She couldn't begrudge them getting together. Tim was a great guy and would probably be good for Erin. She just wasn't ready to see Erin with someone.

"Hey, Gable, you're playing tonight, right?" Carl's voice surprised her.

She looked up to find him watching her.

"You all right? You look like a stunned mullet."

She forced herself to smile. Carl was sometimes just a bit too in tune with her, kind of like her brothers were. "You sure do have a way with words, Carl. I'm fine. And yes, I'm planning on it. It's at Jerry's house tonight, isn't it?"

"Yeah. Are you sure you're okay? You don't look so good."

"Gee, thanks. You sure can turn a girl's head with those compliments," Gable deadpanned.

"Gable…"

"I'm fine. I just didn't sleep very well last night. Look, I gotta run or I'll be late for work. See ya."

She escaped further questions and headed to Meriwether, her drive filled with reminiscences of why she'd not slept yet again. Last night's dream was only a slight variation of the previous evening's.

Erin was wearing a teddy this time, but the end result was the same. Gable awoke aroused and unsatisfied, and unable to get back to sleep for a long while.

Tired or not, Gable fully expected to come out ahead, as she normally did, in the weekly firefighter poker game. Her brother Kelly had taught her all the ins and outs of poker and blackjack and half a dozen other games. He'd taught her how to read other players' facial tics and body language when they looked at their cards, and how to keep her own expression from telegraphing what she had in her hand.

So in short order, she had gotten to know all the regular players well enough to beat them regularly. Carl bit his lip when he got a good hand and drummed two nervous fingers on the table when his cards were exceptionally bad. Don Baum's eyes narrowed ever so slightly when the deal went his way, and Jerry DeYoung played with his chips when he got a sure winner and was anxious to bet.

Oscar Knapp, a thin, reedy farmer, always had a toothpick between his lips when he played, and that ol' toothpick would start to dance at the corner of his mouth whenever he got a pair or better. The more the toothpick moved, the better the hand. All the other players had picked up on his tic, it was so obvious, and they bet or folded accordingly. Oscar always came up short and never figured out why.

The other firefighters who played joined in just now and again, and it was harder to read them. Gable had played with Tim Scott only twice, but that had been enough to discover he was about as good as she was. The last time they'd played, he'd cleaned the table.

She liked a challenge, especially when it came in the form of a payback, so she was initially pleased to see Tim's truck parked among those outside the cabin that was their venue for that night. But her mood deflated when she realized the pickup pulling in behind her belonged to Erin. Much as she wanted to see her again, Erin would be a big distraction during a poker game, and Gable wasn't particularly anxious to share her friend with the guys.

"Hey, Gable! I tried to call you today to ask if you were playing," Erin greeted her as they got out of their vehicles and headed up the walk together.

"I haven't been home. I came straight from work."

"Carl called me and said you needed another hand. So tell me, am I going to lose my shirt?"

Gable cringed inwardly at Erin's choice of expressions. "Depends on what kind of player you are," she said noncommittally.

They knocked and were admitted by a barrel-chested man with dark, bushy eyebrows and wild, unkempt hair.

"Hi Jerry," Gable greeted. "Have you met Erin Richards, our new rookie?"

"Not officially." Jerry offered a hand and introduced himself. "Go on in and make yourself at home." He gestured toward the living room. "Everyone else is here and we're about ready to start. Can I get you both a drink?"

"A beer would be good," Gable said, which prompted a raised eyebrow from her host. She rarely drank when she played cards, and was the exception to the group in that regard. But she had spotted Tim through the archway staring right at Erin, and a drink suddenly sounded mighty good.

"Beer for me too. Thanks!" Erin echoed her, and they went in to take their seats around a large round dining table.

Carl greeted them with a wave and Gable said, "Have you all met Erin?"

"Fresh meat!" Don Baum said. "Hope you brought lots of cash!" He stood and extended a hand toward Erin. "Hi, Erin. Don Baum." The town barber was by far the oldest of the group at seventy, a confirmed bachelor with a stubble of beard and food stains on his clothes.

"Hi, Don." Erin shook his hand.

"Oscar Knapp." The gangly farmer stood and offered his hand. "Don't know if you remember me..."

"Hi, Oscar," Erin took his hand in hers and shook it. "Of course I remember you. You were one of the guys who helped get me out of my basement that day. Thanks again."

"Don't mention it."

"Nice that you could make it," Tim said.

He and Erin exchanged broad smiles and Gable felt that same queasy sensation in her stomach again. Battling butterflies.

Jerry came in with two bottles of Budweiser and handed one to each woman.

"Why don't you sit here?" Tim invited, motioning to the empty chair beside him.

"Well, all right," Erin replied, which left Gable sitting between Don and Carl, directly across from Tim.

"So, Erin, what's your deal?" Don asked. "You married?"

She shook her head. "Divorced."

Gable glanced at Tim to see his reaction to this news, and cringed at the big grin on his face.

"So, are you seeing anyone?" Jerry asked as he started to deal the cards.

Oh great. Both of them? Jerry was single too, but he was in his mid-fifties, at least fifteen years older than Erin, so Gable hadn't really considered he might also be interested in Erin. And she didn't like the way he was looking at her, either, the old coot. *I'm gonna hate this. I'm just gonna hate having to sit here and listen to them hit on her all night.*

"Well, I hope to be seeing several guys before the evening is over..." Erin responded, and Gable nearly choked on her beer. "All jacks and kings, please, dealer."

The guys laughed, and Gable gradually relaxed as they got down to the business of poker.

❖

It was clear from the outset that they had three ringers, all of them out for blood.

Tim and Gable went head to head in almost every hand, betting big and raising bigger, and Erin stayed with them most of the time, but the others just weren't in their league.

It was impossible to tell when Tim or Erin was bluffing, and Gable figured they were having the same problem with her. All three played with reckless abandon, the pots growing much larger than what was typical for the group.

The conversation was friendly and the mood at the table seemed outwardly relaxed despite the intense competition. Only Carl had a hint there was more going on tonight than was apparent.

"You're on fire tonight, Gable," Tim said as she began transforming her latest win—a huge pile of chips—into neat little stacks.

"I'd say we're about even, wouldn't you, Tim?" she replied good-naturedly.

"And the rookie there ain't half bad." He gestured toward Erin.

"Nope. She's got the touch," Gable agreed.

"She's got ears too," Erin added, but you could tell she was pleased with the compliment. It was her turn to deal, so she gathered up the cards and began to shuffle like she'd done a turn or two at the tables in Vegas.

"Come on, deal the cards," Oscar grumbled. He had only enough chips left to bet a couple more hands at the rate he was losing. He said he'd promised his wife he wouldn't lose more than the forty dollars he had in his pocket.

"How about we take a break?" Jerry suggested. "The pizzas should be here any minute."

"Sounds good to me. Maybe it'll cool off these three and give the rest of us a chance," Don said. He stood and stretched, his pants loose on him, held up by suspenders. "Pit stop," he declared, ambling off.

"Can I get anyone another beer?" Jerry got to his feet.

"I'll take another, please," Erin said.

"Me too." Gable held up a hand.

"I need to stretch my legs," Carl said, heading for the front door.

"Translated…he has to talk to his wife." Gable looked at Erin. "He won't admit that to the guys, of course. They'd rib him about it. But he's on that cell phone with her at least a dozen times a day."

"Not all men are afraid to admit they can't stand to be away from the women they love," Tim said, and Gable knew he was being sincere.

That was the awful thing. She liked Tim, she really did. He was honest and honorable. A sweet man and a genuine hero, though he didn't like to talk about his experiences as a firefighter. She'd heard the stories from the other guys on the squad.

"Is that right?" Erin asked him with a bemused smile.

"That's what I hear," he said, smiling back at her.

"Well, you'll let me know if you run across one of 'em," Erin said. "Cause they're a rare breed." She glanced at Gable. "Can you direct me to the restroom?"

"Through the archway, down the hall, second door on the right."

As soon as Erin departed, Tim got up and came around the table to sit beside Gable.

"Gable, we're friends, right?" He had a fresh-faced eagerness about him, like a teenaged boy with his first car.

"Of course, Tim. Good friends." Gable leaned back in her chair and crossed her arms, and gave him a cocky smirk. "But I'm still gonna take all your money."

"Oh, I don't care about that," Tim said, shaking his head. "I was hoping you'd put in a good word for me with Erin."

Her smile disappeared, and the butterflies in her stomach became stampeding buffalo.

"Put in a good word for you?"

"Yeah. I'd like to ask her out, but she doesn't know me from Adam. I know it'd help if you vouched for me."

Gable was momentarily speechless. *How can I say no? He is my friend, and he's asking me for a favor. And I think he'd really be good for Erin. How can I deny her that chance for happiness? Just because it's killing me?*

"Gable?" Tim's voice told her she better find an answer soon if she didn't want to make it obvious she had feelings of her own for Erin.

"Sure, Tim. I'll put in a good word for you, not that what I say will necessarily make any difference on who Erin goes out with." She was proud of how calm and composed her voice sounded when she was dying inside. "I'm going to get a breath of fresh air." She got to her feet and hoped Tim wouldn't read anything into her rapid departure.

She went out the front door and sat on the steps. Carl was in the street, still talking on the cell phone while he paid the pizza delivery guy who'd just pulled up.

Gable held it all in as he approached her, heading back inside, juggling three pizzas in one hand while he stuck the phone in his jacket with the other.

"Hey there, Lucky," he greeted her. "You're sure on a hot streak tonight."

"Yeah, lucky me," she echoed with halfhearted enthusiasm.

"You okay?"

"Fine, Carl. Get in there while the pizza's still hot. I'll be right in."

"Whatever you say. But I'm here if you want to talk about it later." He went inside and Gable put her head in her hands and let the weight of the evening fall on her.

The gnawing in her gut threatened to unleash the beer she'd consumed earlier onto the tidy hedges that surrounded her. She was angry as well, and where had that come from? *Not angry. I'm jealous, that's what I am.*

She hadn't recognized what it was immediately because it had never really happened to her before. This wasn't a crush at all. No sir, not by a long shot. She was jealous as hell. And that could only mean one thing. She was falling in love. At forty-six, she'd finally found the real thing. Just with the wrong person. And as Erin's confidante and Tim's good friend, she'd have a front-row seat for much of their courtship.

Her eyes grew moist at the thought of it. And she did lose her beer then—her stomach heaved and sent it flying over the narrow railing and into the bushes below.

Her game went all to hell after that. She was determined to continue on as if nothing had happened, but it was impossible. Tim was grinning all to hell, and Erin looked so damn cute. Gable suffered in silence as her pile of chips began to shrink.

"Well, someone's tide certainly has turned," Jerry observed with commiseration from the sidelines. He had pulled out two hands earlier, leaving only Gable, Tim, and Erin playing. Oscar, Carl, and Don had gone home.

"Hey, Gable, I need to run to Home Depot in Cadillac and pick out a couple of ceiling fans for my place," Erin said as Tim dealt the next hand. "Want to ride along? Maybe this weekend?"

Now's your chance. You need some distance. This is the perfect solution. She considered it and made her decision all in the space of a second or two. And when she answered, her voice betrayed none of her inner turmoil. "You know, you should get Tim to give you a hand. He'd know better than I what to look for, and I bet he'd even put 'em up for you. Didn't you tell me you rewired your cabin yourself, Tim?"

"Yup, sure did. Pretty handy with plumbing too, if you have anything in that area you need help with, Erin. And I've got a flexible schedule. We can go tomorrow, if you like."

"Well, if you're sure…" Erin glanced first at Tim and then at Gable, her eyebrows cocked in confusion.

Gable did her best bluffing all night, making it look as though she was real happy about the whole proposition.

"Great," Tim said. "What time shall I pick you up?"

"How's nine?" Erin answered.

"Fine with me."

"Well, since you're assigned to my zone, I would bet you know where my house is, right?"

Good thing Gable had turned down that second beer. The buffalos in her stomach were back, and they'd brought their friends. If she was going to feel this awful seeing them together, how would she ever get through Erin's training? And working at the firehouse?

She was glad the pharmacy was busy the next day. It helped to keep the images of Tim and Erin together at bay, at least for a while. After work, she drove home slowly with the radio playing, not anxious to be alone with her thoughts.

It was agony. But there was a spark of something wonderful there too. *I'm falling in love.* Words she'd never been able to say. Was beginning to doubt she'd ever say. *Still may not ever say them aloud.* The thought of that made her even sadder.

She pulled into her driveway, and when the two-track crested a small rise she could see a flash of red through the trees near the house. Her heartbeat picked up. As she got nearer, she saw that it was…*Yes! Erin's truck!*

"Hey there," Erin hailed her from the screened-in front porch, where she was sitting on an oversized wicker chair.

Gable mounted the steps and opened the door. "Hi. Didn't expect to see you today."

"Well, I got everything done that I needed to do. I knew you had to work, so I thought I'd bring you some dinner. They got a new Chinese place in Cadillac." She held up a large plastic bag. "Needs to be reheated, though."

Gable took the bag and unlocked the entry door. "Awful nice of you. Come on in."

Erin followed her inside and looked around while Gable zapped the food in the microwave and got out plates, silverware, and napkins. "Nice place, Gable. Really nice. Feels really comfortable and cozy in here."

Gable's single-story home was decorated in earth tones: dark brown furniture and a tan Berber carpet, hunter green curtains, and the accents around the living room—rugs and pillows—followed the spectrum of autumnal color. The room was a seamless extension of the forest outside the door.

An overstuffed sofa and matching easy chair and ottoman provided comfortable seating in a space where the predominant feature was books. Built-in floor-to-ceiling bookcases covered most of three of the four walls of the expansive living room, and the shelves were crowded with books, framed photographs, and items found on a walk in the woods. Wild turkey feathers. Porcupine quills. Enormous pinecones. Unusual rocks.

The handsome coffee table and end tables, and the matching entertainment center that held the TV and stereo, all were made of maple, and all by the same careful hand. A cast-iron woodstove sat in one corner, on a hearth made of brick and slate. Illumination was provided by wall sconces and indirect lighting, which lent a subtle warmth to every surface.

Gable had furnished the room with the sole purpose of her own enjoyment, as she seldom had any visitors except family. But she was thrilled that Erin was here, and very pleased she seemed to like what she saw. She wanted her to feel welcome so she'd visit long and often.

But she had to know what had happened. "So how was shopping?"

"Good. Got a lot done. Tim put both the fans in. One in the main room, and one in my bedroom. We had lunch at the Chinese place, and I got takeout for us. They have a great menu. I hope cashew chicken and Mongolian beef are okay."

"Two of my favorites."

"So tell me about Tim," Erin said, taking a seat at the opposite side of the table.

Gable froze, but just for a second. *Oh great. Make me extol his virtues.* "Did he ask you out?"

"Yeah. I told him I'd think about it."

Gable took a deep breath and let it out. "Tim's a good man. He's been a firefighter for…fourteen years, I think." She dished food from the containers onto her plate, but she didn't have much of an appetite. "He was married for ten years, but his wife passed away a couple of months before I moved here. She had breast cancer. He took it very hard, the other guys say. Beth used to play poker with them, even though she wasn't on the squad. Tim hasn't played much since she died."

"That's so sad. He seems like a really nice guy," Erin said, digging into the chicken.

"He is. The genuine article. Tim's seen a lot of fire and been in some bad situations—he's lost count of his saves and had some close calls himself. Most of that was in Chicago, where he was a paid firefighter. He's been a volunteer here about five years, I guess. You know he's an EMT, right?"

"Yeah, he did tell me that. But he really didn't talk much about himself today. He kept asking about me."

"It's obvious he likes you," Gable said. *But I'm falling in love with you.*

"I haven't been on a date since I can't remember when. And first dates, especially, can be pretty awful."

"I don't think Tim has seen anyone since Beth died," Gable told her. "So he's probably as out of practice as you are. I don't think you need to worry about that. He's an easy guy to talk to. I know from all the driving around we did during my SAR training."

"You sound like you're trying to convince me to go out with him." Erin had stopped eating and she was watching Gable intently.

"No. That's your decision. I'm just saying that if you're interested… you could sure do a lot worse."

"You have no idea how right you are," Erin said without elaboration. She put her fork down. "I guess I had a bigger lunch than I thought. I can't eat any more."

Gable had hardly touched hers, either. She was too preoccupied with wondering what Erin's hair would feel like, sliding through her fingers. It was lustrous and shiny—a blend of coppery red and golden blond.

"Well, I better run." Erin rose and slid her chair in. "I have a full day of training tomorrow. As I recall, you're in the first aid sessions with me that begin tomorrow night, right?"

"Yup." Gable followed her to the door.

"Good. I'll see you then. And maybe we can get together this weekend?"

"We'll see. Thanks again for dinner."

Erin paused at the doorway. "Thanks for the chat." She reached out and hugged Gable. "I'm so glad we met."

Gable hugged her back, allowing herself the brief thrill of holding her.

"Me too," she whispered after Erin had gone.

Tim corralled her the next night as she was getting out of her Jeep at the firehouse. "Thanks, Gable. I owe you big-time."

"Oh, you don't either, Tim. Just be good to her, okay?"

"You don't have to tell me that."

"She say yes to your date?"

"Yeah, this afternoon. We're going out to dinner and a movie Friday night."

Too much information, Gable thought, picturing them at a romantic candlelit table. Tim with his arm around Erin in a darkened theater.

"That's great. We better get inside, don't you think?" She led the way into the large conference room, where Erin was chatting with two other firefighters, both men. There were about a dozen other people milling about, none of whom Gable recognized.

"Okay, looks like we're all here," Chief Thornton announced, motioning everyone to the folding chairs that had been set up. Erin came over to sit between Gable and Tim.

"We're happy to have Leslie Franks with us. Leslie is with the local Red Cross and will be doing the training with us this week."

Leslie, a tall, thin woman with graying hair, stood and waved. "Hi, folks. Glad to be here. Don't be afraid to ask questions as I go along."

"And for those of you who don't know him, Tim Scott..." The chief motioned toward him and Tim waved his hand. "Tim's an EMT with the county ambulance service. He'll be going around and helping out, making sure everyone is doing everything right."

The chief then acknowledged the strangers among the gathering. "I'd also like to say welcome to the teachers from the Pine River schools who are joining us tonight to get their CPR certification. Okay, I think we're ready to get started. Leslie?"

"Thanks, Roger," Leslie said. "Okay, folks, tonight we're going to cover CPR—that's cardiopulmonary resuscitation, as most of you know...and AED, that's how to use an automated external defibrillator. I'll be back tomorrow and Thursday to teach Standard First Aid and Preparedness, and how to administer supplemental oxygen."

Chief Thornton wheeled out a TV and VCR on a stand while she was talking and set it up in front of the chairs, then plugged them into a nearby outlet.

"First I'm going to show you all a video. Then we'll do some hands-on training. Can someone get the lights?"

"Haven't you done this already?" Erin whispered to Gable while they waited for the video to begin.

"Yup, back in Tennessee. But my certification was going to run out in a couple of months anyway. I thought I'd take it again with you, in case I could help you out." She glanced past Erin at Tim and forced herself to smile. "I didn't know you'd have your own EMT at the ready."

The video interrupted any further discussion. It was a good thing Gable knew CPR as well as she did, because she missed the entire screening. She kept glancing sideways at Erin and Tim in the dim light cast by the TV, expecting to see them holding hands or something. When it was over, Leslie hit the lights.

"Okay, first we're going to practice on Resusci-Andy," Leslie said, gesturing toward a flesh-colored mannequin the chief carried in and laid on a mat in the front of the room. "He was developed especially for CPR training. You can actually do the breathing on him and watch for the rise and fall of his chest. Plus, he's got an air-pressure device in him that will help you gauge how hard to press when you do the compressions. When all of you have had a turn with him, we'll split up into pairs and you can practice on each other so you can get a feel for what to do with a real person. Okay, who's first?"

After they had all had their turns, they cleared away the folding chairs and set up mats on the floor.

"Okay, if you'll all split up into pairs now," Leslie said. "You can take turns practicing on a real person. Remember the key elements. A-B-C. Airway, breathing, and circulation. Simulate the breathing, and don't really press during the compressions. We don't want any cracked ribs tonight!"

Erin looped one arm through Gable's, claiming her as her partner for the exercise.

Gable couldn't mask her surprise. "Don't you want to work with Tim?"

"I can't, I have to mingle," Tim said before Erin could answer.

"You want to be victim or rescuer first?" Erin asked.

"Rescuer," Gable said.

Erin lay flat on the mat and Gable went through the process, reciting what she was doing aloud so Erin could follow along. "Gently tilt the head to clear the airway. Look, listen, and feel for any sign of breathing. Clear any airway obstruction." Her hands were shaking slightly as she touched Erin's face and neck. She hoped to God Erin didn't notice.

"Now the breathing." She put her mouth near Erin's, and simulated the technique, turning her head to watch for the rise and fall of Erin's chest. She could see the faintest outline of Erin's nipples through the thin material of her T-shirt, and it made her pulse quicken and her mind go hazy for a moment.

She snapped back to what she was doing. "The victim is unresponsive," she said, her voice higher than usual. She put two fingers on Erin's neck near her windpipe, feeling for the carotid artery. Erin's pulse was strong, but a bit faster than normal. "No pulse. I'm starting compressions."

She positioned her right hand on Erin's chest below her breasts, feeling for the sternum, and used it to judge where to place her hands. Locking her elbows, she began simulating compressions, all the while trying to keep her mind on the task at hand.

Her former CPR training was certainly nothing like this. Despite her best efforts, she was getting aroused touching Erin.

It only got worse when they switched positions. Erin's lips, so close to hers, were a profound temptation. And having Erin's hands on her, however clinically, unleashed a growing pool of wetness between her legs.

"Okay, everyone had a turn?" Leslie asked. "Good. Now we want to practice two-rescuer CPR. Let's break up into threes so we have a patient for each team."

There weren't enough people to make it work out perfectly, so Tim joined Gable and Erin for the next part.

"I'll be the victim," Tim told the women, lying flat on the mat.

"I'll do breathing first, okay?" Erin looked at Gable.

"Sure." Gable positioned herself alongside Tim's chest to begin compressions.

Erin was trying to be entirely professional about the whole thing, and so was Tim, but Gable caught the shared shy smiles between them just before Erin leaned down to simulate mouth-to-mouth.

They switched places then, and when Erin put her hands on Tim's chest to begin compressions, Gable's overactive imagination found the whole maneuver entirely too erotic.

"Be right back." She excused herself and headed outside, where she leaned against the wall of the garage and tried to regain her composure. *You knew this wasn't going to be easy. You need to get a grip, girl. It's only going to get tougher and tougher.*

The door beside her opened and she half turned, expecting—hoping—to see Erin. But it was Carl.

"When did you get here?" she asked. "I didn't see you come in."

"Just a few minutes ago. Came in to pick up the training schedule. I'm going to work with Erin on the breathing apparatus next week. How's the CPR going?"

"Fine," she lied.

"Gable, what's going on with you?" Carl squinted at her in the dim light as if he was trying to read her expression.

She looked at the ground. "What do you mean? Nothing's going on with me."

"Okay, whatever you say. You know you can talk to me, right?"

"Nothing to talk about," she insisted, still avoiding his eyes.

"Whatever. I'm heading home. You have my number if you change your mind." He turned and headed toward his car.

If Carl can see so easily that something is bothering you, she wondered, *how long will it be before Erin picks up on it too and starts asking questions?*

CHAPTER SEVEN

Gable gritted her teeth and suffered through two more nights of first aid training with Erin and Tim looking increasingly cozy. They all sat together again both nights, so Gable had to listen to the two of them debate at length where they should eat and what movie they should see on their upcoming date.

And Erin, of course, picked Gable again as her partner for all the exercises, so Gable had the added torture of being able to touch her, but only in a clinical and detached way…splinting her arm and bandaging burns, immobilizing her neck and back. Then the tables were reversed and she had to try to remain relaxed and calm while Erin put her hands on her and did the same. *Can she tell how fast my heart beats when she's near?*

Gable couldn't wait to get out of there when the classes ended on Thursday evening. All she could think about was that the very next night, Tim and Erin would be alone together. Anything could happen, and probably would.

It was eating her up inside. Somehow, it sort of felt…*final*. Even though Erin was straight, Gable hoped and believed she occupied a special place in her heart. But she wasn't sure there'd be room in Erin's life for their friendship once she and Tim became an item.

Gable just wanted to go home and crawl into bed with a box of Russell Stover chocolates. Her cure for the blues. But Erin wouldn't let her charge out of there with a quick good-bye, intercepting her as she was getting in her Jeep.

"Hey, Gable!"

Gable rolled down the window and Erin put her hands on the sill and leaned down to talk to her.

"Are you all right? You were kind of quiet tonight."

"Sure. I'm fine. Just got a lot on my mind."

"Anything I can help with?"

"No. Thanks. Mostly work and family stuff." She hated lying, especially to Erin. But she couldn't admit the real reason she wasn't behaving like herself.

"Okay. Well, if you change your mind, you know I'm here for you." Erin smiled at her, such a sweet smile that Gable's heart ached all the more that this woman would always be out of reach.

"Thanks, Erin."

"Hey, I stopped you because I wanted to ask if I could get you to come over on Saturday and help me."

"Help you?"

"Yeah, they're supposed to deliver my new furniture that morning. I know I'll be wanting to move it around, see what works best." She leaned closer to Gable. "I'll fix you lunch if you say yes. Please?"

Gable couldn't refuse. She was secretly very pleased that Erin had asked her and not Tim. Even though it was getting more and more unbearable to be near Erin, she couldn't say no.

"Sure. What time?"

"Noon? They should have come and gone by then."

"Okay. See you then. And have fun tomorrow with Tim." She said the right things and forced herself to smile.

She went through half a box of Russell Stover that night. A new record.

Friday was one of the longest days ever. The pharmacy was aggravatingly slow all day, giving her far too much time to relive every moment she'd spent with Erin and think too much about the dreams that had been keeping her awake.

By evening she was pacing the floor like a nervous father whose daughter was on her first date. She tried to watch television, but nothing held her interest. And she was too keyed up to focus on a book. She settled for eating the other half of the box of chocolates, then tried to go to bed early so the night would pass more quickly.

It was all futile. Thoughts of Erin consumed her.

Saturday Gable awoke groggy from another restless night of erotic dreams and downed four cups of coffee on her porch, waiting impatiently for noon so she could head over to Erin's. She got so tired of staring at her watch that she decided to ride her bike so she could leave her house at eleven fifteen and work out some of her nervous energy.

You're a masochist, you know, she told herself forty minutes later as she pedaled over the rise that led down to Erin's place. *Why are you so anxious to hear about her date with Tim?*

Erin greeted her with her usual bright smile and pulled her into the cabin's great room by one arm. "I can't wait to see how everything's going to look once it's all put in place. Thanks for coming."

"Glad to help," Gable said.

The furniture that Erin had bought during their shopping expedition—bed, futon for the guest room, dresser, desk, bookcases, nightstands—lay scattered around the large space. The only thing missing was the piano, which she special ordered and would take weeks to arrive.

Gable couldn't stop herself. Wondering about Erin and Tim had kept her awake all night, after all. She could think of nothing else. "So how was your date?" She tried to keep her voice steady, but her blood was pounding in her ears.

"Nice," Erin said. "Tim's a very sweet man. Just like you said. We ended up going to that theater in Cadillac that has those classic movie festivals—you know the one I mean?"

"Uh-huh." Her stomach was tied up in knots.

"They're showing *The African Queen*, complete with original trailers and interviews with the actors and John Huston."

"That's a great movie."

"Yeah, Tim likes a lot of the same movies we do. They're showing a bunch of the Hepburn-Tracy movies next month. *Desk Set, Pat and*

Mike. Woman of the Year. We're going to go back."

"So…you hit it off, eh?" The knots in her stomach twisted tighter.

"Too soon to tell. He's a nice guy, and we have a lot in common. So we'll see where it goes." Erin smiled and shrugged. "I've not been real good at picking who to get serious about. It's made me pretty skittish, I guess."

"Well, I'm not one to talk, because I haven't had much success in that department, either." Gable spoke from her heart, knowing Erin wouldn't suspect what she really meant. She took a deep breath and let it out. "I can't say whether Tim is or isn't the right guy for you, but I do hope you find someone who really makes you happy."

"I hope the same for you, Gable. What about you? Ever come close to getting married?"

Erin was looking at her in a way that made Gable feel vulnerable and exposed. She was desperate to change the subject. "Nope. So… shall we get going? Where do you want to start?"

Erin looked around. "I thought we'd get the hardest stuff over with first, okay? Getting that dresser upstairs is going to be the worst, even with the drawers out. I probably should have had the delivery guys do it, but they were in a hurry and I thought we could probably handle everything ourselves."

Gable had good upper-body strength, but the dresser was solid oak and oversized, and getting it up the stairs might be a bit of a challenge. "Well, we can lean it on its side and slide it. It helps that the stairs are carpeted."

They got the drawers out and hefted it over to the bottom of the stairs in stages, moving it a few feet each time before resting. It was a heavy sonofabitch, even if it was a gorgeous piece of furniture.

"This is going in your room?" she asked, catching her breath before they tried to haul it up the steps.

"Yes. Other end of the hall," Erin was winded too, and Gable tried not to stare at the rapid rise and fall of her chest.

They leaned the dresser on its side on the stairway and Erin positioned herself on top, Gable on the bottom.

Gable got a firm hold on the dresser and bent her legs. "You ready?"

"Ready."

"Okay. On three. One…two…three!" Gable pushed upward with all her might, and Erin pulled, and the dresser rose…two steps, three, four. But Gable had to bear the weight of the piece with her legs and back while she repositioned herself to clear the final distance. It was awkward. Unwieldy. She put her all into it to push it up that last slight rise, and when she did, a muscle in her back snapped and burned, extended too far. She cried out in pain and collapsed where she was on the stairs.

"Oh God, Gable, what is it? Did you hurt yourself?" Erin scrambled down beside her.

"Pulled a muscle." She gritted her teeth. Her back burned as though someone had stuck her with a hot poker. "Not a big deal. I'll be fine in a minute." She slowly rolled her shoulder to try to work out the pain.

Erin got behind her and began to massage the area with her fingers. "Here?"

"Ow!"

Erin gentled her touch. "That sounds bad. Maybe you should see a doctor?"

Gable shook her head. "I'll be all right. Just need to put some heat on it and rest, I think."

"Come on, lie down on the couch. We can do all this moving another day." Erin helped her to her feet and led her toward the couch. "Try to relax. I'm going to take care of you," she said once Gable was lying as comfortably as possible.

"I can make it home to my own bed," Gable protested.

"Nonsense. You hurt yourself trying to help me. The least I can do is try to make you feel better. And besides, you rode your bike over. I'll be right back." Erin disappeared up the stairs, then returned a couple of minutes later. "Come on up and sit in the whirlpool for a while. It'll help loosen up those muscles some. And then I'm going to give you a massage."

Gable's breath caught in her throat. *A massage?* "Uh…uh, that's not necessary." She felt almost faint at the thought of Erin's hands on her. "I don't want to put you out."

"Don't be silly." Erin laughed. "I want to. Come on." She helped Gable to her feet and led her up the stairs and to the bathroom, where the tub was already filling.

There was a light scent in the air—lavender, maybe, Gable thought. The room was lit by candles, and soft classical music played from a boom box near the tub. It was so romantic that she forgot completely for a moment about her sore back. She couldn't stop staring at Erin. Lit by candlelight, she was mesmerizing. Gable felt a rush of heat between her legs.

"There's a robe behind the door," Erin said. "When the tub is full, here's where you start the jets." She pointed to the controls and glanced at Gable, but Gable looked away, afraid her desires were all too apparent.

Erin crossed to the door. "Take your time," she said softly, as she closed the door between them.

The hot water and powerful jets did Gable's muscles a world of good, and she lingered there a long while, thinking about Erin and trying to regain her equilibrium. It wasn't easy.

In a few minutes, Erin would be touching her, and Gable would be doing all she could to act as if it was nothing at all but a therapeutic, friendly gesture. She wasn't sure she could handle it. Just imagining it made her incredibly hot. She closed her eyes, and Dream Erin appeared in naughty lingerie. Tempting her. Teasing her. It was too much.

She turned her body so that one of the powerful jets shot its pulsating spray right where she needed it. Her hand followed to finish the job. She couldn't stop herself. She thought it would help ease the building pressure in her loins. But it was as unsatisfying as her dreams.

She emerged sheepishly from the bathroom, suspecting that what she'd just been doing would be obvious.

But Erin gave no sign to suggest that was true. "Go on in and lie down." She gestured toward the guest bedroom, a few steps away. "Off with the robe, and under the covers. I'll get the boom box."

Pausing at the threshold, Gable felt a sense of déjà vu sweep over her. Candles lit this room too, casting it in a soft buttery glow, and the bedcovers on the futon bed had been neatly pulled back. Inviting. Exactly like the setting of her dreams. She was suddenly weak in the knees again. Worse, she felt a gentle push against her back.

"Go on," Erin urged. "I won't hurt you, I promise."

Gable turned to Erin to protest. She couldn't do this. She'd never survive it. But when she looked at Erin, only inches away…When she saw Erin's sweet smile, she caved. She could deny Erin nothing. She nodded dumbly and started for the bed.

Erin thoughtfully turned her back, busying herself with plugging in the boom box while Gable stripped off the robe and slipped under the covers. The sheets were cool against her heated skin, and she welcomed the slight shock to her system. She felt as though she would burst into flame at any moment.

She lay down on her stomach, her arms cradling the soft down pillow Erin had thoughtfully provided for her head. She tried to calm her racing heart, but when she looked up at Erin, it only began beating faster.

How is it, she wondered, *that you look even more enticing every day?*

Erin was dressed in faded jeans and a long-sleeve T-shirt. The sleeves had been pushed up, because she was evidently going to use that bottle of baby oil she had in her hand. She squirted some into a warming ramekin, like the kind you get butter in when you order lobster in a restaurant, and lit the candle beneath it.

Gable stared at Erin's hands as she rubbed them together to warm them. She had imagined those small, delicate hands on her many times, just not quite like this. She willed herself to be strong. But as soon as Erin touched her, massaging the warm oil into her back and shoulders in long, liquid strokes and circles, a soft moan escaped her lips. She couldn't help it.

"So you like that, eh?" Erin leaned over to whisper softly in her ear, with what was surely one of the most seductive tones Gable had ever heard.

"Mmm-hmm. Very much," was all she could manage. It was hard to keep her voice even. "You have great hands." It came out before she realized what she was saying, but Erin clearly wasn't offended.

"Glad you think so. You should learn not to fight me when I want my own way."

"I'll try to remember that," Gable croaked.

"Now relax," Erin encouraged. "This where it hurts?" She found the sore muscle and began working it gently.

"That's it."

After a few minutes, Erin began pressing more firmly, working the muscle until it relaxed. "Better?"

"Much. That feels wonderful."

Erin didn't stop there, and Gable could not encourage her to. Once the pain was gone, she felt only a growing arousal.

Her skin was hypersensitive everywhere that Erin touched her. She could feel the moisture building between her legs.

Erin pulled the blanket back farther, to massage Gable's lower back.

Fingers danced enticingly along the very top of Gable's ass, and she bit her lip to stifle a groan. *God help me.*

Erin's hands worked their way along her sides, fingertips barely touching the soft swell of her breasts where they lay pressed against the sheets.

Another soft moan escaped her lips. She prayed Erin hadn't heard it.

It was forty-five minutes of sheer, sweet torture. Finally Erin pulled the blankets back up, and rested her hands momentarily on Gable's shoulders. "All done. Don't move for a minute. I'll get your clothes."

Somehow she spoke. "Thank you, Erin."

"Any time. Be right back."

Gable closed her eyes and took deep breaths, savoring the last moments of a most memorable massage.

Erin came back with her clothes, neatly folded, and set them on the edge of the bed. "Take your time getting up," she said in a soft voice. "Slowly—so you don't pull anything again."

Gable swore she felt the lightest touch of Erin's hands through her hair. But then she heard the door close, and she was alone again.

When she pulled back the blankets and reached for the clothes, she could smell the heady scent of her arousal, thick in the air. *Uh-oh.* She was suddenly very glad they'd done this in Erin's guest room, and not in the bed Erin slept in.

Erin fussed over her the rest of the afternoon and into the evening. She got Gable comfortably ensconced on the couch and waited on her hand and foot, fetching drinks, a lap robe, and pillows for her back. While Gable surfed through TV channels, luxuriating in the unaccustomed pampering, Erin fixed them both a nice supper, topped off with a homemade cherry pie. Finally, at nine thirty, when Gable reluctantly announced she should be heading home, Erin insisted on driving her, hoisting Gable's bike into the back of the red pickup.

"Are you sure you can manage everything all right?" she asked later when they pulled up in front of Gable's. "I can stay if you want me to."

An offer Gable nobly ignored. "I'll be fine," she said. "My back's feeling a lot better."

They got out and Erin hefted the bike out of the truck and wheeled it onto the porch, Gable falling into step beside her. "I want you to rest tomorrow. All day! No heavy lifting! And if you need anything, call me."

"I will," Gable promised.

"So do you think you'll be able to go to the picnic Monday?"

"Oh sure. I'll probably have to sit out some of the events, but I can certainly pitch in with the food and stuff."

"I'd hate for you to miss it because you got hurt helping me out," Erin said.

"Would you stop apologizing already?"

They were face-to-face on the porch, lingering outside the door, as if both were reluctant to part company.

"Well, I better let you get inside and get some sleep," Erin said, taking a step to plant a quick peck on Gable's cheek. "Sorry you hurt your back. Sleep well. And do call me if you need anything at all."

Gable nodded, relishing the unexpected, brief caress of Erin's lips and the way it had seemed to warm her from within. "Drive safe, and I'll see you Monday."

Despite her sleep deprivation of late, Gable still had trouble dozing off that night. She lay awake for hours, staring at the ceiling. The massage had helped a lot, but her back was still bothering her and she couldn't get comfortable. It didn't help any that she couldn't stop thinking about the way Erin touched her—delicate hands caressing her face, her stomach, her ass. Her imagination was fueled by the massage. Now she had intimate knowledge of how it felt to have Erin really touch her.

She managed to doze off finally at two a.m., and so was still asleep at nine when loud knocking at her front door awakened her. *Erin!* her hazy mind wished, still seduced by her dreams. Throwing on a robe, she stumbled to the door and threw the bolt.

Her brother Stewart stood there holding a cardboard tray with two large Styrofoam cups and a paper bag.

"Morning," he said, grinning as he pushed by her and headed to the kitchen. "I brought bagels. Baked this morning. I know you can't get them up here. And you look like shit, by the way."

"What are you doing here, Stewart?"

"I've been trying to call you for a week, and you're never home." He sat at the table and took the bagels and cream cheese out of the bag. "I thought I might have acted a bit…well, insensitive when you called me."

Gable got plates and knives and sat opposite him. "I check my machine every day. I haven't had any messages from you." Stewart passed her one of the coffees. "And I just got out of bed, how do you expect me to look?"

"Like you got some sleep. Which I seriously doubt from the look of those impressive bags under your eyes. And I never left a message. I wanted to talk to you."

"What about? Has something happened?"

"That's what I want to know. What's happening with Erin?"

"You drove all the way up here to ask me that?"

"No. Yes. Well, I came up to see how you were doing. I hadn't heard from you for a few days, and I knew you were having a hard time. Just wanted to see if you needed a shoulder to cry on or wanted to bend my ear for a while. I won't make fun of your feelings this time, I promise."

"That's very sweet. But I can handle this."

"So you say. Then why aren't you sleeping?"

"Who said I'm not sleeping?"

He gave her a look she knew well, that told her he didn't believe a word she was saying.

"All right. So it's taking me a while to get okay with this. It's gotten a little more complicated." Gable sipped her coffee. "Erin is dating a guy at the fire station."

Stewart gave her a sympathetic frown. "Sorry, honey. I know that must be tough, seeing her with somebody else."

"Not just tough. Almost impossible." She leaned back in her chair and ran her hand through her hair. "Tomorrow is the big picnic at the firehouse. I just know it's going to be more of the same. Erin and Tim will both be there." She let out a big sigh. "I keep thinking I should put some distance between us for a while. I just can't seem to get over feeling the way I do when I'm around her so much. It's only making it harder. Maybe with some time apart we can just be friends and I can handle that."

"Have you got any time off coming? I can take a few days and we can go camping or kayaking or something."

Gable shook her head. "I used it up when I went down to see you after the tornadoes. And I probably shouldn't be doing anything too strenuous. I pulled a muscle in my back yesterday." She stretched, testing it. Still sore, but better. "Getting away isn't a bad idea, though. Maybe we can go somewhere next weekend?"

"Cool. Just let me know," Stewart said. He leaned across the table and put his hand on her arm. "You just have to give it time, sis. And try to keep your mind occupied. That's the best remedy I know."

Stewart did his best to help her do just that until he left for home early that evening. They spent the day together, hanging out and watching TV, and he kept up an endless chatter about family and work in an effort to keep her mind distracted. None of it really helped much. Erin invaded her thoughts at every turn. Gable felt powerless to stop the constant flurry of images and sensations from the massage the night before: Erin's fingers skimming along the edge of her breasts, the top of her ass. The way she looked in the soft amber glow of the candlelight.

Gable knew she had to try to bury her attraction for Erin if she was to ever keep her as a friend. But her mind and body simply refused to obey. Erin made her feel *alive*. How could she willingly give that up?

CHAPTER EIGHT

The Fourth of July picnic at the Plainfield Township Fire Station was one of the major community events of the summer, drawing in hundreds of locals from the surrounding area and a good number of holiday tourists. They came largely for the food—a massive outdoor barbecue of chicken and burgers and hot dogs, accompanied by several tables of salads, side dishes, and desserts, provided by the firefighters and their families and friends. There were also the usual family-style games—piñatas, a three-legged race, water-balloon toss, tug-of-war—with blue ribbons and bragging rights going to the winners. The finale was a fireworks display, the biggest one for several miles around.

It was a fun day for all and a worthwhile event for the firehouse, which used the proceeds to purchase firefighting equipment, as well as smoke detectors for low-income and elderly residents.

The year before, Gable had been a brand-new rookie with the department, which had guaranteed that she'd be drafted for every event and introduced to half the surrounding populace. This year, she knew, it would be Erin's turn.

The day started out pleasantly enough. Gable had originally been tapped to help set up the hose and ladder demonstrations that would later entertain the gathering, but the chief reassigned her to the food area when she confessed that she'd hurt her back. It just so happened that Erin was assigned there as well, so they worked side by side the first couple of hours, dishing out food and helping senior citizens and small children carry their plates to their tables.

She wasn't crazy about the way that a few of the single guys looked at Erin as they went through the food line, but for the most part, she enjoyed watching her interact with the steady stream of visitors. She envied the way Erin could engage nearly anyone in easy conversation, especially the kids from her school.

"Lee, is that you?" Erin feigned wide-eyed wonder as she greeted a fair-haired young man of about eleven. "I hardly recognized you, you've shot up so much since school ended! If you don't watch out, you'll be taller than I am by September!"

The boy blushed, and Gable could see how delighted he was with the comment. *Bet you have a crush on her too. Who doesn't?*

"I can't believe how big this event is," Erin said, plopping down onto a folding chair beside Gable to catch her breath during a rare lull at the food tables. "I didn't think there were this many people in the entire county."

"The chief says it gets bigger every year. This time the proceeds are going toward a new pumper."

"Well, I was hoping to get to spend some quality time with you today," Erin said, looking right at Gable with such a sweet grin that her heart turned to mush. "But we've hardly had a chance to breathe, let alone get a chance to chat."

"Should get easier now, since most everyone has eaten and the games will be starting soon. We'll just get the stragglers and the teenaged boys who never seem to stop eating." *And who keep coming by for another look at you*, Gable thought, admiring the way Erin's tank top and denim shorts showed off vast expanses of smooth, inviting skin. Her eyes lingered on the hint of cleavage she could see. *No one would ever guess you were thirty-nine.*

And Erin's appeal went far beyond her youthful face and figure. It was in the warm and familiar way she interacted with the people she met, extending an arm to steady a frail senior citizen, hugging one of the teachers she worked with in greeting. *She's much more physically demonstrative than I am.*

Gable recalled Erin's frequent hugs good-bye and last night's peck on the cheek. *I wonder what makes some people more touchy-feely than others.* She certainly enjoyed being the recipient of Erin's tactile hellos and good-byes, though each made her mourn its brevity.

"I still feel so bad that you hurt your back," Erin said. "Frankly, I was counting on you to be my partner in the three-legged race. I thought we'd make a great team."

The thought of being tied to Erin, their arms around each other, brought a flush to Gable's cheeks. "My back really is feeling a lot better, but I probably *should* play it safe today."

The chief silenced the gathering with an announcement on the bullhorn. "We're ready to start the games, everyone. Pick a partner and line up for the wheelbarrow race!"

Gable turned to Erin, reconsidering her negative response, but before she had a chance to speak, Tim appeared with an outstretched hand.

"What do you say, Erin?" he said. "It's tradition—the rookie has to be in every event."

Erin glanced at Gable, who gloomily confirmed, "I had to do the whole lot last year."

"Well, all right, then. I hate to break a time-honored tradition." Erin allowed Tim to lead her away, with a backward glance at Gable that looked like genuine regret.

Nah. Couldn't be.

Erin and Tim didn't make it even halfway to the finish line. First they tried using Tim as the wheelbarrow, but Erin couldn't support his weight for long so they switched positions, with only marginally better results. Though Erin had good upper-body strength, she kept collapsing in laughter, and they gave up after several efforts, along with a half dozen other laughing pairs of contestants.

Gable brooded from behind her sunglasses, oblivious to everything but the way Tim looked at Erin and the way that he was making her laugh.

Once the ribbons were handed out for the event, the chief announced that next up was the water-balloon toss.

To Gable's surprise, Erin trotted back to the food tables as pairs of combatants began lining up.

"C'mon, you can do this one with me," she urged. "I think those Jell-o salads can watch themselves for a minute or two."

Uncommonly pleased that Erin had ditched Tim for her, Gable followed her to the double row of paired contestants, and they faced each other, grinning, a scant ten feet apart for the first toss. Gable was handed a filled red water balloon, slightly bigger than a softball, the elastic stretched taut.

"Ready?" she asked.

"Ready."

Gable gently tossed the balloon underhand the few feet that separated them. Erin caught it without difficulty, as did all the other contestants on either side of them. They moved ten feet farther apart, and repeated the process, with Erin successfully tossing the red balloon back to Gable. Four other couples weren't so lucky and were eliminated when their balloons broke.

Next they moved to twenty-five feet apart, a distance which eliminated more than a dozen other pairs of contestants. But Erin gently scooped the balloon into her outstretched arms, and they advanced to thirty feet.

"Great catch!" Gable encouraged, seeing there were only four other couples left.

Thirty feet looked incredibly far, but as they set up for the toss, Erin gave her a grin and a wink of reassurance. The balloon sailed through the air, and Gable cradled it like a baby, breaking its fall with her large hands, and suddenly they were one of only two pairs still in the contest. The other was a duet of tall teenaged boys Gable recognized. They were fraternal twins, and the stars of the local high school basketball team.

"Nice hands there, Gable," Erin hollered. "We can do this!"

They moved another five feet apart, a seemingly impossible distance, and the crowd began to cheer on their favorites.

"Okay, Gable, put it right here." Erin cupped her hands in front of her chest.

Gable was distracted by the cleavage displayed just above those wonderfully delicate hands, and perhaps that was the reason she tossed the balloon a tiny bit too hard. It burst with an impressive splash, dousing Erin's tank top. Erin gasped in surprise at the cold soaking, failing to notice that her top was now clinging to her, outlining her breasts and her suddenly rigid nipples. Gable, on the other hand, couldn't pry her eyes from the sight until Tim came up behind her and slapped her on the back.

"Aw. You almost had it there, you two. What a shame," he commiserated.

Erin finally noticed that Tim and several of the other men standing around them were staring at her, and she glanced down and saw why. "Oh my." She crossed her arms over her chest as color blossomed in her cheeks. "I think I better go and try to dry off some."

"Here, take this," Gable slipped off the long-sleeved denim shirt she had on over her T-shirt and offered it to her.

"You're always saving me, aren't you?" Erin said as she took the shirt with a smile and headed off toward the restrooms.

"Dang," Tim whispered under his breath as they both watched Erin leave. He turned to Gable and grumped, "Spoilsport."

Despite herself, Gable had to laugh.

Things went steadily downhill after that.

When Erin emerged from the firehouse wearing Gable's shirt, she was immediately intercepted by Jerry DeYoung and led off toward the next event—the tug-of-war, which pitted the volunteer firefighters against men and women from the community they served.

Gable knew it was another event she'd better pass on, so she returned to the food tables to watch.

The thick rope was stretched over a muddy trench, six feet wide, which separated the two sides. Erin, as the rookie, was given the spot on the rope nearest the trench. If the firefighters lost, she'd be the first one to get filthy, just as Gable had been the year before.

It was a slightly closer contest this time, despite the fact that the townspeople had drafted the same two big bricklayers who routinely anchored their team to victory. It lasted a full three minutes before the firefighters began slipping slowly but surely ever closer to the mud pit. Erin dug in her heels all the way, the strain showing on her face, but when the inevitable happened and she was pulled into the quagmire, she took it with the same good humor with which she seemed to take everything.

After the tug-of-war came three events for the kids—the watermelon seed–spitting contest, the egg-in-spoon race, and the piñatas—one for the little kids, and one for the older ones. Gable was hoping that Erin might come over and watch with her, but she had obviously been corralled by the four men who were now crowded around her, vying for her attention—Tim Scott, Jerry DeYoung, and two others Gable didn't recognize. Every now and then, she glanced through the crowd in Gable's direction, but she seemed to be having fun if her smiles were anything to go by.

I should go home, Gable thought, her mood darkening further when a fifth admirer joined the group around Erin. She didn't know his name, but she recognized the rather attractive fifty-ish bachelor as the proprietor of the Pine River Lumberyard, where she shopped on occasion. *He's got money*, she thought, recalling the gossip when the village's first Hummer had appeared on Main Street.

The chief announced it was time for the three-legged race, and Gable could see from a distance that Tim had somehow won the animated five-way discussion over who would get to be Erin's partner.

They lined up side by side at the edge of the field near the food area. Gable had a perfect view. She felt a sudden twitch of jealously as she watched Tim curl his arm around Erin's shoulder, and it grew into a gnawing ache in the pit of her gut when Erin's hand snaked around Tim's waist. She frowned, holding back tears that sprang from nowhere.

"On your mark..." the chief hollered through the bullhorn.

Erin looked directly at Gable.

"Get set..."

The smile on Erin's face evaporated as she registered that Gable didn't look quite right.

"Go!"

Erin stumbled briefly as Tim lurched their joined legs forward, but her attention snapped back to the race and they quickly joined the other competitors dashing toward the other end of the field. Couples tripped and fell, but Tim and Erin had a steady, smooth rhythm going that edged them just ahead of the others. The firefighters in the crowd roared approval as the couple lunged toward the finish line and collapsed in a laughing heap of arms and legs on the other side.

Gable didn't have a great view when Erin and Tim got their blue ribbons—they were too far away for her to read their expressions. But she was seeing much more than she wanted to, anyway. After the ribbons were handed out, Tim scooped Erin up in his arms and twirled her around, then planted a big kiss on her to the cheers of the crowd.

Why are you torturing yourself? Gable decided it was time to leave. She would be in no mood for fireworks tonight.

That night, she stared at the ceiling for a long while, unable to sleep. Seeing Erin with others was killing her. She needed some distance. Maybe she should avoid her for a while. The prospect only made her feel even worse.

❖

When she got home from work the next night, Gable found a message from Erin on her answering machine.

"Hi, Gable! Sorry I didn't get a chance to say good-bye yesterday, hope everything is okay. I know you're not home yet, but I wanted to call and invite you over for dinner. Nothing fancy. Just lasagna and garlic bread. And I promise I won't make you move furniture! Tim helped me, so it's all done. Call me."

Tim was at her house. Helping her move her bed into her bedroom. Gable could picture it with all-too-vivid clarity. The two of them together, getting more and more comfortable with each other. *Did he kiss you some more? With all that privacy, did he make a move?* That thought led her mind to a dangerous place. She closed her eyes and imagined what it would be like to kiss Erin, to feel those soft lips beneath hers. It would be wonderful, she had no doubt. An ache blossomed in her chest with the realization it could never be.

Gable debated with herself a full ten minutes on whether to return the call at all, but her ingrained sense of common courtesy wouldn't allow her to ignore it. So she had to call. And she would have to lie. She hated that part. But there was no alternative. *Distance, remember? You can't see her. It will only drive you crazy.* Maybe she'd wait a couple of hours, so Erin couldn't talk her into coming over. *You can say you stayed to have dinner in Meriwether with some people from work.*

The phone rang a half hour later as she was munching on a tuna sandwich. She let the machine get it. "Hi again, it's Erin. Thought you'd be home by now, and maybe just missed my message. Anyway, call me!"

Gable felt like a heel. Her appetite gone, she tossed the remainder of her sandwich out the door for some lucky raccoon or possum to find. *It's all for the best. You can't go on like this.* But she was unable to convince herself it was the right thing to do. She was deliberately hurting Erin, and there was no way she could feel good about that.

She forced herself to wait two hours before calling Erin back. *Keep it short and sweet.* Her hands trembled slightly as she dialed the number she had memorized. She had actually rehearsed what she would say, afraid her voice would betray her, afraid Erin could tell she was lying.

After they exchanged hellos, she said, "Sorry, I just got home and got your message. I stayed to have dinner with some friends from work."

"No problem. I kind of figured you must have done something like that. It's okay, it was a spur-of-the-moment thing anyway."

"I appreciate the invitation."

"How about tomorrow?"

Gable hadn't foreseen this possibility.

"Come to dinner tomorrow," Erin blithely continued. "I have tons of lasagna left, and it's always better the second day anyway."

No excuse at the ready, Gable stammered. "Uh...well...Let me think...oh, wait! I promised one of the women I work with that I'd help her with something tomorrow when we got off. I'm not sure what time I'll be home. Maybe late." *Brilliant. Just brilliant.* It sounded like such a terribly lame excuse that Gable was certain Erin would see right through it. But if she did, she gave no indication.

"Oh, well, that's all right. How about Thursday?"

Shit. Shit. Shit. "Sorry, I've got plans on Thursday." *Now she knows I'm lying.* Gable didn't even try to come up with a reasonable excuse. She just wanted to get off the phone.

"Oh. Okay."

She heard the hurt in Erin's voice and hated herself for causing it. "Look, I've gotta run," she said. "I'll talk to you soon, okay?" *But not too soon.*

"Sure. Good night, Gable. Sleep well."

Being apart from Erin didn't work. If anything, it was worse. She had a powerful imagination, and it worked overtime wondering how much time Erin was spending with Tim and what they were up to.

Erin hadn't called her again all week, and Gable wondered whether she'd put so much distance between them that their budding friendship would be irrevocably harmed.

On Friday morning as she fixed herself breakfast, she glanced at Erin's training schedule, tacked up on the refrigerator door. Erin had a session with Tim from two to five that afternoon to go over portable extinguishers and fire inspection practices. *They get off at five. It's natural they'd go out to dinner somewhere after. Then maybe a movie. And back to her place. That's what I'd do.*

There was a message on Gable's machine when she got home from work shortly after six that night. Her heart skipped a beat when she saw the red number one on the digital display. Maybe she'd been wrong, and it was Erin calling.

Much as she feared having to make more excuses, she missed hearing Erin's voice. She pressed the button and held her breath.

"Hi, sis. Just calling to confirm I'll pick you up at nine." Stewart's voice. "I've got all the camping gear we need. Just bring your clothes and fishing gear and we can catch breakfast on the way up to the bridge."

They were going to spend Saturday fishing on a lake Stewart knew near Saint Ignace. Then on Sunday they would take the ferry to Mackinac Island and poke around the fort and the fudge shops before heading home.

On any other occasion, Gable would have looked forward to spending some time with her brother. They always had a blast when they went fishing together. But all she could think about was how far away she'd be from Erin. She stared at the answering machine, wishing she hadn't erased Erin's messages, so she could play them again.

There was a knock at the door.

It's her. Gable knew it was. She wasn't sure how she knew. But she was certain of it. Her resolve flew out the window and she couldn't get the door unlatched fast enough.

"Hi." Erin had a look of uncertainty on her face, as though expecting to be turned away. She held a large paper grocery bag in her arms.

Gable wanted to hug her, she was so happy to see her again. She managed to restrain herself, but she couldn't stop grinning like an idiot. "Come on in, I just got home."

Erin's uncertainty dissipated and she smiled back at Gable as she crossed the threshold. "I took a chance and brought you dinner."

"You shouldn't have done that."

Erin had started toward the kitchen but she froze at Gable's words and looked at her. The smile disappeared. "Why? Do you have plans?" *I don't want to hurt you anymore. And I don't think I can lie to your face.* "Nope. No plans. I only meant you shouldn't have gone to all this trouble."

Erin's face brightened. "No trouble. I missed you!" She continued on to the kitchen. "Go on and change," she called out over her shoulder, "and I'll get dinner started."

"God, I missed you too," Gable whispered, watching her go.

She decided then and there that it was useless to try to distance herself from Erin. It would do nothing to change the way she felt about her. It would only hurt Erin, and that was simply unacceptable.

Gable couldn't decide what to change into for dinner. She'd tried on half her wardrobe. *In my own home, for Pete's sake. And for what is probably a hamburger and fries from a fast-food joint.* She'd paid no attention to the bag Erin had been carrying, having been too busy admiring how well Erin's rust-colored blouse complemented the color of her hair. Not to mention how nicely it hugged every contour of that beautiful body.

Gable herself would never wear a form-fitting blouse or a tank top like Erin had worn at the picnic. But Erin was more comfortable with her body than she was—that was obvious not only in what she wore, but in the way she carried herself. *She certainly wasn't self-conscious when she was trying on clothes.*

Gable closed her eyes and swallowed hard, remembering the way the dressing room mirror had gifted her with three Erins, in cream satin bra and panties, all smiling at her. *Oh yeah.*

There was a soft knock at her bedroom door. "Gable? Everything's ready."

"Be right there." The navy button-down shirt and faded jeans would have to do. Gable ran her hands through her hair, took a deep breath, and steeled herself for an evening of impossible temptation.

It was immediately apparent it was going to be far worse than she imagined. A spicy aroma filled her nostrils as soon as she opened the door. She couldn't identify it, but it sure as hell wasn't burgers and fries.

Erin had set the round oak table with Gable's best plates and china. Two wineglasses held a burgundy liquid. Merlot, she guessed. They had discussed their favorite wines the night of the tornado. Daisies overflowed a petite crystal vase that Erin had tracked down from under the sink. Brass candlesticks taken from the mantel had new red tapers in them, which cast the table in a soft, hazy light.

Erin sat waiting for her. Watching her. Smiling at her.

You look so wonderful by candlelight. Gable wanted to freeze that moment in her mind's eye, so she could replay it over and over. It would be fodder for dreams to come, she was certain. There was such joy in Erin's face, and such open affection...*and she looks so damn irresistible*...that Gable—just for a moment—considered telling her everything.

Her indecision must have been written on her face, for Erin's smile faded.

"Gable? Is something wrong?"

She pasted a smile on her face. "No, not at all. I'm just surprised. You really shouldn't have gone to all this trouble."

"It's not much. Come sit."

Gable took a chair next to Erin and watched her ladle up two big bowls of chili, thick with chunks of tomato and beef and garnished with cheddar cheese and red onions. Her breadbasket was filled with slices of a crusty French baguette, and there was a small mixed-greens salad with mandarin orange segments and glazed almonds, dressed in a sweet-and-sour vinaigrette.

"This is quite a spread," Gable said.

"I just warmed up some chili I made last night," Erin said. "It's better the second day too." She smiled as she said it, but she looked at Gable as if hoping she would comment on the reference; would somehow explain why she was so busy she couldn't see her all week. It wasn't a hard push, more of a nudge, but it was a sure sign that Erin knew she wasn't hearing the whole story.

Gable dug into the chili, grateful for the distraction. She didn't know what to say.

Erin wasn't going to let it go. Her voice was subdued. "Gable, did I do or say something to upset you?"

Gable took a sip of wine and tried to show no reaction at all to the question. "No, why would you say that?" *Just because I've been acting like a total basket case since the first time I laid eyes on you?*

"I thought maybe you were avoiding me."

"No, I..." Gable cleared her throat, buying time to try to think up an excuse that wasn't really a lie. "I've had a lot going on, that's all. A lot on my mind."

"Anything I can do? Would it help to talk about it?"

"Not really. But thanks for asking."

"I'm not just saying that, you know," Erin pressed. She put down her fork and reached across the table to place one hand loosely on Gable's forearm. "You've done so much for me. Been such a good friend. Not only the night of the tornado, although that was certainly a hell of a how-do-you-do." She looked into Gable's eyes and smiled. "I want to be there for you every bit as much as you've been there for me. You can tell me anything, you know. Anything. I'm a good listener."

"Thanks, Erin," Gable managed, too acutely aware of the small, soft hand on her arm. "I know you mean that, and I'll keep it in mind."

"Good. I hope you do." Erin withdrew her hand and resumed eating with a more relaxed demeanor, apparently satisfied with the exchange.

"So how has your training been going?" Gable didn't want to come right out and ask about Tim. A part of her didn't want to hear explicit details about how their relationship was going. But another part couldn't stand *not* to know, either.

"Real good. I think I'm catching on okay. I was supposed to get my gear this week, but everything they had was too big. The chief had to special order it."

"I'm not surprised. You're such a tiny thing."

"I hope I can do my part when the time comes."

"You will. Don't worry." Gable reached for another slice of baguette. "So what did you learn this week?"

"Well, let's see. I did forcible entries with Chief Thornton and Jerry. That was fun. Yesterday Cliff showed me where everything was on the trucks. Today was portable extinguishers and fire inspection practices with Tim. Pretty boring, actually. I'm looking forward to the physical stuff—the ladder drills, seeing what it's like to work with the hoses."

Gable nodded. *Don't do it. Don't. It'll just eat you up.* She shoved aside her better judgment. "Have you been out with Tim again?" She said it as off the cuff as she could, but she held her breath waiting for the answer.

"Yeah, we went to dinner Wednesday. Just to that pizza place in Pine River. It was nice." Erin shrugged noncommittally. "He's going to come over next week and help me put a fence up so I can have a garden next year."

Gable poured herself a second glass of wine. She held the bottle over Erin's nearly empty goblet. "Care for some more?"

"Please."

When the glasses were full again, Erin raised hers for a toast. Gable clued in and hoisted hers as well.

"To you and to us. To a very special friendship. Thank you for being there for me."

"To our friendship," Gable agreed.

As they clinked glasses, Gable reaffirmed her decision to remain close to Erin regardless of how painful it was for her at times. Erin was absolutely right. They were developing a rare friendship, a special blessing in their lives, and she would do whatever she had to, to preserve it.

They chatted about mundane things as they washed and dried the dishes, regaining the easy familiarity that had seen them through the long night of the twister. Erin didn't mention Tim again, and neither did Gable.

As Erin dried her hands on the dishtowel, she glanced at the clock on the stove. "You know, *Gone with the Wind* is on TV tonight. I haven't seen it in ages." She looked at Gable with hopeful expectation.

"I haven't either."

"Starts in ten minutes."

"Better go warm up the TV while I make us some popcorn, then."

Erin shot Gable a big grin and threw the towel at her before heading off toward the living room. She pivoted on her heels at the doorway. "Hey, it doesn't end until midnight. Mind if I stay over? We can have a slumber party!"

Oh God. "Sure," Gable muttered, turning away toward the pantry so that Erin wouldn't see the blush coloring her cheeks. *And what kind of dreams will you have tonight with her in the next room?*

She remembered then that Stewart was picking her up in the morning, and picked up the phone on the kitchen wall.

Stewart answered on the second ring.

"Hey, bro," Gable greeted him as she stuck a bag of popcorn in the microwave. "Would you be pissed off if we did our weekend getaway another time?"

"No, of course not. Did something come up? Are you okay?"

"I'm fine. Erin showed up with dinner kind of out of the blue, and we're going to watch a movie that runs late."

"Ah. Erin, eh? How are you doing with that?"

"I'm dealing with it. You know what they say. What doesn't kill you makes you stronger."

"I hate to see you unhappy, Gable."

"I'm not unhappy. Actually, I'm the happiest I've ever been, when I'm around her. It's just very frustrating too." She kept her voice low, and shot a glance into the living room to make sure Erin couldn't hear her. She had settled onto the couch and was flipping through channels on the TV.

"Call me if you need to talk," her brother said. "Love you."

"I will. Thanks, Stewart."

Except for the fact that she wanted to reach out and touch Erin all night but couldn't, Gable had a great time. They shared popcorn out of a big bowl, sitting side by side on the couch, exchanging trivia about the movie and reciting their favorite lines along with the characters.

She was not at all tired when Rhett told Scarlett he frankly didn't give a damn, but Erin was fading fast.

"Come on, to the guest room with you, sleepyhead." Gable got to her feet and extended a hand. Erin took it, and Gable pulled her up.

She felt so light, a slightly firmer tug would have brought their bodies together. The very thought of it made Gable take a step back, letting go reluctantly, memorizing the warmth of Erin's hand in hers.

She led the way to the spare bedroom and turned down the coverlet. "Would you like a big T-shirt or something to sleep in?"

Erin yawned and stretched. "Nah, that's okay. I'm fine. Just don't be shocked if I meet you coming out of the bathroom in the middle of the night. I sleep in the buff. Can't stand pajamas."

Oh. Shit. There goes any chance at all of my getting any sleep tonight. "Uh...all right, then. Sleep well, and I'll see you in the morning. Let me know if you need anything."

"I will. Thanks."

As Gable turned to go Erin's voice caught her at the doorway. "Gable?"

"Yeah?"

"I had a good time tonight. I have more fun with you than anyone."

"Me too. Thanks for coming over."

Gable finally did doze off, but slept fitfully, awakening at every tiny sound, imagining it was Erin. Around three a.m. when she awoke, she realized it really *was* Erin this time; the water was running in the bathroom between the two bedrooms. Gable couldn't help herself. She slipped out of bed and went to the door and opened it an inch, as quietly as she could.

She had put a nightlight in the guest room to ease Erin's fear of the dark, and plugged another into an outlet in the hall so Erin could find her way to the bathroom. The latter gave Gable enough light to get a real good look at Erin's incredible body as she stumbled back to bed.

There would be no more sleeping after that.

Gable got up at six, threw on a robe, and made a pot of coffee to wake herself up. She was channel surfing with the volume turned down when her emergency radio blared the signal for a callout. She was on the first-response team.

Gable jotted down the address and hustled to her bedroom, running headlong into Erin in the hallway.

"Was that your radio?" Erin had dressed hurriedly; her blouse wasn't buttoned right.

"Yeah, a house fire. Not far from here." Gable continued to her bedroom without further elaboration, threw on her clothes, and was back in the living room in seconds.

Erin had her shoes on and was waiting by the door. "I'm coming with you. I may not be able to help much yet, but I want to go."

"Okay." There was no time for discussion.

They got into Gable's Jeep, and Gable turned on the emergency flasher as she hit the gas and sped toward the fire.

"I wish I had my gear." Erin looked enviously at Gable's fire coat, turnout pants, helmet, and boots, piled in the back of the Jeep.

The smoke was visible from a couple of miles away—a dark column billowing upward into a clear, cloudless sky. They were first to arrive. The top floor of the two-story home was nearly fully involved. Flames leapt from the south side windows and curled upward, charring a wide black swath to the roof.

As the Jeep screeched to a stop on the gravel drive, a middle-aged woman came running out from behind the house. The turquoise housedress she was wearing was half burned off her, and much of her frizzy blond hair was gone on one side, the charred ends black.

"Help!" she screamed. "My son Peter is up there! I couldn't get to him!" She ran up to Gable as she got out of the Jeep and grabbed at her arm. "Help him! He's only seven!"

"Where is he? Where did you last see him?" Gable scrambled into her gear. She cursed the fact she did not have her SCBA. The air packs stayed with the trucks.

"He's in his bedroom." The woman pointed at the only corner of the second floor that was not engulfed in flames. "I couldn't get to him. The stairs were on fire. Hurry! Please!"

"Do you have a ladder?" Gable asked.

"Behind the house." The woman broke down crying.

With no time to comfort her, Gable and Erin darted around the house, found a tall aluminum ladder, and hurriedly set it under the bedroom window. "I'm going up for the boy," Gable told Erin as she pulled her gloves out of her pocket and put them on. "You wait for the pumper and tell them where I am."

"Please be careful," Erin urged, positioning herself to steady the ladder.

Gable raced up the rungs, mentally going through the checklist that had been drilled into her during her training. *Stay low and go.* The temperature of a burning room was three hundred degrees just a foot off the floor, five hundred degrees five feet up, and twelve or thirteen hundred degrees at the ceiling.

The window wasn't locked. She opened it but kept her face turned away as thick black smoke billowed out and up. She hyperventilated, holding her last big deep breath as she crawled inside and dropped to the floor. She kept one hand on the wall to orient herself.

The smoke was thick, but she caught a glimpse of the door to the hallway across from her—it was closed but on fire, fed into a hot sheet of flame by the rush of air from the open window. *You don't have much time.*

"Peter!" she hollered. She inhaled a lungful of the thick acrid smoke and immediately began coughing.

"Peter! Where are you?" she managed between coughs. The smoke stung her eyes, causing them to water profusely. She had to keep them closed much of the time, taking quick, squinting glances to try to see. "Peter! Answer me if you can!"

There was no response, so she began to search. Crawling along the floor, one hand on the wall, the other extended in front of her. *Children are most often found in or under the bed or in closets.* She came to a dresser and skirted around it. Came to a corner of the room. Beyond it, a nightstand. *The bed!* She searched it quickly but thoroughly, then sprawled flat to grope beneath it, both hands outstretched. Nothing but boxes. Comic books. Toys.

Her eyes were burning and her lungs ached. She sucked in more smoke. *Taking too long*, her mind thought fuzzily as she went into another coughing spasm. But she forged ahead, around the bed. Another nightstand.

She was so close to the fire now she could feel the heat of it and hear the roaring, crackling sound as it consumed the door and spread up into the ceiling above her. *You have to hurry. Not much time.*

She left the safety of the wall to scramble around the door, keeping her face averted from the flames. She groped her way to the opposite wall, her hands finding shoes and toys and discarded clothes…and then, another door. *Closet!*

Please, God, she prayed as she turned the knob. She could no longer see, her eyes raw and burning from the smoke. Her heart fell as she groped her way through the deep closet, finding only clothes, a hockey stick, roller skates. She had almost given up hope when she finally came upon the boy, curled into a fetal position in the back corner.

He wasn't moving.

She grabbed him and backed out of the closet.

The fire was spreading rapidly now, closing in on them—one wall and half the ceiling were aflame. The heat was intense, searing her face and neck. She tried to shield the child as she dragged him across the floor in the direction of the window.

"Gable! Answer me, damn it! Gable!" Erin was at the window, standing on top of the ladder.

Her voice helped direct Gable where to go, and in another moment, she was there. She handed the boy over the sill to Erin and groped her way down the ladder after them. She collapsed at the bottom, struggling to breathe, unable to see.

Gable recognized the sound of tires skidding on gravel as more firefighters arrived, then the wail of the fire engine, growing steadily louder.

"I'm going to move you, Gable. Try to relax." Carl's voice, just above her. He reached beneath her shoulders and dragged her several feet, then slid off her helmet. "You all right?"

"Okay," she managed to rasp out between coughs. "The boy?"

"He's alive. Erin and Tim are working on him. You done good, Gable." Carl had to shout to be heard over the siren on the pumper as it pulled up near them. "Oxygen's here."

The siren died, and a minute later someone set an oxygen mask on her face. Gable still couldn't open her eyes, but it was a bit easier to breathe. All was controlled chaos around her. She could hear Chief Thornton shouting instructions, and recognized the clang of the ladders coming off the truck. Another siren. The ambulance, she guessed. The other sounds around her began to fade as it wailed louder and louder, stopping very near where she lay. The siren died, car doors slammed. She could hear the voices of the paramedics as they tended to the boy a short distance away.

"Gable, are you all right?" Erin's voice, nearby. Kneeling over her.

Gable pulled the oxygen mask away from her mouth. "Yeah. Peter?"

"He'll be okay, they think. They're getting him in the ambulance now. Then they'll bring the other gurney over for you."

Gable shook her head. "Hate hospitals," she rasped.

"It'll be all right. I'll be right there with you. But I'm going to have to drive your Jeep and meet you there. They won't let me ride along, there's not enough room."

"No," Gable protested. She started coughing again, and Erin replaced the oxygen mask.

"Leave that alone, and stop talking! Damn it! Don't be so stubborn!"

"Don't need..." Gable tried to talk through the mask, but it muffled her words.

Erin took her hand and leaned down to whisper in her ear. "Please, Gable. Please don't fight this. Okay? For me?"

Gable absolutely loathed hospitals. Her mother had died in one, three days after her car went off an icy road and struck a tree. But Gable could see it was pointless to try to argue with Erin. She nodded her head reluctantly, and Erin squeezed her hand. "Good. Thanks."

The paramedics flushed out her eyes with saline at the fire scene, and they repeated the procedure at the hospital, so Gable was able to get a good look at the cluster of familiar faces crowded outside the emergency ward as they wheeled her to a semiprivate room. Erin, Tim, Carl, and a half dozen more of her firefighter friends, some still in their turnout gear.

Two nurses fussed over her, getting her an extra blanket, fluffing up her pillows. The other bed in her room was vacant. She was still on oxygen and they'd hooked her up to an IV. She had to move the mask to be understood.

"What's Peter's condition?" Her voice was still raspy, and it hurt to talk.

"Put that back," said the matronly nurse whose nametag read Amy. But she smiled at Gable as she said it. "He's going to be fine. We're keeping him overnight too. Just for observation. You're the one who got him out, right?"

Gable nodded.

"Nice work." Amy smiled at Gable as she loaded a syringe from a small bottle. "I'm going to give you something to help you sleep." She injected the syringe into Gable's IV.

"Can I talk to her a minute?"asked a voice from the doorway that Gable didn't recognize. She turned her head to see the woman from the fire, still in her charred housedress, but with bandages and ointment covering the burns on her face, neck and hands.

"Sure," Amy told the woman. "But I don't want her to talk." She looked directly at Gable. "You just listen. All right?"

Gable nodded as the woman approached the bedside.

"I'll never be able to thank you enough." The woman had tears in her eyes. "Risking your life that way to save my son. I don't know how to thank you. I would've died if anything had happened to him."

Gable reached out her hand. The woman took it, and squeezed hard.

"You've got a lot of other people out there who want to see you too," Amy said. "But you can only have two at a time."

"I'll leave. So your friends can come in," Peter's mother said. She leaned down to kiss Gable on the cheek. "God bless you," she whispered before retreating.

Gable risked incurring Amy's wrath by removing the oxygen mask. "I'll see Erin and Carl," she requested, before dutifully replacing it.

"You got it." Amy signaled the other nurse. "But I'm going to stay right here so you don't try to talk."

Carl and Erin came in, both their faces etched with worry until Gable waved at them with both hands to assure them she was all right. Erin pulled a chair near the bedside and took Gable's hand. Carl stood behind the chair.

"Hey there. How you feeling?" Erin asked.

"She's not supposed to talk," Amy said from the other side of the bed.

"Oh, right." Erin winced.

Gable gave Erin's hand a squeeze and winked at her, and that brought a relieved smile to her face.

"Since they won't let everyone in, I'm supposed to tell you that everybody sends their love and prayers," Carl said. "We're all real proud of you, Gable. That was a gutsy thing, going in there alone without your mask."

She shrugged. It had all happened so fast she really didn't have time to be afraid.

"I felt so helpless," Erin said. "You were in there so long."

Gable reached up for her oxygen mask, but Amy cut her off at the pass, grabbing at her arm to stop her. "Don't you dare," she admonished.

Gable let her hand drop back to her side. "Your voice saved me," she rasped through the mask to Erin, drawing a frown from the nurse.

"If you're going to talk," Amy said. "I'm going to ask them to leave."

"No! She's not going to talk anymore, are you, Gable?" Erin's expression beseeched Gable to agree.

Gable flashed Amy an okay sign.

"All right." Amy turned to Carl and Erin. "Make sure she doesn't. I'm going to check on a couple of other patients, but I'll be right back. She's had a sedative, so she'll be dozing off on us pretty quick."

As soon as she was out the door, Gable pulled the mask off. "Go home," she told them.

Erin slapped gently at her hand and replaced the mask. "Stop that. And I'm not going anywhere."

Gable reached for the mask again, but Erin held her arm down.

"I mean it," Erin said more sternly. "Don't make me get tough with you."

Gable rolled her eyes, and Carl chuckled.

"I'm going to go tell everybody you're okay and send them home," Carl said. He patted her arm. "You did us all proud, Gable. Let me know if you need anything."

She gave him a thumbs-up sign, and the room fell quiet for a moment after he'd gone. Gable could feel the sedative taking effect. Erin took her hand again.

"Go home," she repeated through the mask, although she rather liked Erin sitting there, holding her hand.

"Not a chance. Nowhere else I'd rather be."

Gable yawned. "Stubborn," she said drowsily.

"That makes two of us."

"Not going to sleep until you leave," Gable vowed. She was fighting to keep her eyes open.

"Wanna bet?" Erin smiled as she said it, but then her expression grew serious. "You had me scared for a minute there, Gable." A tremor shook her voice.

"I'm fine. Go home. Stop worrying." Gable needed to close her eyes. *But just for a minute.*

"Stop talking! I can't help worrying, Gable. You're important to me. I don't want anything to happen to you."

"Important to me too," Gable mumbled, fading fast. *So very important.*

CHAPTER NINE

When Gable next opened her eyes, sunlight was streaming in through the window of the hospital room and Carl was seated where Erin had been, engrossed in the sports pages of the *Charlevoix Courier.*

Gable felt a small pang of disappointment.

Her oxygen mask was gone, replaced by a nasal cannula that wrapped around her ears and supplied a gentle air flow into her nose. She had a headache, and her throat felt like she had swallowed sandpaper. Sooty, ashy, *nasty* sandpaper. *Yuck.*

"Hey, Carl. What time is it?"

"You're awake!" Carl grinned, set the paper aside, and looked at his watch. "A few minutes before eight."

"What are you doing here?" she asked.

"Thought I'd stop by and see how you were feeling."

"Thirsty."

"I can fix that." Carl poured a cup of water from a pitcher on the bedside table and handed it to her. "How's your head?"

"Hurts."

"Carbon monoxide," he said. "You might feel it a couple of days. Aspirin will help. Any nausea?"

"Yeah."

"Want me to get the nurse?"

"In a minute. When they gonna let me out of here? Do you know?"

"Erin said the doctor was supposed to see you at eight thirty and decide then."

"Erin? Erin was here?" Her pulse quickened. Only then did Gable realize she was hooked to a monitor that was beeping out her heartbeats.

Carl had heard the change too. He glanced at the digital read-out on the monitor. It read 79. 80. 81. An odd smile came over his face. He studied Gable intently for a moment, then said, "Erin is *still* here. I made her go and get coffee. I think she bribed the nurses to let her stay overnight since they kicked me out at ten."

He was smiling at her like the Cheshire cat in *Alice in Wonderland*, and Gable didn't like it one bit. "Well, you can both go home. I'm fine," she said. She could feel her embarrassment beginning to color her cheeks. She looked over at the monitor. Beepbeepbeepbeep. 83. 84. 85.

"Oh, I doubt you can get her to leave." Carl smirked.

"There's no reason either of you need to stay."

There was a long silence.

"She doesn't know, does she?" he asked gently.

Gable froze. "Doesn't know what?" She tried to inject innocent conviction into her tone, but he wasn't fooled. They both knew he had it figured out.

"You can talk to me, you know," he said. "I understand better than you think I do."

She looked at him then.

"My niece Ruthie is a lesbian. She's twenty-one and goes to Juilliard. Brilliant girl. Gifted. She's educated me, you might say."

"I see," was all Gable could manage.

"Ruthie didn't tell anybody in the family until she turned eighteen, though she knew long before that. She said she was worried about how everyone would react, but at the same time, she hated keeping it from all of us. Felt like she was living a lie—not telling the people closest to her." He paused, a trace of hurt evident in his eyes. "She said it was like they couldn't really know who she was."

"Carl, I'm kind of a private person," Gable said. "I don't feel the need to share that information with a lot of people."

"I understand that. But I think there's a difference between telling the squad you're gay and telling your best friend, who seems to be open-minded enough to understand."

"You don't know that about her."

He shrugged. "Maybe not. It's just a feeling. We chatted last night a good long while, and I got to know her. She obviously thinks the world of you. She talked about you practically nonstop."

"We're close."

"But you'd like to be closer."

Gable sighed. "She's *straight,* Carl."

"Yeah, I know. So maybe you can't have the kind of relationship you'd like to have with her. But I think you'd be happier if you at least told her you were gay."

Gable shook her head. "I don't think so. I don't know."

"Will you at least think about it?"

"Yeah. I can do that. Would you do me a favor?"

"Sure."

"Ask a nurse for some aspirin, will you?"

"You bet."

"And get them to take me off this heart monitor before Erin comes back!" she hollered after him.

Erin stuck her head around the door a few minutes later as the doctor was finishing up his visit. Politely, she hovered a few feet into the corridor as he removed the oxygen tube from Gable's nose.

"Okay, I'll sign you out," he said. "I want you to take a couple days off work and rest. Take the antibiotics and call me if there are any complications."

"I will, Doc. Thanks."

"You have someone to drive you home?"

"Yes, she does." Erin stepped into the room.

"Good." He scribbled on his prescription pad and gave the paper to Gable. "Get that filled at the hospital pharmacy before you leave. Lots of fluids, lots of rest. Bland food for a while. Nothing spicy."

"All right."

The doctor departed and Erin hurried to the bed, smiling at Gable, wearing the same clothes she'd had on for two nights running with the exception of a brand-new navy sweatshirt that had *Michigan* embroidered on it in gold. Her hair was slightly mussed. Gable thought she looked adorable.

"I thought you got your bachelor's at Western and your master's at Michigan State. When did you go to U of M?"

Erin glanced down at her sweatshirt and shrugged. "All they had in the hospital gift shop. I was getting chilly."

"Why didn't you go home?"

Erin shrugged. "Thought you might like to have a friendly face nearby when you woke up. I know you weren't keen on coming here."

"I hate hospitals."

"I figured. And I hate confined, dark spaces and you helped me with that, so here I am."

"You know, you're probably going to run into a lot of confined, dark spaces when you start going out on callouts and get trained to go into buildings," Gable said. "Have you thought about that?"

"Yes, I have," Erin said. "I'm optimistic I can deal with it when there's a job to do and I'm focused on that. Whenever there are distractions in a situation like that—like when you talked to me the night of the tornado—that really makes it easier."

"You know if you run into a touchy situation and I can help, don't hesitate to ask."

Erin grinned at her. "I know that. And I want you to know the same goes for me."

An attractive nurse with short hair the color of copper came into the room with a clipboard in one hand. "Hi, hero," she greeted Gable as she approached the bedside. "Just got done signing out the boy you saved. You're next."

She handed the clipboard to Gable and raised the head of the bed until Gable was sitting up, then she leaned forward until she was close enough to point at the paperwork. "I need you to sign here," she turned a page, "and here."

The nurse didn't move away while Gable signed; her proximity seemed somehow *familiar*, enough so that Gable looked directly at her when she handed the clipboard back.

The nurse gave her a big smile and held her eyes a little too long as she took the clipboard. "My name is Sheri," she said. She was not in a hurry to leave. "Let me know if there's anything else I can do for you, won't you? If you need a ride home, I get off in a couple of hours."

What the hell? Oh my God, this woman is hitting on me! Gable couldn't find her tongue for a moment. She blushed, which only made the nurse smile more.

"I'm fine, really." She shot a glance at Erin, who was watching the exchange with an unreadable expression. "I have a ride."

"All righty. Well, if you change your mind, I'll be at the nurses' station." The nurse headed for the door. "Hit your buzzer when you're ready to leave, and I'll wheel you out."

"I can take care of it," Erin said coolly. "If you'll bring a wheelchair by."

"I can walk out," Gable said.

"Hospital policy," Sheri informed her. "Your friend can take you out. I'll get the chair."

"Need help getting dressed?" Erin asked Gable after the nurse had gone.

"No!" Gable said, a bit too quickly. "Uh…I can manage. Where are my things?"

"Carl took your turnout gear with him. Said he'd get it to you later. The rest of your things should be here." Erin went to a tiny closet and opened it. "Whew!" She grimaced as she brought Gable's jeans, shirt, bra, socks, panties and shoes to the bed.

Gable could smell it too, from several feet away. Her clothes absolutely stank of smoke. But she didn't have many options if she wanted to get out of there. She eased her legs off one side of the bed and slipped to the floor. One hand held her clothes tight to her chest. The other held the hospital gown closed over her bare bottom. She padded slowly to the room's tiny bathroom and went inside to change.

Would you still offer to help me get dressed if you knew I was gay? she wondered as she pulled up her jeans. Her thoughts strayed to the nurse. *Maybe I just need to get laid. Maybe that will put out this fire that's been burning inside me since I first set eyes on Erin. Maybe.*

They didn't talk much on the ride home in the Jeep. Erin insisted on driving, and Gable was happy to let her. She was preoccupied thinking about what Carl had said. *You'd be a lot happier if you at least told her you were gay.*

Would she? Attempting to be rational, she weighed the pros and cons of coming out to Erin.

If you tell her, it could change things. That was her greatest fear—that telling Erin would irreparably harm their friendship. *No matter how cool she appears to be, you just never know how someone's going to react. She might treat you very differently once she knows you're gay.* Gable didn't think it was likely that Erin would completely turn her back on their friendship, though she'd heard of that happening to others. *But she might stop confiding in you. Start keeping you at arm's length. Do you want to chance that? Risk the closest, dearest friendship you might ever have?*

She stole a glance at Erin, who was singing along with the radio, which was tuned to a station that played familiar classic pop tunes. It was easy to tell she was musically inclined—she always sang harmony to the theme, usually a perfect fifth below or above the melody.

If you tell her, you're going to have to work even harder not to let on how you feel about her. You'll have to be on guard all the time. Gable stared out the window. *But not forever,* she amended. *Just until you get over wanting to rip her clothes off.*

She glanced at Erin again. Erin felt eyes on her, and turned to smile.

The longer you keep this from her, the harder it will be to tell her. And you will have to tell her someday. You know you will. You can't dance around it forever. Your evasions will trip you up, or she'll find out some other way—maybe by accident. Gable's mind flashed again to the flirtatious nurse.

If you wait to tell her, or if she finds out on her own...she'll be really hurt. She'll think you didn't trust her. Gable sighed. *The bottom line is, you just hate lying to her. Carl was right about that, wasn't he? You won't feel right until you're honest with her.*

They pulled into her driveway.

Okay, so you're going to tell her. Now you just have to decide when. And how.

"I appreciate your staying with me," Gable said as they stopped in front of the house, next to Erin's pickup. "And your driving."

"Don't mention it." Erin cut off the engine and handed the keys to Gable. "And you're not dismissing me. I'm coming in to fix you something to eat, and then I'm going to tuck you in bed."

Gable got out and shut the door of the Jeep but didn't go inside. "That's not necessary. You can go home now. I know one kitty who's going to be pretty pissed at his mommy."

"Earl Grey will be fine. He has plenty of dry food, and I'll give him extra Fancy Feast when I see him." Erin started walking toward the house. "You're supposed to be resting, not arguing with me," she called over her shoulder.

Gable really didn't have the heart to protest further. She wanted one more night of Erin not knowing. One more night where she didn't have to worry about whether Erin would pick up on her feelings. One more night of the way things were. Because even though it wasn't all that she wanted, it was so much more than she'd ever had before.

She headed up the walk after Erin. *Better enjoy it while you can. Nothing will be the same after you tell her.*

Erin got her comfortably settled on the couch, feet up and pillows behind her back, then warmed up some chicken soup and made a pot of tea.

"Don't forget to take your pills with your food," she said as Gable sampled the soup.

"Erin, I'm a pharmacist."

"Oh, right. Brilliant, Erin." A slight flush infused her cheeks, and Gable thought it quite endearing. But she could see that Erin also had circles under her eyes from having stayed awake half the night at the hospital. It was time to send her home.

"You really don't have to fuss after me anymore, you know. I can manage to put these in the sink and get into bed by myself."

"You sure?"

"Positive. Go! And thanks again for everything."

"Any time." Erin got up but detoured to the back of the couch before she left to hug Gable around the neck. "Get some sleep. Call me if you need anything."

"I will."

"I'll check on you tomorrow. What do you want for dinner?"

"I've got stuff here I can cook," Gable said.

"The doctor told you to take it easy for a couple of days, and I'm going to make sure you stick to that. I'm going to Cadillac tomorrow, so I can bring back any kind of takeout you like. What sounds good to you?"

Gable smiled. "Whatever. I'm easy."

"I'll surprise you, then."

No, Gable thought. *I'll be the one surprising you.*

CHAPTER TEN

Erin, there's something I should tell you. Not that it's any big deal, but we're good friends and getting to be better friends all the time, and I just think it's something you should know about me that you probably don't. I'm gay."

Erin didn't say anything right away, but her eyes got big and Gable heard the sharp intake of breath at the news. It was clear the announcement was a total surprise. Her stomach was tied up in knots.

"You're gay?" Erin repeated after a full minute had passed.

"Yes."

"I see." Erin got up and walked to the window and looked out. She didn't say anything more for the longest time, and she didn't look at Gable.

"I...I had no idea. None." Erin still wouldn't look at her, and there was something about the tone in her voice that Gable didn't like.

"Gable, I...I don't know what to say to you. It's just...*wrong*. I can't condone it. I can't be your friend anymore." She shook her head. "I have to go." She was out the door and in her truck almost before Gable could blink.

Gable hurried after her and caught up with her as she started to pull out of the driveway. "Erin, wait!" She ran alongside the pickup, tapping desperately on the window, but even though she was certain Erin heard her, the truck only picked up speed.

"Erin! Come back!" she screamed. "Please come back!"

Gable sat bolt upright, coming awake in an instant, her heart thumping loudly in her chest. She looked at the bedside clock. It read

4:12 a.m.

She prayed the dream was only her anxieties working themselves out in her subconscious, and not a premonition of things to come. There would be no more sleeping until she talked to Erin.

❖

Gable paced back and forth, glancing out the front window every now and then, listening for the sound of Erin's truck. She was wound up tight.

The woods outside her home were alive with birds—bright yellow goldfinches and indigo buntings, rose-breasted grosbeaks and her favorite of all—ruby-throated hummingbirds, mesmerizing in their aerial acrobatics. But today Gable was oblivious to all of it.

When she finally heard the familiar rattle of the red pickup as it bounced up the rutted two-track driveway, a rush of anticipation skittered through her, a mixture of fear and excitement.

"Hi there! How you feeling?" Erin said when Gable opened the door.

"Better. But bored. Come on in."

"I brought you something for that." Erin stepped through the doorway and held up a DVD. "I rented us *The Terminal* since we both like Tom Hanks. Have you seen it yet?"

Gable shook her head.

"And I know the doctor told you to keep to bland food, so I got us macaroni and cheese for dinner. Some rolls, and cottage cheese and fruit. Hope that's all right." She held up a paper bag.

"Sounds great. Can I at least pay you back for all this?"

"Yeah, right. I'll put it on your tab." Erin rolled her eyes. She was wearing a low-cut V-neck blouse that hugged her breasts much too provocatively for Gable to keep her mind entirely on the task at hand.

Why do you do this to me? She groaned inwardly, and for a brief moment considered delaying her revelation for a day when Erin didn't look quite so delectable. *Yeah, right. Like that's gonna happen any time soon.*

"Are you hungry?" Erin asked. "Or do you want to wait a while?"

"Let's wait, if you don't mind. How about I make us some tea?" Gable couldn't eat until she got this over with.

"I'd love some, but let me make it. I know where everything is. You go sit and relax."

"Erin, I can boil water."

"Indulge me for another day. I want to play Florence Nightingale."
Erin headed for the kitchen and Gable took a seat on the couch.

They made small talk as they sipped their tea, sitting a few feet apart on the couch. Chief Thornton and Carl both had called to check on Gable. Erin had run errands in Cadillac, picking up more essentials for the house. Gable waited for the right opening, gathering her nerve, but it was a good half hour before she steeled herself for her leap-of-faith pronouncement.

"Erin, there's something I've been meaning to tell you." She was forced to take a sip of tea; her mouth was parched.

Erin seemed to sense something was up. She set her tea down and gave Gable her full attention.

"I don't want to make a big thing out of it," Gable continued as offhandedly as she could. She took a deep breath and let it out. "And I hope it won't in any way hurt our friendship, which means an awful lot to me." She heard a slight tremor in her voice and took another sip of tea. *Damn, this is hard.*

Erin stiffened.

"Look, I'm making a bigger deal out of this than I should. It's just that you never know how someone is going to react."

"Gable, what is it?" Erin was looking at her curiously, her body rigid, tense.

"I just thought you should know that I'm gay." *There it is. You've done it. You can't take it back now.* Gable held her breath. She couldn't look directly at Erin. She felt too vulnerable. She watched Erin out of the corner of her eye.

Erin didn't immediately respond, but her posture relaxed slightly as the news sank in. Gable took that as a favorable sign.

"I know it's got to be difficult to share that information with someone you haven't known very long," Erin said. "So thank you for trusting me with it." She sipped her tea. "And I want you to know—and I only say this because I'm sure you've had some bad experiences—it makes no difference to me whether you're gay or not."

Gable let out a long breath as relief washed over her. "Good. Glad to hear it." *I hope that's the truth, Erin.*

There was a short awkward silence.

"Do you mind if I ask you a couple of questions?" Erin said.

"Sure." *As long as you don't ask me how I feel about you.*

"Have you always known you were gay?"

"Pretty much. I tried to ignore it when I was younger. I dated boys the first year or two of high school, trying to fit in and be like everybody else. But I knew something was wrong...missing."

Erin tilted her head in thought. "I haven't really known anyone who was gay. Or if I did, I didn't *know* they were gay." She poured them both more tea. "But I guess I'm pretty dumb in that regard. I had no idea you were."

"It's not something I volunteer right off the bat. I'm pretty private by nature, and I've always found it hard to talk about real personal stuff unless I know somebody well." Gable felt as though a huge weight had been lifted. Erin seemed more curious than disturbed by her revelation.

"Gable, was that nurse at the hospital hitting on you?"

Gable could feel herself blushing. "Yeah, I guess she was."

"I wondered. I thought so...but then I didn't think you were gay, so it really seemed kind of odd to me." She looked at Gable and cocked her head in confusion. "How did she know you were, if I didn't? She'd barely met you."

Gable shrugged. "Beats me. Some lesbians have a kind of 'gaydar' and can pick out another gay woman a mile away. But that's sure not the case with me. I'm usually pretty clueless."

"That's got to be rough. I mean, not knowing whether someone you're attracted to...whether they..."

"Play for your team or not?"

"Yeah, something like that." Erin grinned.

You have no idea. "It's not easy," Gable admitted. "Particularly when you're shy. I've always had a problem approaching women I was interested in."

"So who else knows? Do the guys at the firehouse?"

Gable shook her head. "Carl guessed, but he's the only one. Otherwise, pretty much only family, and friends back in Tennessee. I haven't told anyone since I moved here."

"Then I feel especially privileged that you felt you could share it with me," Erin said. "You know, Gable, I don't think there's anything you could tell me that would make any difference in how much I care about you and respect you."

Gable could tell she meant it. "Thanks, Erin." *Thank God.*

Just as Carl had predicted, she felt suddenly a lot happier and less anxious. It had been a freeing experience to come out to Erin. One less secret to keep from her. Even though she would have to be even more careful now not to let her feelings show, she was very glad she'd made the decision to tell Erin.

"Ready for some dinner?" Erin asked.

"Sure." Gable's stomach had calmed considerably. She was suddenly ravenous.

The evening reassured Gable that she had done the right thing. She and Erin had their usual great time, sharing a bowl of popcorn and exchanging obscure film trivia as they watched the movie. Erin was every bit as warm and sweet as she'd been before.

In fact, as they chatted over decaf lattes after the movie, she opened up more to Gable than she ever had. It was as if a barrier between them had gone, and that in revealing the most private parts of herself to Erin, Gable had deepened their level of trust. It seemed this encouraged Erin to expose some of her own innermost feelings.

"Hasn't it been hard for you?" she asked, setting down her cup and turning sideways on the couch so she could look at Gable. "Not telling anyone here that you're gay, I mean?"

Gable shrugged. "Sometimes, I guess. I started to tell June—she's a woman I work with—well, I started to tell her once or twice. And I've been tempted a few times to tell some of the guys at the station. But then I start blushing like crazy even *thinking* about telling them, and I always put it off. I am *way* too shy, I know. I often wish I was more outgoing, like you are."

Erin shook her head. "Don't wish to be like me." Her expression grew serious. "I'm okay in social situations, I guess because of my teaching background. I can mingle in a crowd just fine. But it's an entirely different thing when it comes to one-on-one relationships." She paused and looked at Gable. "It's easy with *you.*"

She frowned and fell silent, apparently chewing this over. There was a trace of bemusement in her expression, as if she had just discovered something she barely knew about herself. "Or a lot eas*ier,* anyway," she murmured, almost to herself. "But I have a really hard time talking about my feelings to someone I'm *dating*. It's not shyness so much..."

Gable didn't say anything, intrigued by Erin's sudden need to draw close instead of drawing away. It was the last thing she'd expected, even after Erin's insistence she was fine with Gable's sexuality.

Erin's gaze had turned inward, unfocused. "I'm not entirely sure why it happens, but I think it has a lot to do with my nightmare of a marriage." She blew out a breath. "I think that kind of crippled me. I find it very difficult to really get close to anyone." Erin glanced at her with an unreadable expression. "Tim is a sweet, attractive guy, and he's really interested in me."

He'd be a fool not to be.

"I like him. He's got a great sense of humor and he's fun to be with." There was another long pause. "But it feels like something's... *missing*. Like the chemistry really isn't there. I don't know, maybe I'm not really giving it a chance. Maybe my past is getting in the way."

"You're the only one who can figure that out," Gable said gently. "My brother Stewart always says to go with what your heart tells you."

"That's good advice. Well, Tim and I are going out again next week. I'll keep you posted."

Not too much detail, please. Gable stifled a yawn. The lack of sleep the night before was catching up to her.

"I'm going to run so you can get to bed," Erin said. She leaned over and hugged Gable before getting to her feet. "I had fun tonight. And thanks for trusting me enough to confide in me."

Gable followed her to the door. "Thanks for...well, I guess just thanks for being cool about it...not letting it matter."

"Gable? Can I ask you another personal question?" Erin was only a couple of feet away, looking at her intently.

Gable held her breath.

"Are you...seeing anyone?"

Gable shook her head, not trusting her voice.

"Ah," Erin said, turning to go. "Just curious."

❖

For the first week or so, it seemed as though Gable's revelation hadn't altered their relationship at all. On Sunday she and Erin took a shopping excursion to Charlevoix for groceries and odds and ends. Two days later they shared a rented movie and home-cooked meal at Gable's house, and on Thursday they did the same at Erin's. And they talked on the phone nearly every evening they weren't together, catching up on events of the day.

It was still hard for Gable to keep her feelings for Erin hidden, but she was immensely relieved that Erin's behavior didn't change. So she was surprised when Erin didn't call her Saturday night as promised, after her date with Tim. Erin had planned to be home by nine; they were going to a late-afternoon movie and then dinner because Tim had an early EMT shift.

A change in plans; she got home later than she expected, Gable decided the next morning as she made herself a pot of coffee. *Or maybe Tim stayed over.* The thought depressed her. She should be getting used to the idea by now that she would never have Erin. But it just got harder and harder. *How will you fall in love with anyone else when you feel this way about her?*

Her doorbell rang. It startled her so much she jumped. She glanced at the clock on the stove. Seven forty a.m. Too early for a casual visitor. She belted her robe over her pajamas as she headed for the door. Early-morning phone calls always made her think *Someone's hurt! Someone's dead!* Early-morning visitors were usually tourists—snowmobilers or hunters or fishermen—who'd had a breakdown or accident near her remote home.

But it was Erin at the door of the screened-in porch, looking as though she hadn't slept much. Tousled hair and slightly puffy eyes, like she'd been rubbing them. She had a white paper bag tucked under one arm.

"Hi. You were awake, right? I saw your lights on."

"Sure, I just made some coffee. Come on in." Gable stepped aside and Erin came a few steps onto the porch and turned to face her.

"I hope you don't mind me coming over this early without calling first. I couldn't sleep, so I took a drive. I brought some donuts." She held up the paper bag.

"Great. Have a seat and I'll pour us some coffee."

Gable poured two mugs full and doctored Erin's with Equal and half-and-half. She set them on a tray with two small plates and napkins and carried them back to the porch.

Erin sat in one of the big wicker chairs, watching the profusion of wildlife outside the screen. The feeders Gable had hung from the eaves were crowded with birds, and a dozen squirrels chased each other for the seed that fell to the ground.

"So you couldn't sleep?" Gable asked, hoping it would start Erin talking. Something had obviously happened. Erin wasn't her usual upbeat, confident self. She seemed withdrawn. *I'll kill Tim if he's hurt her.*

"No. I just got to...thinking about things. Got my mind going and couldn't shut it off."

"Anything you want to talk about?"

"No." Erin shook her head. "Not yet, anyway."

"Okay. Well, I'm here for you if you change your mind." Gable hid her disappointment.

They sipped their coffee and munched on donuts in silence. Gable caught Erin surreptitiously watching her a couple of times, but each time she glanced at her, Erin would quickly look away. It made her a little paranoid. *Is it Tim? Or is it me? Does she suspect how I feel about her?*

"Gable, have you ever been in love?" she asked abruptly. "I mean, where you thought...this is *it*!"

Gable nearly choked on her coffee. Her mind raced. *How the hell do I answer this?* She set her cup down on a small table between them. She didn't want Erin to see her hands were shaking, so she leaned back in her chair and folded her arms across her chest.

"Well, I'm not exactly Miss Experience in the romance department. I had crushes, of course. Infatuations. And I've dated a few women, but I wasn't with any one woman for very long." Gable steeled her nerve. "I did...fall in love. Once. I mean, where it really felt...different. Special." She couldn't look at Erin. "But...she didn't feel the same. It wasn't reciprocated."

"So...you thought you knew. But you were wrong?" Erin asked.

"Yeah, I guess you could say that."

"I'm sorry. That had to be very hard for you."

Gable shrugged, unable to answer. *Why are you asking me these questions?*

"I don't know that anybody can give me any answers." Erin set her mug on the table beside Gable's. "I told Tim last night that I wanted to just be friends with him."

Gable's pulse quickened at the news. "You did?"

Erin stood up and stepped to the screen. She stood there stiffly and stared out. "I may have made a mistake. Not given him enough of a chance. I don't know."

It has nothing to do with you. Don't get your hopes up. Gable bit back her disappointment.

"I'm so confused." Erin's voice was subdued. After a long silence, she said, "Tim's a marrying kind of guy. He was getting too serious too soon." She closed her eyes. "I don't think I can give him what he needs. But I don't know that I would recognize true love if it bit me on the butt."

Gable tried to dispel the erotic image that popped into her head. *Get your mind out of the gutter.* "I wish I knew what to say, Erin."

"There's nothing you can say, I guess. I just have to figure out what the hell is going on with me." She let out a rueful sigh and then turned to face Gable. "I'm gonna go. Thanks for listening."

"Any time." Gable got to her feet. She had an odd sense that Erin wanted something from her. She vacillated, trying to decide if she should delay her on some pretext.

In the end, Erin hugged her good-bye, as she often did, but Gable could have sworn something was different this time. Erin held on just a little longer, embraced her just a little tighter.

Gable felt vaguely ashamed of herself the rest of the day. She was *glad* that Erin wasn't seeing Tim anymore. She knew she shouldn't be. It was obviously upsetting Erin, and she hated to see her friend so morose and confused. Tim might have made her very happy.

But she couldn't help feeling relieved that for the moment, anyway, there would be no competition for Erin's time and attention.

They chatted on the phone several times during the next few nights, but Erin's mood did not change. She was subdued and withdrawn, reluctant to share any more of what she was going through, though Gable tried her best to draw her out. Their conversations were brief and focused only on mundane things. Gable proposed they do dinner and a movie one night at her house, but Erin declined, saying she hadn't been sleeping well and was going to try to turn in early.

There was a growing distance between them, and by the end of the week Gable wondered whether Erin might be reconsidering her decision to stop seeing Tim. There was no answer when she tried to phone her Friday night.

She got her answer on Saturday, when she drove to the fire station for a day of drills with the ladders and hoses. She was looking forward to seeing Erin and getting a firsthand look at how she was doing, but it was Tim who intercepted her as she entered the building.

"Hey, Gable. Have you talked to Erin?"

"Why? Isn't she here?"

"Not yet. Do you know what's going on with her? I'm kind of worried about her, frankly."

"Worried? Why?"

"Well, she told me last weekend she didn't want us to date anymore. I was disappointed, you know…I had a lot of fun with her and thought it might lead to something. But I told her I understood, and it was okay."

"I know that must have been tough for you." Gable commiserated.

"Well, she called the chief right after that and cancelled all her training this week. Said she wasn't feeling well. But I went by her house to check on her, and she wasn't there."

"This is news to me. I spoke to her on the phone a few times, and she didn't say anything about any of this." Gable got a sick feeling in the pit of her stomach with the realization that Erin wasn't telling her everything.

"Is she going to be here today?" Tim asked.

"I don't know. I presumed she would be."

"Gable, do you know why she broke it off with me?"

"You'd have to ask her that, Tim."

"I did. She told me she didn't want to get my hopes up that there might be a future for us…but I think there's something else going on."

"What makes you say that?"

He scratched his chin thoughtfully. "I don't know. She just was really withdrawn during our last date, from the moment I picked her up.

Like she was somewhere else. It was really weird, because she'd been just the opposite the week before—happy, relaxed."

"You have no clue what's happening with her?" Gable pressed. She wanted to know for herself.

"I tried to find out...That's when she told me she thought we should just be friends. But I got the impression it wasn't really about me. It kind of seemed like she was blowing me off just to get me to stop asking questions. I thought maybe she told you what was bothering her."

Gable shook her head. "I don't think I can help. I don't know any more than you do, but I'll try to talk to her when she gets here. *If* she gets here."

Erin did, in fact, show up for the training, but she arrived just as they were getting things going, and there was no time for pleasantries with anyone. She waved hello at Gable, and Tim too, but kept to herself, standing off to one side, as the chief explained the drills they would do that day.

After the briefing, they split up into teams of three to rotate among the ladders and hoses. Gable started toward Erin at that point, but Erin quickly positioned herself with Carl and Don, as if deliberately avoiding her. They all suited up in their turnout gear and adjourned to the training grounds situated behind the fire station—a four-acre plot that contained several concrete block buildings and a small obstacle course.

Gable had a hard time keeping her mind on what she was doing the rest of the morning, her frustration growing each time she would catch Erin's eye, only to have her look away.

I'm not imagining it. She's avoiding me.

By the time they broke for lunch, she had convinced herself Erin was having a delayed and very homophobic reaction to the revelation that Gable was a lesbian. It made her heartsick. And quite unexpectedly, it also made her angry. She had worked up quite a head of steam by the time she cornered Erin in the women's locker room.

"What's up?" Gable asked.

"What do you mean?" Erin was stripping off her shiny new turnout jacket. She had on a T-shirt under the heavy fire coat, and it was drenched in sweat from the rigorous morning. It clung to her, outlining her breasts. Gable couldn't tear her eyes away. A little of her anger dissipated.

"Erin, are you avoiding me?"

"No." But Erin wouldn't look at her. And Gable noticed her hands were shaking as she stripped off her turnout pants.

"Erin, what is it? Talk to me!" Gable reached out and put one hand on Erin's shoulder.

Erin shrugged off the hand and turned to Gable with tears in her eyes. "Talk to *you*?" She spit out the words. "That's a laugh. Like you talk to *me*, you mean?" She slammed the door of her locker shut and stormed out.

Gable remained rooted in place for several seconds, unprepared for Erin's sudden outburst and completely bewildered by it.

By the time she ran out to the parking lot, Erin's truck was gone.

She tried to call Erin several times that afternoon and evening, but her machine kept picking up and Gable didn't want to leave a message. She didn't know what to say. All she knew was that she was feeling empty inside, and desperate to reconnect with Erin, repair whatever it was that had caused this rift.

But you know what it is, don't you? Somehow she found out how you feel about her. And she doesn't like it one bit.

On Monday, after several more abortive attempts to reach Erin by phone, Gable finally left a message. "Erin, it's Gable. Please talk to me."

Her phone remained maddeningly silent.

On Tuesday, she drove directly to Erin's cabin from work. There were lights on inside—she could see Earl Grey's silhouette in the front window, but Erin's pickup was gone and there was no answer to her knock. She left a note tucked into the screen door that read simply:

Please call or stop by. Any time. We need to talk.
Gable

She left another phone message the next night. This one just said: "Erin, I miss you."

Waiting was excruciating. She couldn't sleep. It began to sink in that she might have lost Erin altogether.

CHAPTER ELEVEN

The next day at work, Gable was so fatigued that she actually fell asleep for a moment in the back of the pharmacy. Fortunately, she was out of the view of any drugstore patrons. She dozed off at her desk, hunched over a pile of paperwork, and only came awake when the buzzer at the counter sounded, announcing someone needed a prescription filled.

She shook herself awake and yawned, and glanced over the half-wall partition that separated her from her customers. Erin stood alone at the counter, nervously biting her lip, holding a large plate of something covered with plastic wrap. Cupcakes, it looked like.

Relief poured through Gable as she stood. "Hey, Erin."

"Hey, Gable." Erin's eyes met hers, and the edges of her mouth twitched upward in an embarrassed smile.

"It's good to see you." Gable stepped around the partition.

Erin held out the plate. Her expression altered from embarrassed to hopeful. "The school band is having a bake sale to raise money for uniforms. I thought a plate of cupcakes might be a good way to say I'm sorry I bit your head off the other day."

"No need to apologize." Gable accepted the plate and set it down. Gently, she asked, "Are you all right?"

Erin leaned against the counter and brushed some nonexistent dirt off the top as she considered her answer. "Yes. I just…had some things to sort out. I'm sorry I haven't been in touch. I should have called you."

"Is there anything I can do?"

Erin looked at Gable for a long moment, and her eyes shone with tears. "Can you forget I've been such a jerk?"

"I never thought that in the first place. You're entitled to have an off day."

"Thanks for understanding."

An elderly woman pushing a walker came up behind Erin, interrupting them.

"Good morning. May I help you?" Gable asked.

The woman dug in her purse and pulled out four empty prescription vials. "I'd like these refilled, please."

"Certainly." Gable glanced at the labels. "It'll be a few minutes, if you'd like to take a seat."

"I'm going to let you get back to work," Erin said, once the woman had moved away. "I've got a training class soon."

Gable stuck out her lip in a disappointed pout, which drew the first genuine smile from Erin since she'd arrived.

"Come to my house for dinner tonight?" Erin asked with a hopeful expression.

Gable smiled back. "I'd like that. I've missed you."

Erin looked at her for another very long moment. "I've missed you too." Then she was gone.

That evening, Gable detoured home long enough to change into a T-shirt and jeans. When she drove up Erin's driveway shortly before seven, she spotted Erin waving to her from a portable gas grill set up a few feet from the cabin. It was a warm late-July day, but there wasn't much humidity, and the steady breeze and shelter of the trees made it seem much cooler than eighty-eight degrees.

"Perfect timing," Erin said as Gable got out of the Jeep.

Gable sucked in a big whiff of…steak? Her mouth started watering as she approached. "Something sure smells good."

"It's not Outback Steakhouse, but I splurged and got us a couple of filet mignons at the butcher shop. Medium rare, right?"

"Oh yeah, exactly right," Gable replied, pleased that Erin remembered.

"Go on in and help yourself to a beverage." Erin gestured with the tongs in her hand. "There's beer and soda in the fridge, and an open bottle of wine on the table. These will be done in a minute."

"Okay."

Earl Grey had evidently been watching Gable's approach from his perch in the window. He was crouched just inside the door and pounced on her as soon as she entered, then raced away, hoping she would chase him as she had when he was staying at her house. Gable's eyes followed the cat until he passed the dining area, where her attention shifted to the beautifully laid table. White china and crystal stemware rested on place mats and napkins in a deep emerald green. Between the settings rested a pair of candlesticks and a vase filled with the delicate miniature daisies that grew rampant along Erin's drive.

She always makes meals an occasion, Gable thought, recalling the other times Erin had prepared dinner for her. But she noticed there was a subtle difference this time, in addition to the extravagance of the filets mignons. The place settings were laid opposite each other, instead of at right angles as they had always been before. She and Erin would face each other tonight as they ate.

Erin was just flipping over the steaks when Gable joined her outside with a glass of wine in her hand. "How was work?" she asked, and Gable was struck for a moment by the pure, sweet domesticity of that moment—Erin in her oversized barbecue apron, grinning up at her and asking how her day went. Gable knew she was only indulging an impossible fantasy, but she would savor the moment nonetheless.

"My day got considerably brighter when I saw you standing at the counter," she answered honestly.

Erin smiled broadly at the comment.

"The table looks great." Gable gestured toward the cabin. "And I can't believe you got us these steaks."

"Well, I wanted to do something nice for you. And this happens to be one of those many wonderful indulgences that we have in common, so I benefit too."

I wish we had more in common at moments like these, Gable thought, swallowing hard. It wasn't getting any easier at all to be this close to Erin without being able to touch her. *You just look so damn kissable. How is it that you seem to get cuter every day?*

Over the course of their friendship thus far, Gable had greatly enjoyed being able to steal frequent long looks at Erin whenever Erin was preoccupied—cooking dinner, doing dishes, shopping, watching television. She relished every chance she got to admire, unobserved,

Erin's face, her hands, her body, and the way she moved. And ordinarily, she got plenty of opportunities to do just that.

But not tonight. Tonight, Erin seemed much more keenly aware of Gable's surreptitious scrutiny. Nearly every time she stole a glance as they ate, and cleaned up, and later watched a movie together on television, she found Erin was either already watching her, or else she would quickly seem to sense Gable's eyes and look up.

Gable always glanced quickly away, afraid that Erin would discover the depth of her feelings. Erin never said a word about it, but by the end of the evening Gable had severely curtailed her efforts to observe her in secret. She didn't want to risk putting distance between them again, though Erin acted as if everything was fine now.

"I'd like to reciprocate and invite you to dinner tomorrow," Gable said as the movie credits rolled. "Do you have plans?"

"I'm all yours," Erin said, a pleased smile lighting her face. "I've got training, but I'll get done before you do. What time should I come over?"

"Give me until six thirty to get home," Gable said, suppressing a yawn as she got to her feet.

Erin followed her to the door. "You got it."

Gable turned to say good-bye and found herself unexpectedly enfolded in a hug.

"Sorry again I was such a pain," Erin mumbled into her chest.

"Stop apologizing," Gable returned her embrace, then took a step back. "See you tomorrow, then. Sleep well."

Erin gave her a long look. "You too, Gable. Pleasant dreams."

As she drove home, Gable reminded herself not to get too used to spending evenings with Erin. Soon enough, she reckoned, some of the guys who'd been hovering at the picnic would ask her out. Just as soon as word got around that Tim was out of the picture. *Enjoy it while you can.*

"So what are your plans for the weekend?" Erin asked the next evening as they sat on Gable's porch after dinner, sipping coffee while watching the approaching dusk paint the sky with brilliant shades of pink and lavender.

"I have to work tomorrow until five," Gable said. "James took the day off for his daughter's wedding."

"James? Have you told me about him?"

"Guess I haven't," Gable said. "James is our part-time pharmacist. He's semiretired now, and just works Saturdays and whenever else I need an extra hand."

"Well, that bites," Erin said resignedly, the disappointment evident in her voice. "I have a training class tomorrow night, so Saturday's out altogether. What about Sunday?"

"No plans," Gable replied.

"Let's do something fun," Erin proposed. "Maybe take a drive up the Lake Michigan shore—hit a few antique shops, grab dinner somewhere?"

"Sounds great. Count me in."

They had another pleasant, relaxed evening together, and Gable was treated to another impromptu hug good-bye when Erin departed for home. Once again, Erin seemed to be much more aware of Gable's eyes on her than she used to be. *What's up with that?* Gable wondered.

Erin picked her up at ten on Sunday morning as they'd arranged, but begged a stop at her school before they set off on their excursion. "I lost all my lesson plans in the tornado," she explained as she pulled out of Gable's drive and headed toward Pine River. "I've got some stuff at school that will help me try to recreate them, and I realized this morning I better get going on it. School starts pretty soon."

She pulled into the school's empty parking lot a few minutes later. "Want to come in? Might take me a minute to find everything."

"Sure," Gable replied.

Erin had a key to the outside door of the band room, where she had a file cabinet and locker for her supplies. As she started going through files, pulling out what she needed, Gable took a look around. Wide shelves on one side of the room held an assortment of music cases, containing trombones and flutes, French horns and saxophones and a variety of other instruments.

"Do all these belong to the school?" she asked Erin.

Erin glanced up from what she was doing. "Mmm-hmm. Most of them have been donated over the years." Her face suddenly lit up. "Say! I know what would be fun." She joined Gable and scanned the shelves of instruments. "There it is." She pulled down a black case shaped like a hatbox and unlatched the top. Inside was a snare drum. "As I recall, you said you always wanted to play drums in school, right?"

Gable smiled. "I did indeed."

Erin took the drum out of the case and set it on a stand, then searched among the shelves for a pair of drumsticks. "Ah! 2Bs. Perfect. You'll get a good bounce with these, and they're a good weight for beginners. Okay, hold out your hands. Right one first."

She stepped to Gable's side and took Gable's hand in hers, placing one of the drumsticks in her palm, cradled in the crook of her thumb. "Hold it loosely, like this," she demonstrated, but Gable was finding it hard to concentrate with Erin holding her hand and standing so close.

"Now there are two ways to hold the left stick," Erin continued, gesturing for Gable's other hand. "There's the traditional grip, like this…" She laid the drumstick in Gable's upturned palm and showed her how to cradle it with her thumb and fingers. "Or the newer one is like this." She demonstrated the second type. "Frankly, I prefer the traditional grip." Her small hands enfolded Gable's larger one, and she looked up into Gable's eyes. "But you should go with whatever feels right to you."

Whatever feels right? Gable's mind repeated blankly, as her body registered how much it liked being this close to Erin—shoulder to shoulder, hand in hand. A flush of warmth spread through her, and she froze, unwilling to break the contact.

When she didn't respond immediately, Erin released her and stepped back a step, a playful grin on her face. "Gable? Something the matter?"

"Uh, no! Nope, everything's fine," Gable stuttered, as her attention snapped back to the sticks in her hands.

"Go ahead, give it a try," Erin encouraged, and Gable hit the snare a few times, tentatively.

"You can do better than that," Erin challenged.

Gable relaxed into it, then, and happily whaled away at the drum for a minute or two, getting a feel for the grip and trying to control how the sticks bounced off the drumhead.

"Very nice," Erin said, watching her. "Want me to teach you a couple of basic strokes?"

Strokes? Gable's mind repeated. *Why does everything you say sound sexual?* "Uh, sure. That'd be great." She held out the sticks for Erin to take, but Erin shook her head.

"No, you hold them." She stepped behind Gable and wrapped her arms around her waist, resting her hands lightly over Gable's. "Ready?" she asked.

Gable nodded her head, not trusting her voice. She tried to keep her hands from shaking, but a shudder ran through her as Erin's body pressed closer still. She stopped breathing for a moment.

"Now, when you're learning how to do rolls," Erin explained, "you want to try to control the sticks so that the bead at the end bounces off the drumhead twice. First one stick, then the other. If you go back and forth five times, that's a five-stroke roll. Like this." Erin lightly gripped Gable's hands in hers and slowly tapped out the rhythm on the drum. "And this is a seven-stroke roll." She demonstrated the difference.

Gable could feel her heart pounding in her chest. Their nearness was excruciatingly delightful.

"And a nine-stroke roll." Erin demonstrated, her fingers cradling Gable's hands with a gentle warmth. "Get the picture?"

Gable nodded again. Her mouth was dry. She felt a sudden twitch in her lower abdomen when Erin pressed slightly harder against her.

"Here's a long roll." Erin tapped it out. "You have good hands to play drums," she added in a soft voice as she withdrew her hands and stepped away. "Nice strong hands, good dexterity, nice flexibility in the wrists."

Gable felt herself blushing, so she pounded away at the drums to hide her embarrassment, practicing the rolls.

Erin stepped over to the shelves of instruments and pulled out a long case and laid it on the floor near the drum. Gable stopped playing to watch her.

It was a trombone, and Erin had it put together in under a minute. With a twinkle in her eyes, she held the instrument up and asked, "Ready?" then put the mouthpiece to her lips.

"Ready for what?" Gable asked, puzzled, and Erin launched into a driving riff that she recognized immediately. *"Wipeout."* Like every other wannabe drummer in the world, she had played along with it on many occasions over the years, but always with just her hands, or a couple of pencils on a desktop. *Oh cool.* A big grin splashed across her face as she waited for Erin to get to the drum solo part.

When it arrived, she banged away, right on cue and not too badly, truth be told. But she was not so self-absorbed that she failed to notice how brilliantly Erin played the trombone.

"God, that was fun," she said when they finished. "And I have to tell you, I am really impressed! I've never personally known anyone who could play an instrument like that. You're quite a musician!"

Erin smiled at the compliment. "Thanks, Gable." She pulled the trombone apart and put it away.

Gable felt a pang of disappointment that their jam session was apparently over, and it must have showed on her face.

"You want to play some more, don't you?" Erin smiled up at her.

"Kinda," Gable admitted, in a singsongy voice like a child's.

Erin laughed. "Okay. Hit away, and I'll join you in a second."

While Gable practiced rolls, she watched Erin pull several instrument cases down from the wall and line them up along the floor, assembling the instruments inside so she could play whatever struck her fancy. A piccolo, a French horn, a trumpet, an alto saxophone.

They played for half an hour, a variety of songs and rhythms. Marches and show tunes, TV theme songs and old pop standards. Erin would play a snippet of a song on one instrument, then switch to another, selecting the accompaniment that best fit the tune. "The Stars and Stripes Forever" on piccolo, the theme to *The Simpsons* on sax. Gable played along as best as she could, amazed at Erin's versatility as a musician.

"I can't believe how good you are on all of these," she said as they put the instruments away.

"Well, if you want to see me at my very best, you'll have to come over to my house tomorrow," Erin replied. "They're supposed to deliver my new piano!"

"Oh, I bet you're excited! I know you've missed having one."

"I really have," Erin agreed. "I hated waiting so long, but I wanted the same kind of Baldwin upright I had before, and they're made to order."

"I look forward to hearing you play," Gable said.

"Then I'll expect you for dinner tomorrow."

"I'll be there."

They spent the rest of the day poking around in antique stores and flea markets they stumbled across as they drove up the Lake Michigan coastline. The sky was a deep blue and cloudless, and the great lake shimmered silver in the sunlight. On their way back, they stopped for dinner at a charming seafood restaurant that had great walleye and a breathtaking view of the sunset over the water.

They lingered there over coffee until it was well past dark, neither apparently in any rush to end their time together. It was only when they realized the restaurant was getting ready to close that they headed back to Erin's pickup.

They were on a deserted stretch of road a few miles farther down the coastline when Gable caught a shimmer of color in the sky out her window. "Erin, stop! I think I see northern lights!"

Erin pulled off onto the shoulder and cut the engine, and they both got out. They were miles from the nearest city, so they had an unspoiled view of the night sky, brilliant with stars. To the north, a shimmering curtain of green appeared, stretching from the horizon to the sky above their heads, faint at first, then all at once, alive with movement.

"Wow!" Gable breathed.

"Oh!" Erin gasped.

"Isn't it incredible?"

The curtain grew, expanding as if unfolded by an unseen hand, and traces of yellow mixed with the green, then a flash of red. They watched for several minutes, awed by the phenomenon. Every now and then, a particularly vivid or startling manifestation would prompt an exclamation from one or the other.

"Cool!"

"Look at that!"

"Whoa! That one is amazing!"

Another car approached and slowed to a stop when it got to where they were standing. "Car trouble?" a man in the passenger seat asked.

"Nope, we're fine, thanks. Just watching the northern lights," Erin explained with a wave, and the car continued on.

It took a few moments for their eyes to readjust and regain some night vision. Gable rubbed the back of her neck, which was beginning to ache from looking up. "We're going to feel this tomorrow."

"You know, we're still close to the beach. Want to go watch from there?" Erin asked. "I have a tarp in the back of the truck we can lie on."

"Sure," Gable answered, and they found a deserted stretch of public beach not far away and unrolled Erin's small tarp near the water. It was just big enough for both of them, lying shoulder to shoulder.

The sky above was a dazzling display of color, changing from moment to moment. A curtain of green, then a large whorl of yellow, then streaks of pink and red. In the distance, a chorus of crickets lent a resonant counterpoint to the gentle constant lapping of the surf against the shore near where they lay. With Erin pressed up against her side, Gable could hardly imagine a more perfect moment.

"Have you ever seen anything this beautiful?" Erin asked, her voice soft and full of wonder.

"Never," Gable answered in an equally hushed tone. "I've seen the northern lights before, but it was never like this."

"Sure makes you feel kind of small."

"Yeah, I know what you mean. Gets you thinking about things like, what's our place in all this?"

As if in punctuation to her statement, a shooting star flashed across the sky, and they both gasped.

They watched in silence for another few minutes as the vibrant spectacle continued unabated.

"Gable, do you believe that there's one person that we're supposed to be with? Or do you think there's lots of people out there who could make us happy?"

It took Gable a long moment to answer. "I've always kind of believed in the soulmate thing," she admitted. "One special person for each of us. But I always expected that when it happens, it would hit you between the eyes, and you'd recognize it immediately. You know? Bam!" She took a deep breath and let it out. "But maybe it's not like that at all. Maybe it takes a while sometimes to know it. And I wonder whether you can miss it when it happens, if it doesn't happen just exactly like you always imagined it would."

"So you think it does always happen...I mean, that you will eventually meet that right person...but you just don't always recognize it?" Erin asked.

"Something like that, yes. Maybe they won't look at all like you thought they would. Maybe they can't fulfill every single one of your expectations. But that doesn't mean they can't make you happier than you ever imagined."

There was a very long silence between them then, and Gable wondered whether she'd said too much, given too much away. But there was something about the magic of that moment under the stars that told her to speak from her heart.

The northern lights began to fade, and in a few moments there was only a mere hint of what had been—a thin transparent veil of green, near the horizon.

"It's very late, and I know you have to work tomorrow," Erin said, sitting up. "But I'm very glad we stopped and got to share this."

Gable got to her feet. "Me too."

Erin extended her hand in a silent plea for help getting up, and Gable happily complied. Once she was pulled to her feet, she hugged Gable around the waist. "Thanks for a wonderful day."

"It sure was. Thank you for suggesting it."

They gathered up the tarp and headed back to the truck, walking close together, saying nothing. They were mostly silent on the way home too, but it was a companionable quiet, neither strained nor awkward. More the result of their sharing such an awesome and rare celestial display.

"So I'll see you tomorrow night, then?" Erin asked as she pulled up in front of Gable's at half past eleven.

"I'll be there. Can I bring anything?" Gable offered, turning toward her.

"Just yourself." Erin paused. "Gable, I...I..." She opened her mouth, then quickly shut it again.

Gable waited, one hand on the door handle, but Erin gave an embarrassed laugh and shrugged. "Never mind. I'll talk to you tomorrow."

"You sure?" It sure looked as though she wanted to say something else, and Gable's curiosity was piqued.

"Go," Erin said, giving her a playful shove and a smile. "I've kept you up too late already."

Gable opened the door. "I wouldn't have missed a minute of it," she said, getting out.

Erin nodded thoughtfully. "Me neither, Gable. Good night."

Erin had seemed so relaxed and happy during their Sunday together that Gable wondered what the heck must have happened in the hours since to make Erin so nervous and jumpy on Monday night.

It had been a slow day at the pharmacy, so Gable had had much time to reflect on their previous day. *I'd give just about anything for a lot more days like that,* she thought, as she pulled into Erin's drive for dinner. She was becoming quite used to…and immensely fond of… Erin's hugs, and rather hoped she'd get one tonight too.

But right from the get-go, it was obvious that Erin had something on her mind. She barely made eye contact with Gable when she answered the door, and she seemed harried and anxious about dinner, where she was usually the picture of calm.

"Go on in and make yourself comfortable. I'll get you a glass of wine." She gestured toward the couch, then headed off toward the kitchen. In a tone that fell short of humor, she called over her shoulder. "You may need it—dinner isn't turning out quite like I planned. I shouldn't be trying a new recipe."

"Hey, I'm sure it's fine," Gable called after her.

Earl Grey came running full-tilt out of Erin's bedroom at the sound of Gable's voice and bounded down the stairs toward her. She scooped him up and scratched him under his chin while she glanced around, waiting for Erin to return. The dining table was set as before, with candles and flowers and carefully laid formal place settings. The house was spotless. And there against one wall of the great room was the new piano, beautifully handmade of mahogany and polished to a high gloss. Gable stepped over to it, admiring the craftsmanship. Erin joined her, a glass of merlot in each hand.

"It's beautiful," Gable said, setting down the cat to take one of the glasses.

Erin skimmed one hand lightly along the keys. "Yes, isn't it? I am so glad I insured the other one, or it would have been a long time before I could have afforded this."

"So, do I get to hear you play?"

"Later," Erin said. "After I subject you to my first attempt at a soufflé. I should say first and last attempt, as it looks nothing at all like the photo in the cookbook, but I swear I followed every direction to the letter."

It was true that the soufflé looked rather flat and unappealing, but it actually tasted all right, and Erin had made a Caesar salad to go with it so there was plenty to eat. But Gable could tell that Erin was unusually flustered that everything hadn't gone according to plan.

"Well, I promise I won't make you my new-recipe guinea pig anymore," she apologized again as they did the dishes together.

"Will you stop? It was fine!"

"It wasn't fine. I should've just gone with something I'd tried before," Erin groused.

"Erin, please! It was fine!" Gable couldn't keep the amusement out of her voice, and it seemed to relax Erin slightly.

"All right. I'll let it go," She dried the last plate and set it in the cabinet. "Thanks for washing."

"Any time. Thanks for cooking." Gable rinsed out the sink. "So now do I get to hear you play?"

Erin took a deep breath, as if gathering her nerve. She nodded her head. "Now or never," she answered, almost to herself.

Gable took a seat on the couch while Erin settled onto the piano bench, staring down at the keys for a moment as if considering what to play. Gable liked her vantage point—she could stare unabashedly at Erin in profile from where she sat, seeing every expression, every graceful movement of those wonderfully petite hands over the keys.

Erin started off with a medley of Cole Porter songs, all Gable's favorites: "I've Got You Under My Skin," followed by "You Do Something To Me" and "You'd Be So Nice To Come Home To," and finally, "Easy To Love." A few lines of each song, just enough for Gable to identify it.

She played with feeling, eyes closed, her hands skimming effortlessly over the keys, her face and body one with the music, adding nuances and flourishes that told Gable she was indeed most accomplished on piano.

When she finished, she opened her eyes and looked toward Gable for a reaction, her face expectant and hopeful.

Gable smiled and politely applauded. "That was wonderful. Just wonderful. You play beautifully."

Erin smiled back, but Gable sensed her heart wasn't entirely in it—she almost looked…disappointed? But instead of saying anything, she launched into another medley of old standards—Gershwin this time, another favorite of them both. "How Long Has This Been Going On" was followed by "I've Got a Crush On You," a song Gable had thought of many times, thinking of Erin, in the past few weeks. "Our Love Is Here To Stay" was next in the lineup, then "Embraceable You." Gable had thought of that one a lot lately too.

A chill ran up her spine.

With the closing strain, Erin glanced her way again, the same expectant look on her face…and something else. Something in her eyes that wasn't there before.

Gable held her breath. She couldn't speak. *Is it? Could it…?*

Erin smiled like something in Gable's expression told her what she needed to know. Her eyes closed again, and her fingers danced over the keys. "Only You" gave way to "I Only Have Eyes For You," then "I'm In The Mood For Love," and finally, "All of Me."

Gable's heart was pounding in her ears. She didn't dare believe it.

Erin saved the best for last. It took Gable a moment to place it. An old Doris Day tune, from one of her movies. "Secret Love."

Oh my God. Gable began hyperventilating. When she looked up, she found Erin watching her. This time, neither one of them looked away. Gable felt exposed in that long, unbroken eye contact, as though Erin was looking right through her.

Tears came to Erin's eyes, and she smiled and nodded, and it was then that hope began to dawn in Gable's heart.

"Good Lord, Gable! I thought you were *never* going to get it." Erin turned on the piano bench to face her. "I've been trying to tell you for days."

"You have?" Gable asked dumbly. It still wasn't quite sinking in.

Erin let out an exasperated groan. "I *told* you I have a hard time talking about my feelings. And first I had to be sure how *you* felt.

Though I don't know why I didn't see it before. You wear your heart on your sleeve, you know," she said, almost matter-of-factly.

"Do I?" Gable tried to swallow. Her mouth was as dry as sawdust.

"Mmm-hmm." Erin's eyes sparkled. "I'm sorry it's taken me so long. I've been having a bit of a tough time figuring it all out."

"And you've figured it all out now?" Gable was glad she was sitting down.

"The important parts, anyway." Erin's cheeks colored. She got up and joined Gable on the couch. They sat a foot apart, facing each other, but not touching. "I think I figured out who you fell for. I hope I have."

"You have?" Gable hardly recognized her voice. Erin's face was so enticingly close, her eyes now full of mischief and mirth. Her mouth, so tantalizingly kissable.

"And you're wrong, by the way. About the reciprocal part."

"I am?"

"Yup."

Gable's mind went blank. Her head swam. "Golly."

Erin laughed. "*Golly*? Gable, no one says *golly*."

Erin was smiling at her—*for* her, *just* for her—and Gable felt an uncommon joy fill her, surround her, lift her. Her heart soared, and she realized how incomplete her happy life had been until that moment.

"How about…" She sighed. "I'm in shock?"

"I'll buy that." Erin laughed again. "There's a lot of it going around."

"So…let me get this straight…uh, I mean, about the reciprocal part," Gable stuttered. "Does that mean…"

"Does it mean that I'm lusting after you like I think you've been lusting after me?" There was amusement in Erin's voice. "The answer is most definitely *yes*. Oh, yes."

Lusting after me? As Gable's mind wrapped itself around the words, a flash of hot desire warmed her body. "So…how did you… *when* did you…"

"When did I realize it was you I wanted?"

"Yeah." *She wants me!*

"Well, I knew from the beginning that there was something special about you and me…I was really drawn to you, and curious about you. And I trusted you completely right away…which is really unusual for me." Erin's voice shook, and she lowered her eyes while she searched for the right words.

"When you came out to me, it started me wondering what it must be like to be gay. I've never been with a woman, and honestly, I…I'd never even really considered it before. But once you told me…Well, I started thinking about how I felt about you…and how it would be if *you* and *I* got together…You know…like *that*…"

It was the first time Gable had heard Erin stammer so, and she found it reassuring that the younger woman was apparently as nervous about all this as she was.

"Well, I found *that* mental picture awful damn *hot*, to put it bluntly," Erin confessed.

"Yeah?" Gable was seeing it too, in her mind's eye…and the image of the two of them together turned her arousal up another notch.

"And then I couldn't *stop* thinking about it." Erin laughed. "I swear, sometimes I thought you had to be able to see it in my face! I couldn't keep my eyes off you!"

"Well, talk about dense!" Gable shook her head ruefully. "I *thought* you were looking at me an awful lot, the last few days especially. But I was just worried you were catching *me* looking at *you!*"

They laughed, then Erin's face grew serious. "Gable, why didn't you tell me how you felt?"

Gable managed a chagrined half smile. "I didn't want anything to muck up our friendship. I was worried it would make you feel uncomfortable around me—knowing I was mooning over you. It was terrifying enough just to tell you I was gay! I was afraid coming out to you might change how you feel about me."

"Well, it certainly did *that*," Erin admitted, her cheeks pink. "But not quite the way you thought it might!"

Gable reached out and took Erin's hand in hers, and they shared happy, silly grins.

"So why didn't you tell *me* right away?" Gable asked.

"Well, I was really confused about all those feelings at first. It was sort of like traveling to a foreign country. Exciting, but awful scary. You know that last time I went out with Tim? I did it because I thought maybe I should give that a real chance. That maybe my feelings for you were a phase or something. Did I really want to abandon the kind of life I knew…that was familiar…for something totally unfamiliar?"

"I remember that night. You didn't call me like you promised you would." She looked down at their enjoined hands. Erin's thumb lightly caressed her palm—Gable was amazed at how sensual such a simple touch could be.

"I knew right away that Tim wasn't for me," Erin said. "Once I'd considered how it would be with *you*...I knew I'd never be happy with him, and I didn't want to lead him on. After he'd gone home, I started thinking about whether I should tell you how I was feeling."

Gable didn't interrupt. Erin's thumb continued its gentle caresses as she spoke.

"I drove around a lot that night. I've always done that when I wanted to think." She paused. "First I had to decide whether I could *do* this...I mean, it's kind of a major deal to all of a sudden realize, at age thirty-nine, that you're apparently *gay*, when you never have even *thought* about it before. It's like someone secretly rewired me or something while I slept!"

They shared another silly grin. Gable thought the air around them seemed charged with electricity. *I want to kiss you so much.*

"Once I decided my feelings were too strong to ignore anymore, that I had to tell you," Erin cleared her throat, "then I considered how you might react to the news. Would you be happy? *I* didn't want to do anything to hurt our friendship, either."

Gable squeezed Erin's hand.

"Somewhere around three a.m., I guess, it occurred to me kind of out of the blue that maybe you felt something for me too. It was sort of like...looking back, I began to wonder if I hadn't been missing clues that you'd been sending me. I caught you looking at me kind of funny sometimes. You were constantly blushing that day in the dressing room...and you *really* got embarrassed when you caught me falling off the ladder."

"Well, I did often wonder how in the world you couldn't see how much I was just *longing* to be with you," Gable said.

"Were you? Are you?"

"Most definitely." Gable nodded with enthusiasm, and Erin blushed again.

"Well, I'm very glad to hear that."

"So, all this thinking you did...that was the morning you came over to my house real early, right?" Gable asked.

"Yeah. I had kind of decided that you probably *were* attracted to me and I'd just not picked up on it. But I wanted to be sure. That's why I asked you if you'd ever met somebody special."

"Ah." *Talk about clueless. How could I have been so incredibly blind? Am I that out of practice in the romance department?*

"I hoped it would prompt you to be honest with me, if you *did* feel something for me," Erin said. "I was disappointed you didn't."

"I'm sorry. I was afraid it would freak you out and make you start acting weird around me."

"Well, I got depressed after that. Kind of shut myself away for a while, wondering what I was going to do. And then I got pissed at you for not being honest with me."

"Which is why you were so angry at me in the locker room, and didn't answer my messages."

"Yeah. I guess I wasn't done stewing about it," Erin said. "You sure have left me all stirred up and flustrated, I can tell you!" The blush returned.

Gable laughed. "So what made you come to the pharmacy?"

"Well, I got to missing you somethin' fierce. I played back your phone messages a jillion times just to hear your voice."

"You did?" Gable's heartbeat filled her chest. She felt light-headed. This had to be a dream. Erin saying these things to her. *Lord, please don't let me wake up.*

"And I put your note on my refrigerator and read it about every two minutes! Anyway, I decided I was throwing away the best friend I ever had, and that I might have acted too hastily," Erin continued. "I was just so sure that you did feel something special for me that I had to find a way to tell you how I felt, and really give us a chance." She smiled. "Sorry it took a few days to work up the nerve to say anything, and even then I had to resort to song titles."

"Thanks for being brave."

"But I have to warn you, Gable. I want you like *crazy*—it's all I can think about! But it's still really scary to me." Erin looked away. "I'm a mess with relationships anyway. And I don't know how to… well…how to be with a woman, you know? I mean…" Her eyes met Gable's. "I don't want to disappoint you."

Gable relished the words. *She wants me like crazy!* She took Erin's hand in both of hers. "Erin, I've not been great at relationships either. If it makes you feel any better, I'm probably just as terrified and nervous as you are. I mean, I don't want to disappoint you, either."

"Maybe we can just take this one step at a time, then?" Erin asked.

"We can do that."

"But not *too* slow," Erin added with a grin. Her blush deepened. "I mean, my fantasizing muscles have sure been getting a workout lately, and I'm afraid if we wait *too* long I might spontaneously combust!"

Gable laughed, but her body felt suddenly overheated too. "I'll let you set the pace, then," she said. "How's that?"

There was a short silence, and then Erin met Gable's eyes. There was mischief there, replacing the embarrassment that had tinted her cheeks. "In that case," she said, "I'd like to make a date with you for Saturday."

"Saturday?" Gable whined. "That's five whole days away."

"You didn't let me finish," Erin said. "I'll see you before then, but I'd like to make a date for Saturday as in…a *date*. As in, your next day off? When there's plenty of time?" Erin moistened her lips, and Gable's body heated up another ten degrees.

"Plenty of time?" she repeated weakly.

"Mmm-hmm," Erin gazed into her eyes with heart-stopping candor. "I want our first time together…like *that*…to be really special. Unhurried."

"You mean?" Gable stuttered, as Erin's face moved an inch closer.

"Is that too soon for you?" Erin moved another inch closer, then two. Three.

Gable shook her head vigorously as her pulse quickened.

Erin grinned. "You are *so* slow to take a hint sometimes, Gable. Will you please kiss me?"

She barely got the words out before Gable covered Erin's mouth with her own, their lips meeting in a sweet, soft kiss. She wanted so much to remember that moment that time seemed to stand still. The kiss was tentative at first, a gentle pressing together—then barely apart for a millisecond to reposition before they came together again, this time with much more certainty.

No one's lips can be this incredibly soft.

Gable extended the tip of her tongue to caress Erin's lips—slowly, languidly. Memorizing every centimeter of that oh-so-inviting mouth.

She had stared at it for hours and dreamed of kissing it for weeks. But the real thing far surpassed the fantasies she'd entertained.

Soon, Erin responded to her moist, gentle caresses by meeting Gable's tongue with her own, and the kiss deepened, igniting a fire in Gable's lower belly and making her head swim. When they finally parted to breathe, Gable found it hard to focus.

Erin looked equally discombobulated. "I get it now," she sighed happily.

"Get it?"

"Yeah. *Golly!*"

Gable exhaled a long hum of contentment. "It *is* pretty amazing—how it can feel so different with the right person."

"No kidding! I can't begin to tell you what you do to my body when you kiss me."

"I have a pretty good idea. Five days suddenly seems like an eternity!"

Erin grinned. "It'll pass before you know it. At least, I hope it will. You know I have training tomorrow night and Wednesday night, right?"

"Training?" Gable wailed.

"Yeah, I had to reschedule those sessions I cancelled. I probably won't finish until pretty late. And I have one on Saturday morning, but I'll be done by early afternoon."

Gable stuck out her lip in a pout.

"We can see each other on Thursday and Friday, though," Erin offered. "Maybe go out to dinner one night?"

Gable groaned. "Thursday and Friday are out too. We're doing inventory at the drugstore after we close."

"Oh no!"

"Yeah, major bummer. Gonna seem like a long time until Saturday afternoon."

Erin leaned forward to whisper in Gable's ear seductively. "Well, there is something to be said for anticipation, you know."

The warm breath against her skin sent a shudder through her. "I've already been anticipating for weeks," she said. "I'm not sure how much more anticipating my body can take!"

"Well, I'm right there with you," Erin admitted. "So much so, in fact, that if you don't get headed home pretty quick I may be very tempted to ask you to stay the night."

Gable's body temperature shot up several more degrees. "Oh, it is so not going to be easy to wait," she said, getting to her feet. "All right, I'll be on my way. It is getting late."

Erin walked her to the door, and drew her into a good-bye hug. They lingered long like that, reluctant to part, their arms wrapped around one another.

"Thank you for telling me how you feel," Gable whispered.

Erin nodded, her face against Gable's chest. "Kind of felt like I didn't have much choice." She pulled back to look up at her. "Pretty powerful."

Gable dipped her head to kiss Erin again, a gentle and sweet kiss good-bye, brief enough that it wouldn't leave them both any more stirred up than they already were.

"So…Saturday?" she said as they parted.

Erin smiled at her. "It's a date."

The words bounced around in Gable's head the rest of that night and all the next day at work, like they had a mind of their own. They became the words to any tune that happened to cross her mind, however ridiculous the fit. The William Tell Overture:

It's a date, It's a date, It's a date, date, date!
It's a date, It's a date, It's a date, date, date!
It's a date, It's a date, It's a date, date, date!
It's a daaaaaaaaaaate! Yes! It's a date, date, date!

CHAPTER TWELVE

Though they couldn't be together during the next few days, they spoke often on the phone—each call ratcheting up the sexual anticipation between them.

On Tuesday night, the phone rang just after Gable got into bed, intending to read until she got drowsy.

"Well, one day down," Erin greeted her when she answered. "Only four to go."

Gable laughed. "How was training?"

"I wore myself out rolling and unrolling hose, so I should sleep pretty good tonight."

"It took me a while to fall asleep last night, after everything," Gable confessed. She had driven home in a daze. *Is it really happening?* she'd asked herself over and over ever since. *Can you just wake up one morning and find that all your dreams...even the dreams you never knew you had...had all suddenly come true?*

"It took me a long time too," Erin said. "I kept thinking about Saturday. Picturing us together. It kind of put every nerve ending in my body on high alert."

"Oh, thanks a lot," Gable muttered. "Now I'll never get to sleep!"

The next evening's phone conversation turned up the heat even more.

"I would never have believed a day could drag on like this one did." Gable was in bed again, waiting by the phone, and answered it on the first ring. "I swear to God it's like time stood still."

"I know what you mean. I couldn't stop thinking about you. Just three more days."

"So what time do I get to see you on Saturday?" Gable asked.

"I'm supposed to be done at two. Why don't you come over at two fifteen? That'll give me enough time to get home and get changed."

"Can I bring anything?"

"Nope. Got it covered. Just bring yourself. Oh, and try to get caught up on your sleep between now and then. You'll need your rest."

"Will I?"

"Mmm-hmm. And don't expect to get home early. Or at all. I want to take my time finding out what turns you on."

Gable groaned as a rush of liquid heat infused her body. "You know what you're doing to me, don't you?"

"I sure hope so, because I'm dyin' here! I'm about ready to just come over there right now and ravish you!"

"Ravish me?" Gable gulped. "Oh, great. Thanks for that mental picture. There goes any chance of me getting any rest tonight!"

Thursday night she got into bed almost as soon as she got home at ten. But though she was beat from her long day doing inventory, she still had to talk to Erin before she could sleep. And she found that despite her exhaustion, her body responded to the sound of Erin's voice as soon as she came on the line.

"Just two more days until you get to have your way with me," Erin teased.

"You can be a cruel woman, Erin. You really like getting me all hot and bothered, don't you?"

Erin chuckled. "Fair's fair. You do it to me too. Guess what I did today?"

"Tell me."

"I did some searching on the Internet."

"For?"

"Lesbian literature. You wouldn't believe the stories I found online!"

"Oh, really?"

"Yeah, very *explicit* stories. Let's just say I have some new favorite authors. And I picked up a few ideas for Saturday."

"You're killing me, here," Gable complained good-naturedly, throwing off the bedcovers to cool her overheated body.

"Just one more day," Erin said the next night when Gable answered the phone. "Actually, only sixteen hours or so…not that I'm counting, mind you."

"Worth the wait," Gable said.

"I hope you think so. I hope I can please you…"

"Don't be nervous about that. I *really* don't think that's going to be a problem, believe me."

"You don't?"

"Erin, I get so incredibly turned on just *thinking* about being with you that I'm more worried that I'll…uh…let's just say I'm worried that it will all be over much too fast!"

"Well, if that happens, we'll just have to practice until you're *entirely satisfied* with the timing."

"Oh God, girl, you're making me *crazy*." Gable couldn't help it. Her hand strayed to her nipple, rigid and sensitive, and began stroking it lightly. She could feel the dampness building between her legs. It wouldn't take much for her to relieve this sexual tension.

"Good! It's only fair that we suffer this deliciously *torturous* anticipation together."

Suffer is right. Gable forced herself to stop. She knew only Erin's hand…or mouth…could bring her any real satisfaction.

❖

Finally, it was Saturday.

Gable was so excited she couldn't sleep past seven. She got up and made coffee and showered and dressed. She went online and checked her e-mail, absently munching on a bowl of cereal. Then she decided she didn't like what she had chosen to wear, so she went through her closet and tried on another half dozen outfits, finally settling on khakis and a caramel-colored shirt with a tunic collar.

Glancing at the kitchen clock as she poured herself a second cup of coffee, she was appalled to discover it was only just eight. She tackled every mindless chore she could think of to pass the time. She did the dishes and laundry, made out a grocery list, fixed a broken chair, balanced her checkbook, cleaned out the refrigerator, and filled bird feeders. But the clock mocked her efforts and slowed to a crawl. *Now I know where the expression* killing time *comes from. I'm about ready to throw that damn thing against the wall.*

She surfed through her entire roster of 100-plus satellite channels, but nothing could hold her interest. Grabbing her keys off the counter, she headed to the flower and gift shop in Pine River, where she stared at floral arrangements for several minutes before settling on a bouquet of long-stemmed red roses.

That took up nearly another whole half hour.

She fixed herself a fluffer-nutter sandwich for lunch but decided as she sat down to eat it that her stomach was in too much turmoil to get it down. By twelve thirty she was pacing, impatient as hell, unable to distract herself further from any thought but of Erin. Never in her life, she was certain, had she been so incredibly, *unbelievably* primed and ready to go. *I won't last two more hours.*

But the closer it inched toward two, the more nervous she got too. *I don't want to let her down. Please don't let her regret choosing this. Choosing us.*

Her phone rang and she nearly jumped out of her skin. *It's her! I know it's her!* She leapt for the receiver. "Hello?"

"I can't wait any longer. I'm going to explode."

Gable laughed. "Oh Lordy. Me too. Where are you? Aren't you supposed to be in the middle of something?"

"I'm home. I fibbed and said I didn't feel well and wanted to quit early. Wanna come over and make me feel better?" Erin's voice was so incredibly seductive that Gable's body was instantly atingle with anticipation.

"Don't think me rude, but I'm hanging up now." As she fumbled to put the receiver in its cradle, she could hear Erin laughing.

❖

Gable checked her reflection in the rearview mirror when she pulled up to the last stop sign before Erin's cabin. Her pupils were dilated and she was grinning from ear to ear, like she'd lost her mind. She hardly recognized herself. She ran a hand through her hair to smooth down an errant strand, and took several deep breaths to try to calm herself. Her stomach was doing somersaults, and her senses all seemed hypersensitive, as if to fully appreciate the feelings swirling around inside of her.

In her forty-six years, she could not remember feeling this happy. This excited. And certainly never this *aroused*.

Erin was waiting for her in the open doorway, reclining against the frame, Earl Grey in her arms to keep him from getting outside.

Gable had, from the first moment, thought her an incredibly attractive woman. But she'd never thought her more beautiful than at that moment. Erin was barefoot, clad in faded jeans that had molded themselves to her and a navy T-shirt, left untucked, that was thin enough to let Gable know she wasn't wearing a bra. She had a glow about her, and Gable could see undisguised desire in her eyes.

They watched each other, smiling shyly but not speaking, as Gable slowly mounted the steps with the roses held at her side. Her whole body was trembling.

Erin moistened her lips as Gable neared, and in a moment they stood two feet apart. Erin made no move to step aside so Gable could come in.

Gable reached out with her free hand and scratched Earl Grey under the chin, but her eyes never left Erin's. "You know that I just *have* to kiss you first thing, don't you?"

"I sure hope so," Erin said, smiling up at her. "Because I'm not letting you inside until you do."

Gable lifted her hand to caress the side of Erin's face, just before she dipped her head and brought their mouths together.

Five days of anticipation fueled the kiss.

Erin moaned and opened her mouth, inviting Gable in, and the heat in Gable's belly became a bonfire. When their tongues met and began stroking…tasting…exploring…her head began to swim. Her body moved of its own accord toward Erin's, and Erin's moved toward her.

Earl Grey *rowled* loudly when he got pressed between them, and struggled to get free of Erin's arms.

They broke apart, chuckling at the cat. Erin tried to calm him while Gable struggled to focus. She put a hand on the doorway and leaned against it. Her breathing was ragged and she felt unsteady on her feet.

"Your kiss sure packs a punch," she said.

Erin blushed, but she had a very pleased smile on her face. "Does it? I'd tell you something along the same lines, but I'm finding it impossible to think coherently at the moment." She nodded her head toward the bouquet of roses at Gable's side. "Are those for me?"

Gable held them up, smiling sheepishly. "Sorry, forgot all about them. You turned my brain to mush."

"Flatterer. Get in here and I'll find something to put them in."

Gable followed Erin to the kitchen on shaky legs.

"Would you believe I found this in the rubble? It was my grandmother's." Erin held up a large crystal vase for her inspection. "It was buried under a collapsed wall. Not a scratch on it." She ran her fingers over the etched surface. "It's amazing how a tornado can take a whole house and break it apart, and yet spare something so fragile." She loosely arranged the flowers in the vase and set it in the sink to fill with water.

Gable came up behind her and wrapped her arms loosely around her waist. "I just *have* to touch you," she said softly, resting her chin on Erin's shoulder so they were cheek to cheek.

Erin shut off the tap and leaned back into Gable, caressing the arms holding her. "You won't see me complaining." She sighed contentedly and they remained like that for a long moment.

Gable inhaled deeply and recognized the clean and slightly floral aroma she had come to associate with Erin—her shampoo, she realized now, nuzzling her way along Erin's neck, then lowering her lips to worship the softness of Erin's cheek.

"Mmm, that's nice," Erin hummed, arching her neck to invite more of the same.

"I want this to be perfect for you," Gable said, before nipping lightly on Erin's earlobe with her teeth. Her lips moved unhurriedly along the underside of Erin's jaw and along the silky expanse of neck, planting brief kisses along a winding, invisible path. Her arms drew Erin closer, until their bodies were pressed tightly together. She was certain Erin could feel how hard and fast her heart was beating in her chest.

Erin made a whimpering sound that reverberated through Gable. "What you're doing is an excellent start." She took a deep breath and let it out. "Except I'm finding it hard to stand upright."

"Perhaps we should lie down, then," Gable suggested in a seductive whisper.

"Oh, Gable." Erin turned to face her, and their mouths met hungrily, shyness and nervousness melting away under the fierce heat of their attraction.

Gable's tongue explored the warmth of Erin's mouth while her hands sought naked flesh. Her fingers stole beneath the bottom edge of Erin's T-shirt and found the soft skin of her lower back. As her hands began exploring, dipping into the waistband of Erin's jeans to tease and arouse, Erin's hands grew bolder too, entwining in Gable's hair at the back of her neck and pulling their mouths tighter together, deepening the kiss.

The sudden blare of an emergency radio drowned out the pounding of her heart, and acted like a shock of cold water on her overheated body. Their lips broke apart, but she and Erin remained knit tightly together.

"Oh God, not *now*!" Erin grumbled, slumping against her chest. She was breathing hard, and so was Gable.

"Damn!" Gable agreed, as she struggled to regain her equilibrium.

"McCoy from dispatch. Respond, tree on power line. 48 Gilmore Street."

"A tree?" Gable moaned, throwing her head back in anguish. "They're pulling me away from you for a tree?" She gave a great sob as she reached for the radio on her belt, and Erin chuckled and hugged her in commiseration.

"I should go too," Erin said, grappling for her own radio. "Why hasn't mine gone off?"

"They won't call you. Not if they think you're sick. Not for something like this."

"Crap," Erin muttered.

They headed to Gable's Jeep.

"Look, I'll call you from my cell if we really need you," Gable said, reaching for the door handle.

Erin stopped her with one hand on her arm, and leaned up to plant one brief but passion-filled kiss on her startled lips. "Be careful. I'll be waiting."

Gable whimpered. "I'll be back as soon as I can." She got in the Jeep and sped to the callout address.

She was first on the scene. The address she was given belonged to a small summer cottage nestled in the woods about a mile and a half from Erin's house. As the Jeep bounced up the rutted two-track driveway, she spotted a woman close to her own age standing propped against a shovel, staring up at the power lines that ran to her home. A hundred feet or so from the cottage, a huge tree had fallen on the dual lines, pushing the still-live wires into the branches of a row of pine trees.

The lines were throwing off sparks wherever they rested against a branch. And beneath the wires was a thick layer of flammable forest duff—pine needles and crispy dead leaves and tinder-dry underbrush.

The woman heard the approaching vehicle, and her face registered relief that help had arrived. Gable braked and exited the Jeep, grabbing her portable fire extinguisher from the back.

"Hi there," she greeted the homeowner. "I'm Gable McCoy. Help is on the way. When did this happen?"

"I'm not sure. It got real windy and my power blinked a couple of times. I thought it was just the wind, but then I looked out my window and saw this. I called the power company, but I was afraid there might be a fire. My hose doesn't reach this far."

"You did the right thing." Gable could hear the wail of an approaching siren. "That'll be the pumper," she told the woman. "We'll hang out with you until the power company gets here."

"Great."

Carl was driving the truck. He positioned it as near as he dared and jumped down off the high seat.

"Hey there," he greeted Gable.

"Hi, Carl."

He took a look at the situation and keyed his radio. "Dispatch from Buckman. On the scene with McCoy. Additional units responding—we can handle this."

"Dispatch clear," answered the dispatcher.

"Power crew should be here soon," he told Gable. "We get to babysit. Why don't we pull a handline off the truck in case we need it?"

"You got it."

Once they had it positioned, they leaned against the fire truck to wait.

"I'm going inside for a few minutes," the homeowner said. "I'll see if the power company can tell me when they can get here."

"So how's it going, Gable?" Carl asked when they were alone. "Last time I saw you, at the ladder drills, you didn't look too happy. Neither did Erin."

Gable felt her cheeks color. She couldn't suppress a grin. "You're awful damn observant, you know," she griped.

"That's why I'm a good 911 director. I have an eye for detail." He appraised her with a smile on his face. "Speaking of which, I'd have to say you're *blushing*, which I take to be a good thing?"

"I will *only* say that I'd rather be somewhere else at the moment," Gable admitted.

Carl laughed. "Good for you." He patted her on the shoulder. "You're a right egg, Gable McCoy. It's nice to see you happy."

The distinctive ring of Gable's cell phone pealed from the Jeep, and Gable hurried to answer it. She heard Carl's laughter as she grabbed for the door handle.

"Hello?" She got inside the Jeep and shut the door for privacy.

"What's happening?" Erin asked.

"Not much. Carl and I are waiting for the power company to get here. Then I can leave."

"Do you have any idea how incredibly turned on I am?"

Gable groaned. "Oh, that's great. Just great. Get me all lathered up again when we can't do anything about it."

"I think I'll wait for you in bed."

"Stop it!"

"With some nice lingerie on."

"Erin, please! You're killing me!"

"Or maybe nothing at all."

"You're a cruel woman. I'm going to hang up."

"Oh, all right," Erin said. "I just wanted to leave you with an image that I hope will get you to hurry back."

"You don't have to worry about that," Gable said. "You just worry about getting any sleep tonight."

A half hour later Gable dialed Erin's number again. "At the risk of your taunting me with more provocative images, I'm calling to tell you they still aren't here yet."

"Argh! I have never seen time *crawl* like it's doing right now. It seems like you've been gone for *hours*."

"Tell me about it."

"If I have to wait much longer, I won't be responsible for my actions when I see you," Erin said.

"Promises, promises."

It took the power company another excruciatingly long, maddeningly frustrating half hour to get a cherry-picker truck to the scene, turn off the power, and cut the tree off the line. Once the line was dead, Carl turned to Gable. "Get out of here. Go have some fun."

"You sure?"

"Go!"

Gable didn't need a second invitation. She ran to the Jeep and punched in Erin's number on her cell phone as she headed back down the two-track to the main road.

"I'll be there in two minutes," she said as soon as Erin answered.

She heard a long sigh that was almost a whisper. The sound sent her body into sensory overload.

"I can't wait," Erin said.

Exactly two minutes later they were kissing hard in the doorway, hugging each other fiercely. It took no time at all for both of them to be right back where they had been before they were so rudely interrupted.

Erin's tongue pushed into Gable's mouth. Demanding. Insistent.

Gable's pulse tripled and the heat building between her legs spread through her body, coursing through her veins and dancing along the surface of her skin. Desire drove her and became all she knew.

Erin broke the kiss. "Bed," she said, gazing up at Gable with half-lidded eyes, her lips red and slightly swollen. "Now."

CHAPTER THIRTEEN

Erin led her by the hand to the bedroom, which had been thoughtfully prepared for the occasion. She paused just inside the doorway, and Gable took in the surroundings. Candles lit the room, casting a soft flickering light on the curved, polished wood of the new sleigh bed, covers pulled back to expose the soft Egyptian cotton sheets that Gable had helped pick out.

Without letting go of her hand, Erin took two steps to her left and hit the play button on her stereo. Soft instrumental jazz. "You Go to My Head."

"This is lovely," Gable murmured, pulling Erin into her arms again and dipping her head for another kiss.

Lost in a haze of desire, she didn't immediately register that Erin was undressing her. Before she knew it, her shirt was unbuttoned and Erin was pushing it off her shoulders and down her arms. Erin broke the kiss to pull the shirt off and gazed longingly at Gable's breasts, barely concealed by a thin white tank top that set off the deep tan of her skin. They were not overly large, but were nicely shaped and well proportioned to her lean and muscular body.

Erin placed the fingertips of her right hand on the flat plane of Gable's stomach, and even through the sheer fabric Gable could feel the heat of her touch. Her stomach muscles twitched under the caresses, and when Erin's fingers dipped inside her jeans and pulled her shirt free, her breath caught in her throat.

Erin pushed the tank top up halfway, both hands splayed across Gable's abdomen for maximum contact with her naked flesh. She paused when her fingertips reached the curve of Gable's breast, and leaning forward, began to plant soft kisses on Gable's neck as her hands drifted upward.

Gable closed her eyes and sighed, relishing the feel of the small hands cupping her breasts, of Erin's delicate fingers as they played lightly over her nipples, which were already hard and sensitive. She wanted more, much more, but she forced herself to let Erin set the pace.

This is new to her. For God's sake, don't scare her off! It took every ounce of restraint she had not to rip Erin's clothes off and take her in a rush of frenzied desire. For though she had been with women before, it had never been like this. She had never felt so totally and thoroughly aroused, so out of control, so desperate to touch and be touched.

Erin seemed to sense her controlled impatience, or perhaps she was feeling an equal measure of need and want. She pulled off Gable's tank top and dipped her head to take her right nipple in her mouth, sucking, nipping lightly with her teeth, as her hands found the clasp and zipper of Gable's jeans and undid them.

Groaning, Gable threaded her fingers through Erin's hair, pulling her closer, encouraging a deeper touch. Erin's mouth sucked her harder, and Gable groaned again, then her jeans and underwear were being pushed down over her hips.

Erin's mouth left her as she stepped out of her clothes, putting one hand on Erin's shoulder for balance. She stood naked in the soft light of the candles.

Erin's gaze appraised her with wonder—and obvious approval. "You have a beautiful body, Gable," she said in a hushed voice, as her eyes lingered on the soft brown triangle of hair at the apex of Gable's thighs.

"I'm awful glad you think so," Gable reached for Erin's T-shirt. Her restraint was slipping. She *had* to touch her. And right *now*. She pulled the thin cotton garment over Erin's head, exposing the full, round breasts that had taunted her in her dreams. "Beautiful," she whispered, her voice unrecognizable.

Erin trembled as Gable undid her jeans and slid them off, along with her cream silk panties. The downy fine hair beneath was a shade lighter than the hair on her head. Gable took her hand and led her to the bed, and they climbed under the covers and faced each other, lying on their sides.

"Tell me what to do," Erin whispered, caressing Gable's cheek with the back of her fingers.

"Erin, everywhere you touch me feels wonderful," Gable replied, leaning in to cover Erin's mouth with hers.

As they kissed, slowly and sensually, Gable slipped her arm around Erin and pulled their bodies together, hot flesh meeting hot flesh, breast to breast, belly to belly. She insinuated one of her long legs between Erin's, and Erin released a soft, sweet whimper into their enjoined mouths when Gable's thigh pressed hard against her.

The wetness of Erin's desire bathed her skin, and it drove her wild. She slipped a hand down Erin's back to cup her ass, and rolled, pulling Erin on top of her.

Now Erin's leg was providing the same delicious friction to her heated core, and the kiss deepened as their desire grew, their bodies rocking against each other. Erin moaned again and dug her fingernails lightly into Gable's shoulder. The roar of her blood in her ears drowned out everything else as their rocking grew more furious and unrestrained, and she worried she would come too soon, even before Erin touched her.

Erin broke the kiss, panting for air. "God, Gable. Oh, God. I can't...Oh! Oh!" She closed her eyes and arched her back, and her body grew rigid as an immense orgasm tore through her.

Gable held her close, her own body trembling and on the brink, until Erin relaxed against her, hear head resting on Gable's chest.

"I didn't mean...I wanted to wait..." Erin stuttered as she fought to regain her breath. "But I couldn't...It was too...too much...too intense."

"I know. It's all right...it's wonderful," Gable answered, her voice gentle but strained. Her whole body thrummed with arousal, and when she caught the heady scent of Erin's climax it drove her higher, pushed her beyond words.

She rolled them over until she was on top of Erin, resting her weight on her elbows.

Erin opened her legs and wrapped them around her, shuddering when Gable settled against her. "Oh, Gable," she moaned, arching her back and rolling her hips for more contact.

A throaty growl escaped Gable's lips as she began a slow descent down Erin's body, kissing her way to the soft valley between those exquisite breasts, then claiming one nipple roughly, sucking on it, nipping at it with her teeth. The same treatment to the other, then back again.

Erin's moans rang in her ears, urging her on, so she shifted her weight and brought her fingertips slowly up the inside of Erin's thigh as her mouth continued to pleasure Erin's breasts.

Touching Erin intimately for the first time, her hand sliding into the soaked silky folds, intensified her own sweet ache. Her body was on fire. She struggled to contain her orgasm.

"Gable! Oh! That feels incredible." Erin writhed beneath her, fingernails raking lightly across her back, as Gable teased and stroked her with increasing pressure. "Please! Oh, *please*, Gable. I want to come—I *need* to come."

The plea drove Gable down Erin's body to claim her wet warmth with her mouth. She massaged Erin's swollen clit with rapid strokes of her tongue and pushed two long, slender fingers against her opening. *So wet for me*, her mind crooned, as Erin opened and took her inside, muscles tightening around her fingers in spasms as she roared to climax.

"Gable! Oh God! Oh my God!" Erin screamed.

Gable gentled her strokes but did not stop, drawing another orgasm from her even before the last had subsided.

"Stop!" Erin panted. "I can't…Enough!" She was trembling with aftershocks as Gable reluctantly withdrew and kissed a slow, tender path back up her body.

"I've never…never like that," Erin gasped, clutching at Gable, holding her fiercely.

"It's never been like this for me either, Erin," Gable echoed, savoring the sweet taste of Erin's desire where it lingered on her tongue. She kissed the delicate hollow at the base of Erin's neck. Never had she felt so much while pleasuring someone else. Never had her blood boiled as it did now.

"Oh, I hope that's true." Erin's chest rose and fell with a deep breath. "And now…" She abruptly shifted her weight, rolling out from underneath Gable. "It's your turn, I believe." She pushed Gable playfully down onto her back, and Gable did not resist.

On her side, head propped up on one hand, she gazed down at Gable. "Tell me what I can do to please you. Tell me what you want."

She skimmed her fingertips over Gable's breasts in lazy figure eights that teased the rigid nipples on every pass.

Gable's body temperature shot up, and her heartbeat went into overdrive. "Everything you do pleases me," she said hoarsely. "I'm so close now it won't take much to make me come."

"Well, I don't want to rush you," Erin drawled. "But I can tell you need some attention." Her fingertips closed in on one nipple, pinching it hard, while her mouth descended on the other for equal treatment.

Gable's hips arched off the bed as a powerful rush of ecstasy tore through her, obliterating all thought. "I can't wait...can't...*please*, Erin..." Her body was screaming for release, and her stomach clenched in anticipation.

Erin was blessedly merciful. Her mouth continued to suck Gable's nipple while her hand descended to bring her to fulfillment. Gable spread her legs and held her breath as Erin's palm stole down her abdomen and across the triangle of hair—the caress firm, the intent clear.

Erin's teeth nipped at Gable's nipple roughly as her fingers slid across her clit and into the wet folds beyond. Gable cried out and pressed against Erin's hand, feeling three fingers slide inside, filling her, turning her body into molten lava. An unrelenting pressure was building inside her, a yearning so intense it brought tears to her eyes.

Erin pumped into her with slow strokes, bringing her higher and higher, and then Erin's thumb pressed hard against her clit and sent her reeling over the edge into oblivion. Her whole body spasmed and shook and her mind went hazy, and she collapsed back against the mattress, breathing hard.

"Golly," she sighed, after a very long moment, and Erin laughed— a throaty chuckle of satisfaction.

"Guess I did okay for my first time, eh?" Erin settled against Gable's side, resting her head in the crook of her shoulder and sliding her arm possessively across her stomach.

"Any better and you might have killed me."

"I never imagined it could be like this. Never." Erin's fingers played along Gable's hip, thigh, stomach. "I can't stop touching you."

A contented smile played across Gable's lips. "I like the sound of that. But it might be a problem when we're out in public. People might stare."

Erin chuckled, and the sound vibrated against Gable's chest. "If this is what it's like with us...I'm beginning to wish I'd figured everything out a lot sooner." Erin's hand began to move with more deliberation, skimming over Gable's breasts and down to the edge of her tangle of curls.

"You know what you're doing to me, don't you?" Gable groaned as the heat began to build again between her thighs.

"I certainly do," Erin said, pinching one of Gable's nipples back to rigid attention. "You came over for dinner, and I'm helping you work up an appetite."

❖

Gable stifled yet another yawn and tried to focus on the paperwork in front of her. It was an impossible task. Her body bore the complete exhaustion of a weekend of nonstop lovemaking, and her mind could think of nothing but Erin.

She glanced at the clock on the wall. Eleven thirty. They'd been apart less than four hours—she'd left Erin's about eight so she could detour by her house to change clothes. It felt like an eternity. *You are in such serious trouble here.* But she couldn't wipe the smile from her face.

June Dunsmore, the sixtysomething cashier who tended to mother Gable, had noticed immediately that something was different.

"*Someone* had a nice weekend," she commented when Gable showed up an uncharacteristic fifteen minutes late, with bags under her eyes and a jumbo Styrofoam cup of coffee from the gas station across the street.

Gable blushed a deep scarlet and took off past June toward the pharmacy counter in the rear.

"Aha! I knew it!" June's voice trailed after her. "I want details!"

Fortunately, the place stayed busy all morning, keeping her from further interrogation. But Gable had been largely unable to focus on her work during the brief lulls between prescriptions.

She stretched and stood and stepped to the counter, intending to restock a display of informational brochures. But she had hardly begun the task when her hands stilled and her mind drifted, revisiting the myriad of times she and Erin had come together in the big sleigh bed. Her body warmed at the memories.

"Penny for your thoughts." Erin's voice, enticing and amused, from four feet away abruptly brought her back to the present.

Gable blushed but grinned broadly as she gazed into Erin's eyes. She saw the same hungry look of desire she'd seen there all weekend. "This is torture."

"Mmm-hmm." Erin nodded her head with enthusiasm, grinning back at Gable.

"I thought you had training until five."

"The chief had to end the morning session early to take care of some personal business. I've got almost an hour. Can you break for lunch?"

"Oh yeah."

They walked two blocks to the Slice of Heaven café, a popular hangout known for its pie menu—thirty-five varieties baked fresh daily by the quartet of elderly sisters who owned the place.

Meriwether wasn't very big, but the café was always crowded at lunchtime. People came from neighboring counties for one of the specialty pies they could get nowhere else…pies with names like Pennsylvania Dutch shoofly, and mocha java chocolate, and brandied peach custard.

Every table was occupied, and it looked as though everyone was either waiting for their food or had just gotten it. They wouldn't be sitting down any time soon, and there were no real alternatives within a short drive. They looked at each other with resigned frowns.

"We might be able to get pie and coffee," Gable apologized.

"I'm not really that hungry," Erin said. "I just couldn't wait until tonight to see you."

"Gable? Want to sit with us?"

Gable and Erin both turned toward the voice. Two women in their thirties waved at them from a table in the near corner. One was an attractive blonde, the other a striking brunette with a vaguely familiar face.

Gable looked at Erin. "Well, we won't be alone, but…what do you think? The one on the left—the blonde—is Emily Fairfield. She's the librarian in town."

Erin shrugged. "Sure. Fine with me."

They headed over to the table.

"Thanks, Emily," Gable said as she reached for one empty chair, while Erin took the other, across from her. "Erin Richards, meet Emily Fairfield."

"Pleasure to meet you," Emily said.

"And you as well," Erin responded. "Thanks for sharing your table."

"This is Lindsey Carter," Emily introduced her tall, attractive friend.

"Have we met?" Gable inquired.

"I thought you looked familiar too," Erin said.

"I'm on TV," Lindsey explained. "I'm a reporter with Channel 6 News in Traverse City."

"Oh! Okay, right," Gable said. "I've seen you. Nice to meet you."

"Same here."

The four women chatted amiably over lunch. Gable was a regular in the Meriwether library, and both she and Emily ate at the café at least three or four days a week, so they had chatted on occasion about their jobs, and gossip in town, and the latest novel that caught their interest.

Gable tried hard not to stare at Erin throughout the meal, but her eyes kept wandering over to her, lingering on her lips, drifting to her breasts. She caught Erin several times doing the same to her and wondered how obvious they were being to their lunch companions.

"So…how do you two know each other?" Gable asked Emily and Lindsey as they dug into dessert.

Each of them had ordered a different type of pie. Emily chose mile-high lemon meringue, Lindsey went with rosy red rhubarb, Erin selected Grandma's chocolate pecan, and Gable opted for Montmorency cherry.

Both Lindsey and Emily froze at Gable's question, their forks halfway to their mouths. The two women looked at each other; Emily smiled and Lindsey's cheeks colored slightly.

"Well, Lindsey detoured into town last spring for pie," Emily said. "Remember the day we got that big rain and the bridge washed out?"

"I do!" Gable said. "I had to stay with June for a couple of days. I couldn't get home."

"Well, Lindsey got stranded here too. She stayed with me." Emily turned toward Erin. "The library is that big white house down the street," she explained. "I live upstairs."

"We…uh…found we had a lot in common," Lindsey stuttered, her blush deepening.

The light dawned, and for the first time, Gable began to think she just might have this gaydar thing after all. "A lot in common, you say?"

she asked mischievously. "Erin and I have a lot in common too. I bet we *all* have something in common."

The table was silent for a moment as her words sank in.

"Really?" Lindsey looked much more comfortable all of a sudden.

"You don't say," Emily said.

"We do?" Erin asked with a puzzled expression, clearly not understanding.

"Mmm-hmm." Gable nodded, looking at Erin. "You just joined the club a few days ago."

"Oh!" Erin's hand flew up to cover her mouth. Now *she* blushed. She looked at Emily, then Lindsey, then back to Emily. "Well, whattaya know. Small world."

The others all laughed, and as they finished their pie, the four women made tentative plans to get together one night for poker or a movie or some other outing.

Gable and Erin had to hurry back to the pharmacy if Erin was to make it back to the fire hall in time.

"Well, that was sure an eye-opening lunch. You know, I've chatted on and off with Emily for months now, and I never had a clue," Gable said. "And I've even seen her sitting with Lindsey a few times."

"How did you figure it out?" Erin asked.

"It was just something about the way they were looking at each other. Kind of like how you and I couldn't keep our eyes off each other."

"Do you know how much I want to reach out and *take* you, right here and right now?" Erin asked as they neared her pickup, parked at the curb in front of the drugstore.

"Hold that thought until tonight," Gable answered. "I'll be there as soon as I can."

"I miss you already," Erin said, getting into her truck. She rolled down the window. "I've got it bad for you, Gable."

Gable put her hand on the sill and Erin covered it with her own. "I'm glad to hear that. Me too, Erin. See you later."

She thought about the evening the rest of the afternoon. And by the time she got to Erin's place at 6:40, she could feel the moisture between her legs from her fevered anticipation.

Erin flung open the door as soon as she drove up, and bounded down the stairs and into her arms.

They kissed long and hard, pressing their bodies together, the heat between them scorching Gable, obliterating everything else. Erin's body fit perfectly against hers.

"Oh God, you feel so good," she murmured into Erin's ear.

"Inside," Erin answered breathlessly, tugging at her.

They stumbled into the house and to the bedroom, removing clothes as they went, kisses punctuating every other step.

The first time that night was frenzied and fast. After dinner they took their time.

Around midnight, Gable awoke, spooning Erin from behind, her hand cupped protectively over Erin's breast. She didn't move for a long minute, relishing the feel of her skin, the press of her body, the soft, reassuring sigh of her exhalations. *How can I ever sleep alone again?*

They had not discussed the future or their feelings for each other. It was too soon for that—Gable accepted that fact intellectually, and refrained from bringing it up. Erin had made it clear she had relationship and commitment issues, and Gable didn't want to pressure her or scare her off.

But she already knew in her heart that there would be no one for her but Erin. She was so head-over-heels in love she couldn't think straight, and she could no longer imagine living the solitary life she'd been content with for most of her adult life.

They certainly had passion and chemistry between them, there was no doubt of that. Erin had made it abundantly clear she couldn't keep her hands off Gable any more than Gable could resist touching her when they were alone. But as wonderful as the sex was, Gable prayed that it was more than that with Erin. Much, much more.

Plagued by her insecurities about the future, she found it difficult to fall back asleep and slipped out of bed, careful not to wake Erin. She put on Erin's terrycloth bathrobe. It was a little small for her, but it smelled vaguely of Erin's soap and shampoo, and Gable found it reassuring somehow. She went into the kitchen to make herself a cup of tea, then sat staring out the window at the stars.

Her life felt more out of her control than she'd ever imagined it could be. Just a few months ago, she had a clear and certain future, or so she thought. She'd reconciled herself to the notion that the soulmate thing was a fairy tale and that she was meant to be alone. So she found satisfaction and meaning in her life by helping others.

But now Gable knew what profound joy there could be to every single day, when it was shared with someone you truly loved. She could never go back to her old life, her life without Erin.

Thank you for this gift, she prayed. *May I be long worthy of it.*

She returned to bed but remained by the bedside for a moment, studying her lover's face in the moonlight streaming in through the window.

I love you, Erin. With all my heart. Please love me too.

Chapter Fourteen

Sweat poured off Gable as she labored to widen the firebreak, turning over dirt at a furious pace. Her back ached and her hands were blistered despite her gloves, but it looked like they might succeed in containing the fire if the wind held off a while longer.

It was a cool October day, and the twelve volunteer firefighters on Crew 23 had gravity on their side. They were below the fire on a steep hill in the Manistee National Forest. Although it was a densely wooded area, the trees were mostly virgin white pines, tall and straight, the nearest branches ten to twenty feet off the ground. With no wind to blow it up into the high canopy, the fire was confined to the forest floor and it advanced at a walk, feasting on pine needles and dry bracken ferns.

But the weather service was predicting that brisk winds would move in off Lake Michigan, so the firefighters kept a close watch on the treetops as they moved up the hill, cutting a five foot breach with shovels, pickaxes, and chainsaws.

Gable also kept one eye on Erin, positioned twenty feet to her right. Despite her diminutive figure, she had proven to be a very capable firefighter in the weeks since her training, but today was pushing the limits of all of them. Gable could see that her lover was just as bone-tired as she was, and also as determined to continue on.

The fire had already consumed nearly 260 acres, and crews were working on all sides to bring it under control. It was the highest priority callout; Gable and Erin had both missed work to respond, and they were still at it seven hours later.

Crew 23 was the only thing standing between the blaze and a half dozen homes. They were cutting a firebreak from the creek at the bottom of the hill to the rocky ridge at the top, and were more than three-quarters of the way up when the wind began to rise. It wasn't much at first. The crew kept working.

The intermittent breeze quickly became a steady twenty-mile-an-hour blow, with gusts strong enough to send sparks and embers across the breach. The firefighters had their hands full trying to douse the spot fires springing up all around them. Their upward momentum ground to a halt.

Gable felt the heat of the fire increase as the wind sent the flames swirling up into the higher tree branches. She glanced to her right. A back draft sent a plume of smoke over Erin, momentarily obscuring her. Gable held her breath and gripped her shovel more tightly until she reappeared.

Their radios crackled to life. The voice, a shout, belonged to Carl Buckman, who was working at the tail of the line, farther down the hill. "23 off the hill! Move! Move! Another fire below!"

Gable spun around. Three hundred feet down the slope, thick smoke was rising in a column from the forest. They were in deep trouble, trapped between two fires. She hesitated only until Erin reached her. They were already breathing hard as they sprinted diagonally up the hill toward safety.

The fire below them was everything the one above them was not. It sprang to life with a burst of hot energy, fanned by the wind into a blast-furnace train that howled toward them with frightening acceleration.

"Drop your tools!" Carl yelled, and as Gable tossed her shovel she heard the clatter of several others directly behind her.

She didn't turn around. She had to watch every step as they raced upward over the rocky, uneven terrain. Erin kept pace beside her but was clearly struggling to match Gable's long strides. No one spoke. The world turned red around them, reflecting the firestorm. Everything shimmered in the heat, miragelike. It was difficult to breathe.

The heat was so intense the grass beneath their feet burst into flames. Erin stumbled and fell. Gable paused to help her, and Carl was suddenly there too. They hauled Erin to her feet, one on either side of her, as several of the others sprinted by.

They were running for their lives.

The two fires came together behind them, joining up into a wall of flame that extended from the forest floor to the top of the trees. It was a blowout—every firefighter's worst nightmare. The crackling roar of the inferno was deafening, and embers rained down all around them, pelting their hard hats. The stench of burning hair assaulted Gable's nostrils as the trio finally reached the crest of the hill and crossed into the sanctuary of a wide, rocky ridge where the fire could not follow.

Like the others ahead of them, Gable and Erin collapsed once they were safely out of harm's way on the other side. Erin lay on her back, her face a grimace of pain, her chest rising and falling in exaggerated gasps for air. Gable was likewise panting, on her hands and knees, struggling to calm the pounding of her heart.

"Are you all right?" she rasped.

Erin nodded, unable to speak.

They had made it, all of them, but with only feet to spare. Erin and Gable looked at each other with the shared realization of their narrow escape. Gable crawled the few feet that separated them, and they embraced, both shaking in the rush of fear and adrenaline.

"Too close, that one," Gable whispered. Her arms and legs felt leaden.

"Gable, your hair!"

Gable took off her hard hat and ran a hand through her hair. She'd lost a fair amount in back, and it was singed to crew-cut length just behind her left ear.

"You both okay?" came Carl's voice from above them. They pulled reluctantly apart, heads nodding in unison.

"Yeah, we're all right. Everyone else?"

"Yup. All accounted for." Carl's face was almost unrecognizable under a thick layer of dirt and soot and sweat. "That was one I don't want to repeat. We better get moving as soon as we can."

They made it down the other side of the hill and were relieved by firefighters from a neighboring county. The fire claimed four homes before it was finally contained, but no one was injured.

"Stay with me tonight?" Erin said as they were dropped off at the township fire department.

Gable smiled. "I'd like that."

They had fallen into a routine in the weeks since they became lovers. Gable spent two or three nights a week at Erin's, and Erin spent two or three nights a week at her place. Earl Grey spent the night when Erin did, and now had a litter box, toys, and a hammock bed at each home.

The first couple of weeks, they'd spent every night together. But once school started, they were apart one or two nights a week so that Erin could do her lesson plans and correct schoolwork without interruption. Try as she might, if Gable was present, she said she rarely got anything done.

Tonight was to have been one of those schoolwork nights, so Gable was especially pleased she would not be sleeping alone. Her bed was too big and lonely without Erin, and after their brush with death, she needed the reassurance of her lover's body beside her.

They took a quick shower together when they got to Erin's place, then climbed into bed beneath her fluffy down comforter, too exhausted to eat, too weary to do anything but cuddle.

"I bet we're sore tomorrow," Erin said drowsily.

"That's a pretty safe wager, I think." Gable spooned Erin in their familiar way, her front to Erin's back. She loved the way Erin's smaller body fit within the curve of her larger frame, totally enfolded in her arms.

"That was scary today. Thanks for picking me up."

"We all watch out for each other," Gable said. "I was afraid too." She kissed the back of Erin's neck and hugged her closer.

"You make me feel safe," Erin whispered. "From the moment we met, you've been my hero, you know."

"I want to always be there for you, Erin," she murmured. "Always and forever. You mean everything in the world to me. Everything."

Gable could feel Erin stiffen slightly. *Shit. You and your big mouth.* She had been extremely careful not to say anything that might make Erin feel pressured about their future. But she was tired, and unguarded, and feeling particularly emotional so soon after their harrowing escape.

"What you said." Erin's voice was so soft Gable barely heard it, though their heads were nestled beside each other.

"Mmm?"

"Ditto, for me."

Gable's heart swelled, and tears came to her eyes. She kissed Erin's neck again, and her lover relaxed into her arms. They were soon fast asleep.

❖

Gable lay awake in bed the next night, unable to get comfortable without Erin next to her and powerless to stop the images of the wildfire that had been replaying in her mind all day. She ran her hand through her hair, still unaccustomed to the length. She'd kept it fairly short for many years, but not *this* short. It was shorn in the back, to even out the section of hair that had been burned in the wildfire.

They had been very lucky—or very blessed—to have escaped both the tornado and the fire on the hillside. And Gable knew there likely would be more close calls for them as volunteers in the fire service. She had accepted that risk for herself when she decided to join the squad. But the thought of anything happening to Erin scared the living hell out of her. Terrified her far worse than any threat to her own life.

Like Erin's crystal vase, the fire had been a jarring reminder of the fragility of life, the capriciousness of nature. Gable knew all too well how quickly and unexpectedly loved ones could be taken from you. She ached to tell Erin how much she loved her. Needed her. How much she wanted them to share their lives for the *rest* of their lives. If anything were to happen to either of them, Gable wanted Erin to know exactly how much she meant to her.

Maybe I can *tell her. Maybe if I just don't hit her with too much at once. Start with* I love you *and see how it goes. I know she loves me back, don't I? She admitted as much last night, didn't she?* Gable sighed. *Tell her. And tell her soon. Don't let something else happen.* She hoped she was making the right decision. Now she just had to wait for the right opportunity. Or maybe *create* one.

Not certain how Erin would react, Gable decided not to make a big deal out of it. *Better to keep it low-key.* But she wanted it to be special. A moment to look back on. A memorable setting.

The best option, she decided, was right outside her window. The trees were at the peak of autumnal color. A brilliant array of fiery tones, nearly every shade imaginable in the spectrum from deep scarlet to brilliant orange to iridescent yellow, cast against the varied green palette of pines and hemlocks. A blaze of color carpeting the forest floor, and surrounding her on all sides. The evenings were cool, but not cold yet. Exactly the right time for a campfire in the big fire bowl she had dug in a clearing near her house.

She and Erin both lived where they lived because they wanted to be close to nature, and nature was certainly putting on an amazing display for them. *It's perfect.*

The following Saturday afternoon, Gable spent more than an hour laying the fire, erecting a carefully built teepee of twigs—matchstick-sized tinder in the interior graduating to larger and larger branches—and then the whole structure surrounded by a square framework of split logs. It was a work of art unto itself, and Erin, watching the construction from a nearby lawn chair with a goblet of merlot in her hand, nodded approvingly when it was finished.

"It's lovely. Seems almost a shame to light it."

"Old habits die hard." Gable shrugged. "I can't build a fire unless it's a one-matcher."

"One-matcher?"

"Camp Fire Girls take a lot of pride in building a fire that will catch with just one match. Watch." Gable struck an Ohio Blue Tip wooden match against the side of its box and carefully inserted it into the narrow opening she'd left in the teepee, away from the wind.

The tiny flame caught the tight bundle of dry hemlock twigs in the center of the teepee, and the fire spread quickly upward. Soon they had a roaring fire.

Erin sucked in a deep breath. "Mmm. I love the smell of wood smoke."

"I've always been fascinated by fires," Gable said, taking a lawn chair beside Erin's and poking at the conflagration with a long stick. "I love building them, lighting them, watching them. Kind of ironic I now put them out!" She smiled and sighed contentedly. "I can sit by a campfire for hours."

"This was a nice idea," Erin agreed. "It's so pretty out here."

Gable reached for her wineglass, which she'd set on a makeshift table made out of a tree round, set on its end. "I think autumn is my favorite time of year, though spring runs a close second, with all the wildflowers and the baby animals running about."

Erin nodded. "I had two raccoons coming by regularly with their babies. They were *so* adorable, scampering up trees whenever something scared them. Oh! And the baby birds when they fledge and are fed by their parents. People who live their entire lives in a big city don't know what they're missing."

"There's a line in *Walden Pond* where Thoreau says something like…'I went to the woods because I wished to live deliberately. To see if I couldn't learn what it had to teach, and not, when I came to die, discover that I had not lived.' I like that. I think when you live in the woods you are somehow closer to the heartbeat of life."

"Nicely put," Erin said, reaching out to take Gable's hand in hers. "I'm so glad I'm here. With you. That we found each other."

Gable lifted Erin's hand to her lips and kissed it. "Me too. I can't remember ever being this happy."

A comfortable quiet settled over them as they enjoyed the fire and the autumn foliage, and a sky painted with the bright pinkish red of an approaching twilight. Gable fed the fire with split oak logs until they had a deep bed of hardwood coals. She buried two potatoes wrapped in foil into the embers and let them bake. When they were nearly done, she set up a grill over the fire bowl and cooked two rib eye steaks to medium rare.

"Quite the campfire cook you are," Erin commented as she dressed her potato with butter and sour cream. "Why does food cooked outdoors always taste better?"

"Wait until dessert. Have you ever had a banana boat?"

"Don't think so. What's that?"

"You cut a little trough in a banana, and insert marshmallows and pieces of chocolate. Then you wrap it in foil and cook it in the coals until everything melts together."

"Anything with chocolate in it, I'm pretty much guaranteed going to like it."

After they'd eaten, Gable took their plates inside the house and returned with a blanket. She spread it out on the ground near the fire, up against a low log bench she had built for visiting nieces and nephews.

As she gazed down at Erin as she approached her chair, Gable's heart stopped in her chest. "God, you're so beautiful," she whispered.

Erin smiled up at her, the firelight casting a soft warmth over her skin and accentuating the blond highlights in her hair.

And you get more beautiful every day. Gable held out her hand. "I want to sit with you," she said.

Erin allowed herself to be pulled to her feet and led to the blanket. Gable sat with her back against the bench and settled Erin between her legs, leaning against her chest. Wrapping her arms around Erin's waist, she slipped one hand beneath her sweatshirt and T-shirt, and gently caressed the warm, soft skin of her abdomen. "Mmm. That's better," she sighed, resting her head on Erin's shoulder.

"I'll say," Erin agreed, relaxing back into her embrace.

They stared into the fire and listened to the night noises: the *who-cooks-for-yoooou* lament of a barred owl calling for a mate, the sharp shriek of a nighthawk. The rustle of leaves from the dark forest beyond the fire that told them a deer or some other denizen of the night was watching them.

Now or never. Gable took a deep breath. "You're precious to me, you know," she whispered, her lips inches from Erin's ear.

Erin sighed, and caressed the arms enfolding her. "Same back atcha," she replied in a low voice.

Gable steeled her nerve. Her heart was racing. She wondered whether Erin could feel it, they were pressed so closely together. "Erin, I…I want you to know…" Her voice broke. "I just want you know that I love you. With all my heart." She held her breath.

Erin was silent for a very long time. Finally she turned her head slightly, so that she could plant a gentle kiss on Gable's cheek. "Thank you," she whispered.

It wasn't exactly the response Gable had hoped for, but she was relieved her declaration hadn't made Erin pull away. She seemed contented, even if she hadn't replied in kind.

Give it time, she told herself. *Just give it time.*

CHAPTER FIFTEEN

Gable sat on her couch with her feet up, sipping coffee and staring out of her large picture window. Chickadees and goldfinches, woodpeckers and nuthatches darted back and forth from the trees to the feeders positioned about the yard and beneath the long overhang of eaves. A half dozen squirrels and a lone chipmunk scurried about, busily gathering acorns. The first snows of winter would be on them before they knew it.

Yet another reminder of the impermanence of all living things.

The changing of the seasons made Gable feel restless. She dreamed about the day when she and Erin would spend no more nights apart—the day they would share everything: one bed, one home, one plan for the future. And she wanted that day to be soon.

Gable was glad she'd told Erin she loved her, though Erin had made no reference to her declaration in the three weeks since. She felt more at peace with herself now that Erin knew the full measure of how she felt. And Gable was optimistic that Erin returned her feelings, even if she hadn't articulated them beyond her *Ditto for me* admission the night after they escaped the forest fire.

For Erin *showed* her how much she cared in a myriad of thoughtful ways. In the romantic dinners she labored over, in the small notes she stuck into her pockets, and especially in the ways she touched her and responded to her touch when they made love.

"Mind if I join you?" Erin yawned loudly from the bedroom doorway.

Gable glanced around. Her heart melted at the sight of her lover.

Erin's hair was sleep-tousled, and she looked even more delicately petite than usual, swallowed whole by Gable's plush fleece bathrobe. Earl Grey was perched on one shoulder.

When he spotted a new furry mouse Gable had given him the night before, he jumped down and set off on a hunting expedition. He pounced on the toy and batted it high into the air, purring loudly as it rattled.

Gable smiled and patted the couch beside her. "You're up early."

Erin settled next to her and kissed her on the cheek. "Very funny."

"Well, nine thirty is pretty early for you," Gable teased. "Want some coffee?"

"Oh, bless you. Yes, please."

Gable went to the kitchen and poured herself another cup—black, and doctored Erin's the way she liked it.

"What time did you get up?" Erin gratefully accepted the steaming mug, curling her hands around it to warm them.

"Oh, a while ago."

"That means a couple of hours at least. I'll never understand why you get up at the crack of dawn when you don't have to." Erin yawned again, and stretched like a contented cat.

"I'm a morning person, I guess. I love this time of day, when everything is just waking up. Seeing what critters are out and about. Going over in my head what I'm going to do that day."

"I prefer to remain in bed every single solitary second I can." Erin rested her head against Gable's shoulder. "Although it would be eminently more fun if you lingered there with me." She sighed a long, dramatic sigh, which got her a poke in the ribs from Gable.

"I know what happens when I linger in bed with you. We never leave the bedroom all day."

"And you're complaining about that?" Erin pulled back to look at her with mock horror.

Gable laughed. "Never." She put her arm around Erin and nuzzled her neck. "Although sometimes I need a little recovery time, like after last night. By the way, have I told you lately how incredible you are in bed?"

"Same back atcha, Hot Stuff." Erin closed her eyes and arched her neck to encourage Gable's gentle kisses.

She took advantage of the invitation and kissed, licked and nipped her way from Erin's earlobe, down her neck, along her collarbone, to the valley between her breasts.

"Mmm, that feels soooo nice," Erin said in a low throaty voice, running her hand through Gable's hair. "Are you sure you don't want to linger a while in that big ol' comfy bed of yours?"

Gable worked her way back up to Erin's neck, and then her cheek, and finally kissed her softly on the lips. "Well, I *might* could be *persuaded...*" she drawled slowly in the rich Southern accent she'd had as a child. "You *are* impossible to resist." She dipped her head to nuzzle again at Erin's neck. "We just have to remember to give ourselves plenty of time to get ready for the wedding this afternoon." Two of their friends from the squad were getting married, and all the firefighters had been invited.

Gable felt Erin stiffen. She drew back to look at her, but Erin wouldn't meet her eyes.

"I've been meaning to talk to you about that, Gable. I'm not going."

"Not going? Why not?"

"I'm just not." Erin shrugged. "I'm not into weddings."

"But it's not going to be a long service. Or a big one. They only invited their families and a few friends. We can skip the reception if you like."

"You can go, Gable," Erin said, still not looking her. "Just tell Billy and Therese I didn't feel well."

"I don't really want to lie to them, Erin," Gable said. "Why didn't you tell them...and *me*, earlier, that you didn't want to go? It doesn't sound like this is something you only decided this morning."

"I just don't want to go. It's not that big a deal," Erin snapped, clearly annoyed. She got to her feet. "I'm going to take a shower and get dressed. I've got some errands to run today."

"Erin, wait..." Gable started to protest, mystified by the sudden chill in the air. *What just happened?* But Erin was gone, back into the bedroom without a look back.

The atmosphere thawed only slightly when Erin reemerged fifteen minutes later, dressed in jeans and a T-shirt. She found Gable in the kitchen, stacking pancakes on a plate.

The table was set for two.

"Got time for breakfast?" Gable asked gently. She hoped she could get Erin to talk about what was going on—explain why she was suddenly acting so distant.

Erin paused in the doorway as if considering her answer. After a long moment, she came up and gave her a hug and a halfhearted smile. "That's very sweet of you, but I better run. Have fun. I'll call you later." She gave Gable a peck on the cheek and left the room. Gable followed as far as the doorway.

"C'mon, Earl. Time to hit the road," Erin called to the cat, who was sprawled on his hammock by the window.

Earl Grey remained where he was, staring at Erin to make sure she knew he had heard her just fine and preferred to stay where he was. Erin marched over to him and picked him up.

"Erin?" Gable leaned against the door frame and folded her arms. Something told her she was playing with fire, but she couldn't stop herself. "Did I say something to make you angry?"

Erin took a deep breath before she answered. "No, Gable. I'm not mad. Let's just drop it, okay?"

"Does this have something to do with your marriage?" Gable took a stab in the dark. Erin had volunteered only that she'd made a bad mistake when she had married. She'd never told Gable any more than that, although they had shared the details of most all the other noteworthy parts of their lives.

Erin left with Earl Grey without answering.

Gable was puzzled by Erin's sudden mood swing, and unsettled by it. *But it's not the first time it's ever happened*, she realized, going to the window. *It's just much worse today.* At every mention of marriage or commitment whatsoever, Erin changed. Usually it was pretty subtle. But it was like a chill came over her and she withdrew into herself. Gable watched her drive off without a wave good-bye. *What the hell happened to you to make you this way, Erin?*

She fretted about Erin's abrupt departure all morning. She showered and dressed for the wedding in a simple navy pantsuit and white silk blouse, but still couldn't calm her crowded mind. By the time she got to the church and slipped into a pew in the back, she was vaguely nauseous.

She had hoped that attending the wedding together might encourage Erin to talk about her feelings. Might get her thinking favorably about planning their future together. Instead, the occasion had split them apart.

The dull pain in her stomach grew as she listened to Billy and Therese exchange their vows. She ached to one day say those words to Erin, and to have Erin promise to love, honor, and cherish *her* until death parted them. She wondered again what had happened to make her so against marriage.

As she passed through the receiving line outside the church, she put on her best smile and congratulated the happy couple.

"What a wonderful ceremony. Therese, you are positively glowing. And you don't clean up so bad, either, Billy," she kidded the groom, a mechanic who'd managed to scrub away what she could have sworn were permanent grease stains on his knuckles.

"Thanks for coming, Gable." Therese pecked her on the cheek.

"Erin couldn't make it?" Billy took Gable's hand in both of his.

Gable and Erin had made no public acknowledgement that they were seeing each other, but a couple of the guys at the poker table had caught on to the looks between them, and word had gotten around the squad. They'd been the subject of some good-natured ribbing after that, but everyone had been pretty cool about it—even the more conservative guys Gable had thought might create some problems.

"She sends her regrets," Gable replied. She didn't want to say more. She hated lying.

The reception was being held at the VFW Post a couple of miles from the church—Billy was a veteran of Desert Storm. Halfway there, Gable pulled off the road onto a side street and stopped the car. She took her cell phone out of the glove compartment and checked the display. No messages.

She punched in Erin's number at home. The phone rang five times and then her answering machine picked up.

"Hi. Are you there? It's me. I just wanted to talk to you and see how you're doing." She paused, hoping Erin was listening to her and would pick up. It didn't happen. *Well, she did say she was going to run errands.* "I'm headed for the reception. I'll try your cell. Please call me."

She had talked Erin into buying a cell phone a couple of weeks after they'd started seeing each other. It hadn't been too hard to do, though Erin had sworn she'd never get one. With their jobs and Erin's training, they had been playing phone tag. It was much easier for them to reach each other on their cell phones.

"The cellular customer you are trying to reach is unavailable. If you'd like to leave a message, press one."

Gable hit the button. "Erin, it's me. Please call me on my cell. I hope you're okay." She took a deep breath. "Please don't be mad at me. I'm sorry if I upset you." Setting her phone on vibrate, she slipped it into the pocket of her blazer and headed to the reception.

She mingled for a while with a glass of Guinness in her hand, trying not to glance at the watch on her wrist. She lingered in small groups where someone was telling a story, so she could nod her head agreeably and feign interest, all the while obsessed with wondering what was happening with Erin. Her mind was so removed from the reception that she jumped out of her skin when someone tapped her on the shoulder.

"Hey! Easy there. I only wanted to ask you to dance." Carl had a hand extended, palm up. The reception music was provided by a local DJ, whose current CD selection was Glenn Miller's "In the Mood." A half dozen other couples were dancing.

"What will Alberta say?" she kidded him with a smile, setting down her glass and letting him lead her to the modest dance floor.

"She knows how much I love her," he said, sweeping her around the floor in a fast-fast slow-slow swing step.

The words tugged at her heart. "Your wife is a lucky woman," she told him. *I wish I could know so clearly how Erin feels.*

There must have been something in the tone of her voice. Carl led her off the floor and over to a corner away from everyone.

"What's the matter, Gable?" he asked.

"You're very perceptive, you know that?"

He shrugged.

"It's Erin…sometimes I have no idea what's going on with her," Gable said.

"Women are hard to understand, sometimes," he said, and got a smile out of her. "Anything I can do? Want me to talk some sense into her?"

"No. But thank you. I mean that. You've been a good friend and I appreciate your support."

"I think a lot of the both of you." Carl rested a hand on her shoulder and gave it a squeeze. "Let me know if I can do anything."

"You can lead me around some more on the dance floor and get my mind off my troubles for a little while."

He held out his hand. "I can do that."

Gable tried both of Erin's numbers again as she drove home at eight. The party was still going strong, but they'd gotten past the dinner and requisite toasts, and picture-taking, cake-cutting, and garter belt rituals. She had slipped away when the dancing and drinking had begun in earnest, knowing she would not be missed.

Erin was still not answering either phone. Gable started to leave another message, but stopped herself. *Don't pressure her. Give her some time.*

She held her breath as she pulled into her driveway, hoping against hope that Erin would be waiting for her. Gable had given her an extra key, and she'd used it a few times. She had one to Erin's cabin too, but she knew that now would not be the time to use it.

No red pickup was waiting for her.

Gable unlocked the door and let herself inside. The house was quiet. No messages waited on her answering machine. She shrugged off her coat and dropped her keys on the counter, wincing at how loud they sounded in the absolute stillness. The house lacked warmth without Erin and Earl Grey in it.

This is not like you, Erin. You're never out of touch this long anymore. Not since we've been together. She tried to shake off a nagging disquiet.

CHAPTER SIXTEEN

"Y ou look terrible. Are you ill?"
Gable glanced up from the phoned-in prescription she was filling to find June appraising her with a critical eye from the other side of the counter. The drugstore was empty but for the two of them and Max, a high school kid who worked part time stocking shelves and helping out at the cash register.

She knew the sleepless night spent staring at the phone had taken its toll. She noticed the dark circles under her bloodshot eyes when she was dressing for work, and she had been yawning nonstop all morning.

"I'm fine, June. I just didn't sleep very well last night."

"Ah ha! I *see*," June commented as she bent forward and rested her elbows on the counter, her posture and tone implying that she suspected there might be a good story behind Gable's excuse.

"Get your mind out of the gutter, June. I was all by myself. I just couldn't get to sleep."

June's face fell with the news there would be no good gossip arising out of Gable's tired countenance. "Oh." Then her motherly side took over. "Sure you're not sick?"

"No, really. I'm fine."

The bell over the front door sounded and June headed back to her register, sparing Gable further scrutiny.

The four cups of coffee she had ingested during the course of the morning felt like they were burning a hole in her stomach. And she could feel the tension building between her shoulder blades, knotting up the muscles in her back. She had tried Erin's numbers a few more times last night, and again this morning, with no success. She'd begun to contemplate what it would be like to resume her old life. Without Erin. *What if she shuts you out permanently?*

It was unthinkable. Unbearable.

She had no real hope that Erin would be waiting for her after work, although they routinely had dinner at Gable's house on Monday nights. Still, her heartbeat picked up as she neared her house, and she said a silent prayer for the red pickup to be there.

To her profound relief, it was.

The lights were on; Erin had used her spare key and let herself in.

Gable rushed up the steps. Erin met her at the door and hugged her fiercely. "I'm sorry, Gable. I'm sorry I was such a brat."

"Not necessary," Gable hugged her back.

"Yes, it is," Erin insisted, not loosening her embrace. "I have some...some issues, especially on the subject of marriage," she explained vaguely. "I told you that. But I shouldn't have taken it out on you." She looked up at Gable with moist eyes. "Forgive me?"

Gable kissed the top of her head. "Nothing to forgive. I didn't mean to bring up bad memories, or pry. I really didn't. I just want you to know that if you ever want to talk about it, I'm here for you."

Erin hugged her tighter. "I know that," she said in a soft voice.

"I was worried when you wouldn't answer the phone."

"I drove around a long time. I ended up in Petoskey."

"Petoskey?"

"Yeah. I went to see my mother. I told her about us."

Gable drew back and looked at Erin with wide eyes. "You did?" Her heartbeat pounded in her chest.

"She wants to meet you."

"How did she react?"

Erin snorted. "My mother is never what you expect. She was fine with it. She just wanted to know if I was happy."

"And *are* you happy?" Gable's voice betrayed her and broke on the last word.

"I am happy, Gable. As happy as I can be, without some help."

"Help?"

"I'm going to start seeing a therapist. My mother recommended it, and I think she may have something."

Alarm bells went off in Gable's head. *A therapist? A therapist who will tell you you're really not gay, just confused. I bet that's what your mother is hoping for. She's not fine with it at all if she is recommending you see a shrink about it.* Her insides churned with worry. *Just wait. Give her a session or two with a psychiatrist, and Erin will be telling you she can't see you anymore.*

"Gable? Did you hear what I said?"

You can't tell her not to do this. It's not your place. It's her decision.

"Yes. I heard you. You think this will help you?"

"I do. I hope so."

Gable pulled her close. "I hope you're right."

From all outward appearances, things between them resumed as before. They remained virtually inseparable, spending most of their evenings and weekends together, and were certainly no less passionate with each other than they'd been.

They celebrated a quiet Thanksgiving at Gable's house with turkey and all the trimmings, and Erin spoke excitedly about how much she looked forward to spending their first Christmas together.

But Gable felt like she was living on borrowed time.

Erin was seeing a therapist named Karen twice a week, on Tuesdays and Fridays after school. She told Gable when her appointments were and said they were helping her, but she never shared any details of the sessions.

On those days, especially, Gable lived on tenterhooks, expecting the worst: expecting Erin to march in and announce she was straight after all.

It was on a Friday, three weeks before Christmas, that Gable got a phone call as she was about to leave the drugstore. Friday had become pizza night—Gable would pick up a large pepperoni and black olive pizza at the Slice of Heaven on her way home and they would rendezvous at her house. Erin's therapy went until five and Gable worked until six, so more often than not, Erin was waiting for her when she pulled in.

But Erin had other plans tonight.

"I'm glad I caught you," she began when Gable came on the line.

"What's up?" Gable tried to keep her voice steady, but a feeling of dread pushed at her from all sides.

"Do you mind coming over to my house for dinner tonight instead of doing pizza?"

"No, whatever you like. Is everything okay?"

"Everything's fine," Erin said. "I had a good session today and I want to talk to you about it. Karen thought I might be more comfortable if I was at home."

"All right." Gable couldn't breathe. *Shit. Shit. Shit. This is it.*

"I'll see you when you get here, then," Erin signed off.

"See you soon."

For the first time since they'd met, Gable was not anxious to see Erin. Her worst fears were about to be realized, she was certain. She was going to lose the woman she had come to love with all her heart and soul. It was going to be one lonely Christmas.

When she arrived at her destination, she cut the engine and sat in the Jeep a long moment, looking wistfully at Erin's cabin. The warm, inviting glow of the light from the windows. She'd spent so many hours inside, in Erin's arms, in Erin's bed. It had become as much a home to her as her own. *Home is where the heart is, indeed. How cruel to find it, and then have it taken away.*

She forced herself out of the car and walked slowly up to the front door. Her hand trembled as it reached for the knob. "I'm here," she announced, letting herself in.

The stereo was playing "It Had to Be You."

The dining table was set for two, with Erin's best china and sterling silver flatware set on linen napkins and place mats. Delicate crystal flutes, positioned just so. In the center, two slender candles in silver candlesticks flanked a bottle of champagne chilling in an ice bucket.

Gable pulled off her coat and hung it from a hook next to the front door. Her nose caught a whiff of...*something wonderful.* She started toward the kitchen, but Erin's voice from the bedroom doorway stopped her in her tracks.

"Hi. I was changing."

Gable turned and wanted to melt on the spot. Erin was wearing the outfit that was absolutely, positively *guaranteed* to drive Gable wild—the black demi-cup bra and matching panties she had bought at Victoria's Secret that memorable shopping day. *The* bra and panties that

Erin had been wearing when she haunted Gable's dreams.

Gable couldn't breathe. Perhaps she should never have told Erin about the dreams. That lingerie had become Erin's secret weapon. Gable could feel a roar of heat rush over her like a wave, settling between her legs. She was instantly wet.

"What's all this?" Her voice sounded quite a bit higher than usual, and Erin seemed pleased by that.

A big smile spread across her face as she approached and wrapped her arms around Gable's neck. Automatically, Gable gathered her close, arms around her waist, but she was too stunned to speak. This certainly was not at *all* what she expected.

"Gable?" Erin's forehead furrowed as she looked into Gable's eyes. "Is something the matter?"

"I…uh…well, I uh…wasn't expecting *this*," Gable stuttered.

"Why? I can't be romantic?"

"No! I mean, yes! Of *course* you can be romantic. I mean…you *are* romantic. Very. A lot. Like now. This." Gable sounded like her brain was short-circuiting, which wasn't far from the truth. *You can't think straight when she wears that.* "I just mean…I…never mind." *Why are you fighting this, you idiot?*

Her body took control, as it always did when Erin brought out the black bra and panties. She dipped her head and met Erin's mouth hard as her hands smoothed down over Erin's ass and pulled their bodies roughly together.

Erin whimpered and laced her fingers through Gable's hair as she deepened the kiss, thrusting her tongue into Gable's mouth and rocking against her, a slow easy roll of her hips that sent Gable's arousal into the stratosphere.

She had to come up for air. "God, what you do to me," she said hoarsely, as she matched Erin's movements with thrusts of her own.

"Clothes," Erin panted, breaking their embrace to grapple for the clasp and zipper on Gable's navy dress slacks. "You have far too many clothes on."

Gable fumbled for the buttons on her shirt, not about to disagree. She felt like a death row prisoner who had been given a last-minute reprieve by the governor.

Once Gable was naked, Erin quickly stripped off her lingerie and led her by the hand to the candlelit bedroom and into the big sleigh bed.

Their mouths met again—impatient, hungry—as their bodies pressed against each other, breast to breast, pelvis to pelvis.

Erin rolled them until she was atop Gable, then she pushed herself up on her hands and opened her legs, so she was straddling Gable's abdomen.

Gable reached up and cupped Erin's breasts in her hands as she thrust upward with her hips. She could feel the wetness of Erin's desire paint her stomach, and it ratcheted up her arousal another notch. Erin threw her head back and groaned.

Their rocking against each other grew more frenzied, and Gable pinched Erin's nipples hard.

Erin groaned again, louder. Her breathing was ragged. "Oh God, Gable. Please. I need your hands on me."

Gable pinched the sensitive nipples again before sliding her hands down Erin's flat stomach and into the vee between her thighs. Her thumbs rubbed lightly against Erin's clit, and Erin let out a long, throaty growl that Gable felt to her core.

The fire in her belly flared white hot, and she could feel the moisture build between her legs. She'd never been so wet.

Neither had Erin.

Gable slipped two long fingers of her right hand into Erin as her left thumb circled her clit.

Erin gave a startled cry, and then her hips began rocking furiously against Gable's hand. "Oh! Oh, Gable!"

Gable could tell Erin was very close. So was she.

"Erin," she moaned in a ragged plea, her hands pleasuring Erin in ever faster, longer strokes.

"Yes! Oh, yes, Gable!" Erin arched her back and her hand found Gable's clit and rubbed it hard, sending them over the precipice together.

They collapsed against each other, their bodies trembling, both struggling to breathe.

Once their heartbeats had returned to normal, Erin shifted her weight and snuggled against Gable's side, her head in the crook of her shoulder and an arm and a leg thrown over her body. "How can it get better every time?" she whispered, her hand playing lazily with Gable's sensitive nipple.

"We're very fortunate," Gable said, kissing the top of Erin's head.

"Yes, we are. I'm lucky to have you, Gable. You're sweet, and kind, and generous."

Gable warmed at the reassuring words and hugged her lover closer.

"I'm sorry I haven't been able to tell you how I feel about you," Erin continued in a low voice. She pushed herself up on one elbow so she could look down at Gable. "I've been working on that." She resumed her gentle caresses of Gable's breasts and stomach with her free hand.

"You have?"

Erin nodded. "And I'm making progress."

"You are?" Gable held her breath.

"Mmm-hmm." Erin looked away and cleared her throat. "Karen's really helping me to understand a lot of why I am the way I am. Why I have such a problem telling you the way I feel about you. I haven't gotten it all figured out yet, but…" Her eyes rose to meet Gable's. They were bright with emotion. She took a deep breath. "I love you, Gable. With all my heart."

Gable let out a whoosh of air. Relief flooded through her and warmed her from within. "You love me?"

Erin nodded. "Of course I do." A tear escaped from the corner of her eye and fell on Gable's shoulder. "Did you doubt it?"

"No." Gable pulled her into a close embrace. "No, I…I can feel how much you do, when we're like this." She sighed. "I was afraid that the therapist might…might convince you that it was just a phase you were going through or something."

Erin barked out a laugh. "A phase? You think this is a phase I'm going through?"

"No, of course not. *I* know it's not. I mean…I thought that you might be going to a therapist because you weren't sure you were gay. That your mom suggested it because she wanted you to be straight."

"Gable." Erin's tone was reproachful as she rose up again so she could look into Gable's eyes. "I told you my mother was okay with it. She *is*. She wants to meet you."

"Okay." Gable nodded uncertainly.

"I told her how much you mean to me." She caressed Gable's face with her hand. "I never, *ever* have doubted that. Or questioned whether we are supposed to be together."

Gable's heart swelled in her chest until she felt it would burst.

"I told my mother how *frustrated* I was that I couldn't bring myself to tell you how much I love you. I'd get close…but then, something would stop me. I was afraid you might…" Her voice drifted off.

"Might what?" Gable asked.

"Oh, that you might get tired of it…not hearing the words. That you might find someone else who *would* tell you."

"Erin, there is no one else for me. Ever."

Erin sighed and rested her cheek against Gable's chest. "I hope not," she whispered.

"I was terrified that you were going to break it off tonight," Gable confessed.

"What?" Erin exclaimed. "You're not serious!"

"I was afraid of losing you. Every time you went to see your therapist, I worried you'd come back and tell me you were straight. When you told me tonight you wanted to talk to me—here—about your session, I figured the time had come."

Erin shook her head in disbelief. Her eyes held Gable's. "I wanted it to be *here* because I wanted to fix you a nice dinner, have some champagne. Make it a real romantic evening. And Karen thought it might be easier for me to make my 'big declaration' here, where I feel the safest." She grinned crookedly as a soft blush infused her cheeks. "Of course, as six o'clock got nearer and nearer I decided I wanted to skip right to *this* part and do dinner later, and thankfully I was able to convince you." The smile faded. She blew out a sigh of regret. "I'm sorry, Gable. Sorry that you doubted me. I hoped you *knew*, even if I couldn't tell you."

She looked away, staring off into space as if she was gathering her thoughts. Her jaw set with determination and her eyes grew cold. "My…my *husband*"—she spat the word as if it were a curse—"he wasn't very nice to me, Gable."

Gable felt a sudden overwhelming anger toward a man she couldn't put a face to. "He…He really messed up how I function in relationships." Erin paused and took a shaky breath. "I didn't want to screw this up, Gable. *Us*, I mean. *That's* why I'm seeing a counselor. So that you and I can really have a future together."

"I can't imagine my future without you." Gable ran her fingertip along Erin's jaw.

Erin turned her head and kissed Gable's hand. "I'm glad to hear that." She lay back down against Gable's side, and they hugged each other in quiet contentment for a long while.

"So, tell me…" Gable abruptly changed position, moving atop Erin. She grinned mischievously down at her lover before lowering her head to put her mouth between Erin's breasts. Her tongue ran along Erin's cleavage. "What did you cook us for dinner?"

"Uh…Uh…" Erin shuddered, and her body rose to press against Gable's. "We're having baked potatoes, which are being kept warm in the oven. And, uh…oh, *yeah*…uh, salad. Which is in the fridge."

Her eyes glazed over as Gable's mouth closed around a nipple and sucked lightly, rhythmically. "Oh, God. And…ugnh…pie. Cherry pie for dessert. Oh, Jesus, Gable."

Gable nipped the sensitive bud lightly as she trailed her hand up the inside of Erin's thigh. Teasing.

"Steaks," Erin was panting now, her body writhing beneath Gable's touch. "They're fast. Everything can wait."

"Not everything." Gable slid down to taste her lover, to soothe the raging inferno that enveloped them both. "I can't wait. And neither can you."

Chapter Seventeen

It started out as one of the best Christmas holidays Gable had had since she was a child and her parents had both been alive. She could remember the thrill of running downstairs and opening presents with her brothers, turning the living room into a disaster area of wrapping paper and ribbons, new toys and board games and sporting equipment and clothes.

In the thirty years since, she'd spent a Christmas now and then with one or another of her brothers, but most of the time she'd been alone. And she hadn't really minded it at all. She'd put up a tree, build a fire, fix herself a nice dinner, and open the presents her brothers had mailed to her while yuletide carols played in the background. No, she really hadn't minded it.

But everything was different now. Sharing the experience with Erin *more* than doubled the joy of Christmas. It made Gable feel like a kid again, excited and happy and more filled with the holiday spirit than she could remember.

Erin helped her decorate her tree, and she returned the favor. They played Christmas carols and drank eggnog and swapped stories of where their more treasured ornaments had come from. When Christmas Eve arrived, they ate snow crab at Gable's house and opened stocking stuffers, then adjourned to Erin's to spend the night.

"Can't we open just *one* of our presents tonight? Pretty please?" Gable looked longingly at the smattering of presents waiting under Erin's tree as they hung up their coats.

Erin chuckled. "I thought we agreed to wait until tomorrow."

"We did." Gable sighed dramatically.

Erin put her arms around Gable and squeezed her tight. "I'll tell you what, my darling Camp Fire Girl. Light us a one-matcher in the fireplace and I'll let you open one tonight and the rest tomorrow."

"Deal!"

Once they had a cheery fire going, they changed—Gable into men's flannel pajamas and Erin into light fleece loungewear—and curled up on the couch together under a lap robe.

"This is perfect," Gable said, draping an arm along the back of the couch so she could run her fingers lazily through Erin's hair while they stared at the fire.

"I'll second that." Erin closed her eyes and groaned contentedly. "Although if you keep doing that, you'll put me right to sleep."

Gable's hand froze. "Well, I don't want to do *that*, or I won't get to open any presents!" She leaned over to nuzzle Erin. "Not to mention some other plans I have for you later that I really would rather you be awake for."

Erin smiled. "You're incorrigible. All right. You can open *one*."

"So…which one?" Gable asked, eyeing the four packages with her name on them.

Erin sat up a little and pushed her hair back from her face, blinking drowsily. "You can open that." She pointed to the largest one.

Gable hustled over to the tree and picked up the gift. It was lighter than she expected. She held it up and shook it gently as she carried it back to the couch. It made an odd sound she couldn't identify. Tearing open the green and gold paper, her hands came to a large cardboard box. She opened it and found a sea of Styrofoam peanuts. Digging through it, she found a familiar-looking black case, shaped like a hatbox.

"A drum!" she exclaimed with enthusiasm. "You got me a snare drum!" She took the case out of the box and sprang the latches on the lid.

"I knew you had to have one that day in the band room," Erin gave a satisfied smile. "It was you, as I recall, who told me it's never too late."

"Oh, this is so cool!" Gable shook her head in disbelief. Then realization struck. "You wrapped the drumsticks separately, didn't you…so I won't get them until tomorrow! Oh, you're a cruel woman, Erin Richards."

Erin laughed. "There's other drum-related goodies among your gifts, that's all I'll say. I will let you open another present if you like, but I get one first."

"You're so accommodating," Gable pecked her on the cheek. She jumped up and returned with one of her presents for Erin. "I hope you like it."

Erin pulled off the ribbon and bow and carefully undid the gold metallic paper beneath.

"Oh, Gable. It's lovely." It was a music box made of fragrant sassafras wood, and it had Erin's initials carved in the top. When she opened it to reveal velvet-lined compartments for earrings and bracelets, it played "It Had To Be You," the old standard that Erin had been playing the night she told Gable she loved her.

"How? Where did you get this?" Erin ran her fingers over the smooth polished surface of the box, lingering on the delicate carved initials. "The workmanship is wonderful."

Gable blushed. "I'm glad you like it. I made it for you."

"You made this?" Erin gazed at her with her mouth gaping open. "Really? Oh, Gable, it's just amazing. You never told me you could do this."

"Well, as I recall, I think I did tell you that my brother Mason taught me a thing or two about whittling and carpentry."

"Yes, but you never told me you could do *this*." She planted a kiss on Gable's cheek. "How did you ever find the song?"

"Google. I found a company that sells the mechanisms. They had hundreds of tunes."

"Well, it is an unbelievably cool present. Thanks so much. That took a lot of work."

"Glad you like it. So…do I get another present? Hmm?"

Erin laughed. "Oh, all right. You sure you don't want to wait?"

"Erin!"

"Okay, okay. You have a present up in the guest room you can open tonight." Erin had a devilish grin on her face.

"The guest room?" Gable's curiosity was piqued. She thought all of her presents were under the tree. "Why is it in the guest room? Is it too big? Does its shape give it away?"

Erin shrugged. "Guess you'll have to go up and see."

As soon as Gable started toward the guest room, she jumped up and followed at her heels.

Gable turned the knob and pushed open the door. Curled into a ball against the pillow on the bed lay a sleeping kitten: black except for his four white socks and the stark white triangle on his chest.

"Oh, my," she exclaimed in a low voice.

The kitten raised his head and looked at her and mewled a sleepy greeting. When she started toward the bed, he got up and stretched. Gable gently picked him up and held him against her chest, looking down into pale green eyes as she scratched him beneath the chin in the way that Earl Grey favored. The kitten leaned into her touch, closed his eyes, and started to purr, a raspy loud buzzing that seemed to vibrate his sleek body.

"He's so adorable!" Gable gushed. "What splendid markings—he looks like he's wearing a tuxedo and spats!"

"I got him from the shelter in Charlevoix," Erin said, looking on approvingly. "Can you believe someone could abandon this little guy in the snow?"

"No way. He's so *tiny!*"

"I had him checked out with a vet, and he's had all his shots. So I take it I chose well?"

Gable crossed to Erin with the kitten in her arms and kissed her soundly. "More than okay. Does he have a name?"

"Thought I'd leave that to you."

"Hmm. I'll have to think about that a while. Hey! Has he met Earl Grey yet?"

Erin shook her head. "I didn't want to hit him with too much at once. I've kept him in here since I got him a couple days ago. Thought we could introduce them after he's had time to get used to both of us. I know they'll become great buddies."

"How long do you think it will take Earl to teach this one how to get up in the rafters?"

"Two minutes, I'm sure!" Erin laughed.

Earl Grey used the rafters that spanned Erin's ceiling as his own private playground, racing up and down the logs at all hours of the day and night. He had first gained access to the rafters through a dramatic leap from a high bookcase. Erin had then facilitated his way up and down by covering one of the support posts with rough sisal rope, effectively turning it into a ten-foot-high scratching post.

"I have to admit, he'll sure make it less lonely around my house when you're not there," Gable said. "I've gotten to where I almost can't sleep in my big old empty bed anymore without you in it."

The kitten yawned and slumped in her arms. "Back to sleep, baby boy," she said, returning him to his spot against the pillow. "I'll check on you soon."

He curled into a ball and was soon fast asleep again. She and Erin retreated into the living room and resumed their places snuggled up to each other on the couch.

"I know it's not always a good idea to get a pet for someone," Erin said "But I was pretty sure you'd take to him, after watching you with Earl. And I love to see a precious little thing like that one in there get a good home."

"He's a wonderful present," Gable assured her. "All the presents are great."

They remained wrapped up in each other's arms for several minutes, enjoying the Christmas tree, the fire, and each other. Earl Grey turned up from wherever he'd been hiding all night and settled into Erin's lap.

"Well *there* you are," Erin said. "Where were you this time, eh? Are you going to teach your new little friend where all your hiding places are?"

Although it was a relatively small cabin, Earl Grey sure knew how to disappear—curling into the corner of a closet, or hiding under the bed, or in a pile of laundry. Gable smiled, imagining how it would be with the two felines. Quite a family. It was such a serene and loving moment, there in front of the fire, that she decided the time had come to give the gift she most wanted Erin to have. As soon as she made the decision, she could feel the pounding of her heart in her chest.

"I've got something else I'd like you to open tonight." The quaver in her voice betrayed her nervousness. Her palms felt suddenly clammy. She wiped her right hand on the lap robe that covered their legs before she withdrew a velvet-covered ring box from a pocket in her pajamas.

When she heard a sharp intake of breath, she knew immediately she'd made a mistake. Erin stared at the ring box with wide eyes, her face ashen. Gable never got a chance to say a word.

"Don't, Gable. Oh, please don't." Erin whispered. "Can't we keep things as they are?" She lifted fearful eyes to her, close to tears.

Gable put the box back in her pocket without a word and drew Erin into a cautious embrace. They didn't move for a very long moment.

"All right," she said finally, her voice choked with emotion. "We'll leave things as they are. I won't bring it up again."

As the days passed, she tried to be grateful for what she had and as content with their arrangement as Erin seemed to be, and most of the time she was. Erin was everything she'd ever dreamed of in a partner. Kind. Giving. Honest. Funny. Passionate. When they were together, Gable was blissfully happy. And Erin seemed every bit as devoted to Gable as Gable was to her.

But on the nights she spent alone, Gable admitted to herself she wanted more.

And every morning, she started the day with a prayer that Erin would change her mind sometime soon.

CHAPTER EIGHTEEN

On a bitter cold morning in late January, Gable found it more difficult than usual to extricate herself from Erin's warm body to drive to the pharmacy. There had been an ice storm overnight, and on top of the ice was three inches of new snow. Area schools were closed, and Erin had done her best to convince her to call in sick and stay in bed. She nearly succeeded.

The roads were treacherous. Snowplows and salt trucks had not made it that far out in the country yet. In fact, no other vehicles were out at all, and just a solitary set of tire tracks showed on the road ahead of her. The tracks fishtailed badly in several places—sliding off the edge of the road, or into the oncoming lane. *This is really stupid to be out in this. Maybe you* should *have stayed in bed with Erin.*

Gable drove at a crawl, especially as she approached the bridge across the wide Pine River, two miles from Erin's cabin. Her heart leapt into her throat when she saw the broken guardrail halfway across. There was a huge gap in it, and the tracks she'd been following swerved right to it and ended there. *Oh my God! That car's gone in the river!*

Horrified, she pumped the brakes and slid to a stop at the edge of the road. Even before she shut off the engine, she heard screaming.

She got out and hurried as best as she could to the edge of the bridge and looked over. Twenty feet below her and several feet upstream, a boy of sixteen or seventeen was struggling, trying to pull himself from an enormous hole in the ice, but the ice was too thin to support his weight. He was right in the middle of the river, where it was fifteen to twenty feet deep.

"Help! Somebody help me!" he screamed.

"Hang on!" Gable shouted. Her heartbeat kicked up double time.

The boy's head swiveled around and his eyes found her. "Help me! Hurry! Please hurry!"

"Hang on! Was anyone else in the car with you?"

"No!" the boy screamed.

"I'll be right there!" Gable hurried back to the Jeep, slipping and sliding with every step, and switched on her emergency radio. "Dispatch from McCoy. Car off Peterson Bridge at Belknap Road. Driver in the river. Send ambulance and water rescue."

She heard the dispatcher acknowledge her as she clipped the radio to her belt and hustled to the back of the Jeep. There was a pair of hundred-foot lengths of sturdy nylon rope there, neatly coiled. She grabbed them both. She also shoved a screwdriver from her tool kit into the back pocket of her jeans.

The bank was steep to the water's edge, and she skidded down almost on her butt. The teenager had stopped trying to pull himself onto the ice. Now he was fighting just to keep his head above water. His ragged gasps for air sounded loud in the still morning.

"I'm going to throw you a rope! Try to grab it!" Gable anchored the end of one of the ropes beneath her foot and prepared for her throw.

"I can't!" the boy sobbed.

She tossed the coil of rope, and it fell across the hole in the ice. The boy's head slipped under, then popped up again. He started hyperventilating, desperate for air.

"Grab the rope!" Gable urged.

His arms and legs flailed about in clumsy, jerky movements as he tried for the rope.

It was then that Gable got a good look at the boy's hands. They were clubs of ice. Useless. No way could he save himself, and he wasn't going to be able to keep himself up much longer. She had to go after him.

She tried to calm her racing heart with deep breaths as she quickly prepared the ropes. The one across the ice would be the rescue rope; she tied off her end to a large sturdy oak at the water's edge.

The other rope would be for her. One end around the oak, the other around her waist. A strong current swept down the middle of the river, and Gable knew that if she fell through, there was a good chance she'd get swept downstream under the thick ice.

She was quickly out onto the ice, crawling on her belly toward the teenager. The adrenaline rush energized her and brought all her senses into sharp focus. The boy's eyes were huge, pulling at her, beseeching her to hurry. His head slipped under again, and when it popped back up he was on the downstream edge of the hole. He coughed and gulped loudly for air. If he went under again, the current would take him under the ice.

Thirty feet away. Then twenty, halfway between the boy and shore. When Gable was fifteen feet away, she heard a cracking sound beneath her, and her heart began pounding in her ears. She went fully spread-eagle and froze, her face pressed up against the slick, hard surface.

The ice held. Inching toward him, she shouted encouragement. "Keep your head up! Hang on, I'm almost to you!"

Another sharp report sounded as the ice cracked again. This time she could clearly see the thin fissure of separation, directly under the right side of her body. Once more she froze, trying to keep her weight evenly distributed.

The moment Gable actually fell through seemed to take forever. Everything happened in slow motion. One crack became two, then six, then forty—a spider web of fractures beneath her.

The terrifying cracking sounds got louder and louder.

She watched in horrified fascination as the bottom dropped out and she was plunged into the icy water, still a body length from the boy.

The frigid immersion was such a shock to her system that it squeezed the air from her lungs, inducing a long moment of panic as she started kicking. She sucked in air greedily. Pinpricks of pain everywhere, like she had fallen on a bed of tiny nails. Then cold. A kind of cold she'd never experienced before: a numbing cold, relentless. It soaked through her clothing, weighing her down. *Damn. Got to be fast.*

She focused on the boy, taking great gulps of air as she fought through the broken ice to reach him, grabbing the rescue rope on the way.

Though he had seemed to be all done in, the teenager came to life when she got to him. With a final burst of energy he grabbed at her, desperately trying to use her to keep himself afloat.

Gable went under.

The boy tried to wrap his arms around her. They struggled, locked together, until she was able to turn him so his back was to her. She grabbed him over his shoulder in a lifesaving hold as she popped back to the surface, gasping for air.

"Don't fight me!" she barked at him. "Let me help you!"

He went limp, whether in compliance or exhaustion she didn't know or care. She managed to get the rescue rope wrapped around him, but she'd lost the dexterity to tie the right kind of knot. Her gloves were becoming stiff with ice and she was losing the feeling in her hands. She finally got the rope looped around in a couple of half hitches and let the boy's own body weight tighten it. She hoped it was secure enough.

Her legs began protesting the lengthy struggle against the current. She felt as though twenty-pound weights were attached to her ankles, pulling her down. She concentrated all her energy on getting the boy up and onto the ice.

"Try to help me," she gasped, but the teenager was barely conscious. She got under him and tried to boost him up, but the ice cracked away under his weight.

She took up the slack of the rescue rope and tried again, and then again. The ice kept breaking, and she weakened with each effort, but every attempt brought them a foot or two closer to shore, and onto thicker and thicker ice.

Finally, on the fifth try, the ice supported the upper half of the boy's body, and Gable quickly hoisted his legs up as well. She knew better than to try to haul herself up right next to him. The ice would never support them both.

She was beginning to have trouble keeping herself afloat. She managed to kick her way to a spot far enough from the boy that she thought it was safe to try. *Get out. Get out right now.*

Propping herself up on her left elbow on the ice, she grappled for the rope around her waist that linked her to shore. It was slick and hard, covered with ice. She got a good look at her hands, and her blood ran cold. *Oh Jesus. This is bad.* Her gloves were stiff with a thick coating of ice too.

Gable could no longer move her fingers. She couldn't feel them at all. In desperation, she slammed her right hand against the hard ice repeatedly, trying to regain some dexterity and circulation. She fumbled for the screwdriver in her back pocket so she could gain purchase on the ice, but it was useless. Her hands would no longer obey her. The screwdriver sank to the bottom.

The current was relentless. The muscles in her arm and shoulder finally surrendered to it and she slipped back into the water.

Oh shit. Panic was sour in her mouth. *Help is coming. Help is coming. Hang on. Swim. That's it. Just keep swimming.*

Gable couldn't feel her arms, her legs, or her feet. She looked down and was almost surprised to see her legs still kicking away, albeit in the same scary, jerky way the boy's had. She was losing control of her body, and finding it more and more difficult to focus. It was all she could do now to keep her face above water.

The current pulled at her until she was against the downstream side of the hole. She clutched desperately at the edge of the ice to keep from being swept under it. *There's too much rope.* She tried to twist it around her arms to take up the slack but she had no coordination left.

The current was winning.

Her head slipped under and she sucked in a mouthful of water. It startled her and scared her so much she found the strength for one last desperate effort to survive. She fought her way back up, kicking and failing about with limbs she no longer had power over. She caught a glimpse of the boy, still unmoving on the ice.

If this is all for nothing, she thought hazily, *Erin will be so pissed at me.*

She tried to keep herself from going under by hooking her elbows on the downstream edge of the ice. The current held her there for a full minute or more, her head barely above water, long enough for her to feel a burst of hope she might be able to remain like that until help arrived.

But the ice she was leaning on abruptly gave way, breaking off and tipping sideways, throwing her back into the water. Gable managed to gulp a quick breath before she went under.

The current grabbed hold of her and took her under the ice, into the dark void beyond the hole. She drifted until a sharp tug cut into her waist. The rope pulled taut and the current pinned her, face up, against the ice, several feet downstream of the hole.

Gable opened her eyes, surprised at how well she could see, surprised that it was *beautiful*—the way the ice reflected the light from above; the bubbles trapped in the ice acting like prisms, shooting rainbows of color in every direction.

You can't get back to the hole. You have to break a new one. Her training told her what to do but her body was beyond her control now. Her arms flailed uselessly above her head, waving in the current.

Time seemed to stop then, and Gable drifted outside herself, no longer aware of her body, the cold, the river, the current.

How long does it take to die, when you drown? she wondered. *How long does your brain keep working?* It seemed like forever. She had time enough to think of each of her brothers. Her parents—would they be there at the moment of death, waiting for her?

Gable closed her eyes and saw Erin's face. *You made my life complete, my love. I just wish we'd had more time together.*

She fought it until the last—that final exhalation.

When Gable finally did surrender, she had Erin in her mind and in her heart.

She sucked in water, and then she relaxed. A feeling of euphoria poured over her. Lifting her, surrounding her.

Her heart stopped beating.

CHAPTER NINETEEN

S houldn't she be waking up by now?" Gable heard Stewart's worried voice fuzzily, as if from a distance. Much louder were the regular whooshing sound to her right and the steady beeping that was coming from her left.

"We need to give it time," an unfamiliar male voice said. "It's often hard to predict with these types of cases, because there are so many different variables—the temperature of the water, health of the patient, how long they're submerged, how quickly CPR is administered. I don't think we should be worrying quite yet."

The river, she remembered. Her head ached. And her chest. She tried to speak. *What the hell?*

"How long will she be on the respirator, Doctor?" Erin's voice, sounding as tense as her brother's.

"It's a bit too soon to say. There could be a buildup of pulmonary fluids—that'll be our chief concern over the next forty-eight hours. I'll be able to tell you more after we've gotten all the test results back."

"Thank you, Doctor." *Stewart.*

"I'll check in with you again later," the doctor said.

Gable tried to force open her eyes, but it felt like heavy sandbags were weighing down her eyelids. Her arms were heavy too; she couldn't lift them, couldn't signal Erin and Stewart that she was all right. *Just tired. So very tired.*

❖

The next time she awoke, the first thing that hit her was how sore her throat was. She couldn't swallow. Her chest ached too. But that throbbing in her head was better.

She became aware of a gentle pressure in her palm. Another hand, holding hers. A gentle squeeze of comfort. *Erin.* Her eyelids fluttered.

"Gable? Can you hear me, sweetheart?"

Sweetheart? You've never called me sweetheart before.

Gable opened her eyes. Erin was leaning over the bed. Her eyes were puffy, and she had a gaunt, disheveled look, like she hadn't slept in a long while. But her eyes lit up and her face registered her immense relief. "You're awake!"

Gable squeezed her hand.

Erin burst into tears and squeezed back. "You're here with me, aren't you? You know who I am? You remember?" Her voice shook.

Gable squeezed her hand again and tried to nod her head. The respirator restricted her movements.

"Thank God," Erin said. "I'll be back in a second, Gable. Swear to God, just a second. Don't drift off—I'm going to get the doctor." She bent down and kissed Gable's cheek, then disappeared.

Gable glanced around as much as she could. In addition to the respirator, she was on a heart monitor. An IV fed the contents of a clear plastic bag into a needle in her left arm.

From a distance, she heard, "Stewart! She's awake! She remembers! Get the doctor!"

Erin was quickly back beside the bed, and took Gable's hand again. Tears tracked her cheeks, but she had a smile from ear to ear. "You had us worried there, Gable. Welcome back. I love you."

Gable squeezed her hand very deliberately, three times. *I love you.*

Erin's face brightened more, as she got the message. "I know, honey. I know."

Honey. I like it when you call me honey.

"The doctor's going to be here in a minute, and they're going to chase me out of here for a while. But I'll be right outside. Stewart's here too. He's been in touch with your brothers."

Gable wanted to ask about the boy she'd tried to save but didn't know how. She squeezed Erin's hand and blinked her eyes rapidly.

"Stewart? Do you want me to get Stewart?" Erin asked.

Gable shook her head slightly from side to side. It was all she could manage with the respirator, but Erin understood.

"Okay, that's not it. Are you in pain?"

Gable shook her head again.

"Want me to get you something?" Erin tried.

Gable's forehead furrowed as she shook her head once again in frustration.

Erin frowned. "I'm sorry, honey, I don't understand."

Gable pulled her hand out of Erin's and spread Erin's palm open so she could use it as a writing tablet. With her index finger, she spelled out b-o-y.

Erin's face lit up. "Oh! Of course! The boy! Mike Ester. He'll be fine. You saved him. He woke up right after they brought him in, and the doctors say he'll make a full recovery." She bent and kissed Gable on the cheek, then remained like that, with their faces touching, for a long moment before she whispered, "I'm so proud of you, sweetheart."

She straightened just as the doctor arrived with Stewart. Smiling, she released her hand and retreated a step so that Stewart could take her place by the bedside.

"Hi, sis," Stewart kissed her on the forehead. "Glad you're back with us. The boys all send their love."

"Gable, I'm Dr. Erickson," the doctor began, as he approached smiling from the opposite side of the bed. He was an attractive older gentleman with a gray-streaked beard who reminded her of Sean Connery, without the accent. "You've got quite a fan club lined up outside to see you, so we need to get you well in a hurry. Can you understand me?"

Gable nodded.

"Good. Do you remember what happened?"

She nodded again.

"The rescue squad responded about fifteen minutes after you radioed in, and pulled you out by your rope. They administered CPR on scene, but you didn't respond until you were en route in the ambulance. We ran a number of tests, including an EEG and CAT scan—and there was no evidence of brain injury. We warmed you slowly, and we'll keep the Bair Hugger on you for a while longer." He gestured toward an odd blanket that was draped over her: it looked like an inflatable mattress with holes in it. "Because you swallowed some river water, I want to keep you on IV antibiotic therapy for at least another forty-eight hours or so."

Gable grimaced.

"She hates hospitals," Erin said.

The doctor smiled. "I would wager you're going to get treated quite exceptionally well during your stay with us. Now I want to take you off the respirator, but we have to make sure your lungs are strong enough to stay off the vent. Do you understand?"

Gable nodded.

He put a meter on the tubing between the machine and Gable. "I want you to take a few deep breaths, so I can make sure you can pull enough oxygen on your own. Any time you're ready."

Gable took several long, deep breaths.

"Good. Very good." The doctor reached for the junction of the tubing and unhooked it. "Okay, I want you to blow out a big breath for me."

She exhaled, wincing as the doctor withdrew the tube that had been down her throat. She started coughing as soon as it was out, and a spasm of pain rolled through her chest.

"Easy," the doctor said. "Try to relax."

The coughing abated and she sank back against the pillow. Her mouth and throat were swollen and raw, and her chest felt as though someone were sitting on it. "Thanks," she croaked.

"You're welcome." The doctor poured a paper cup of water as he pressed on a foot pedal to raise the head of the bed slightly. "Here, sip this. Just a little." He put a straw in the cup and held it to her lips.

She took a few tentative sips, which eased the soreness in her throat.

The doctor glanced over his shoulder at a nurse who was hovering nearby. "Get some ice chips, will you, please?"

"How long…" Gable coughed again. The doctor gave her another sip. "How long have I been here?"

"The accident was yesterday morning. It's"—he glanced at his watch—"about two-fifteen in the afternoon on Tuesday."

I've lost a whole day and then some. Where was I all that time? Gable couldn't remember anything beyond deciding to finally let go of that last breath.

"You're out of immediate danger," the doctor continued, putting on his stethoscope and warming it before he laid it gently against her chest. "But we want to keep you in here a couple more days and keep an eye on you. Make sure there are no complications with your lungs." He listened for a moment, then took off the stethoscope with a satisfied expression. "Thank God the water was as cold as it was. You should make a full recovery."

"Great," she rasped.

"You got some frostbite on your hands," he said, prompting Gable to glance down at them for the first time. The left one was entirely encased in gauze, the right lightly bandaged, leaving her fingers exposed. She wriggled them. They felt a little stiff but not too bad, all things considered.

"They'll take a while to heal, but I expect no permanent damage. And you have some bruising around your waist from the rope."

Pretty minor stuff when you really should be dead. She glanced at Erin, and her heart filled with joy and gratitude that she'd been spared yet again. *Thank you for giving us more time together,* she prayed.

"That was a very heroic thing you did." The doctor rested a hand briefly on her shoulder. "If you promise not to talk much, I'll let in a few of your visitors. But I'm going to tell them to keep it *very very* short. You need your rest."

The doctor hadn't been exaggerating when he said a crowd was waiting to see her. More than half of the fire squad was there, including Carl and Tim, and June had called in sick at the pharmacy so she could be there when Gable woke up. The most tearful visitors were the parents of the boy she saved.

The nurses enforced the doctor's order and allowed them to visit only long enough to wish Gable well. Once the crowd had gone, Gable sent Stewart on his way too, under protest. He agreed to go home to Kalamazoo only because she insisted, and Erin promised to keep him informed of every development by cell phone.

Once they were alone, Erin sat on the edge of the bed and put her hand on Gable's thigh. "How do you feel?"

"Mmm. Tired," Gable answered. Her eyelids were drooping.

"The doctor said you need to rest."

"Stay with me?"

"You just try to get rid of me."

"Wouldn't think of it," Gable replied. "Come up here beside me?"

"We shouldn't."

"Don't care. If you really want me to get some sleep…"

"What about your hands?"

"They're all right. We'll be careful."

Erin relented and climbed onto the narrow hospital bed next to Gable. She settled gingerly into her familiar position, lying on her left side with her head tucked into the crook of Gable's shoulder. Gently, she draped her arm across Gable's stomach.

"Sore?"

"S'fine. Thanks," Gable mumbled drowsily. She was nearly asleep when Erin whispered her name.

"Gable? You still awake?"

Gable answered but didn't open her eyes. "Mmm-hmm."

"All my life, I always dreamed I'd only get married once. Just once."

Gable struggled to rouse herself. *Erin's talking about marriage. This is important. You have to stay awake.* She wanted to encourage her to continue, but she didn't want to interrupt. Instead, she tilted her head and kissed Erin's forehead.

"My parents were married for fifty-one years. Devoted to each other until Dad died. And you know how it is, growing up Irish Catholic. No one we knew ever got divorced. It just didn't happen. That's the mentality I grew up with." Erin paused for a long moment.

"I guess I just always believed in the fairy tale that you find the person you're destined to be with, and you live happily ever after." She paused again. "But it didn't happen that way for me." She took a long, deep breath and let it out.

"I was right out of college and had just started teaching when I met Phil. I was thirty pounds heavier and hadn't dated much. Very inexperienced sexually—thanks to all those years of parochial schools. Phil was tall, charming, and a year older than I was, and I had no idea what he saw in me when he asked me out."

Gable could feel her tremble at the recollection.

"I didn't have any self-confidence at all, you understand, back then. I was still a kid, really. I was flattered by the attention, and I wanted so much to fall in love that I got swept up in the relationship. We got married less than three months after we met."

She trembled again. Took another long, deep breath.

"Things went downhill almost immediately. Phil was a very jealous guy. He hated to have me out of his sight at all, and if any guy dared talk to me…Well, he'd accuse me of all sorts of things for hours afterward. I didn't know it right away, but I found out later he followed me when I wasn't with him, spying on me to see if I was cheating on him. He even listened in on my phone calls."

Another long pause.

"What started out as gentle lovemaking became constant demands for sex. Rough sex. Whether I was up for it at that moment or not."

Gable was wide-awake now; her anger at the thought of what Erin had suffered was pouring through her.

"He told me from the beginning that he didn't believe in divorce." Erin laughed, but it was a laugh without humor. "I thought that was a good thing, at the time."

She took another deep, shuddering breath. Her voice, when she resumed, had the soft, fearful quality of a child's voice relating a nightmare. "He started drinking more and more. And then he started hitting me, about six months into the marriage."

Gable clenched her jaw. A tear slipped down her cheek.

"He broke my arm the first time. He cried and cried and promised it would never happen again. The second time he blackened both my eyes and gave me a concussion. That's when I left him."

Erin shifted her weight and hugged Gable tighter. "Phil refused to give me a divorce. He went to the school where I worked and made all sorts of crazy accusations, until finally they had to let me go. I don't blame them. They were worried about the kids, and he was clearly out of control."

She sighed. "Then he started showing up at the apartment where I moved. I wouldn't answer the door, and he'd pound on it and make all the neighbors crazy." Another pause. "One night he hid in the laundry room down the hall until I came home and pushed his way in behind me."

Erin was shaking again. "That was an awful night. And next day. During most of it, he kept me tied up and gagged and locked in a closet."

A tear fell and landed on Gable's chest.

"Oh, Erin." Gable's insides were twisted in knots.

"When he sobered up, he let me go, begging and pleading for forgiveness. I called the cops and got a restraining order and a lawyer. Phil was facing a lot of serious charges, but the prosecutor wasn't optimistic the jury would convict him. I was still married to him, after all." Another long pause.

"My lawyer worked a deal. Phil granted me a divorce and agreed to leave me alone, and I agreed not to press charges. I moved again the next day." She exhaled. A long, slow release of air, announcing her relief at finishing the story. "I looked over my shoulder for a long time, but I never heard from him again. So now you know," she concluded. "I haven't let myself think about those times very much. Too depressing. But Karen is helping me to get past the pain and move forward."

"I'm so sorry, Erin, that you had to endure so much," Gable whispered.

Erin shifted so that she could meet Gable's eyes for the first time since she'd started her story. "I'm sorry I've been living in the past. I've let it haunt me much too long."

She kissed Gable—a sweet, soft kiss on the lips.

"Ahem!" the duty nurse interrupted from the doorway. It was the same nurse who had flirted with Gable the last time she was hospitalized.

They broke apart, both turning deep red in embarrassment, but the nurse just chuckled. She checked Gable's IV and then turned to go. "Since you're the talk of the hospital today, I'll pretend not to notice that visiting hours ended a while ago. Call if you need anything. Although I would say you seem pretty content at the moment." She winked at them and pulled the door closed as she left the room.

"I should let you get some sleep," Erin said, settling back against Gable's side.

"Thank you for telling me," Gable whispered.

"I trust you, Gable. In a way I've never been able to trust anyone before."

"That's the way I feel about you too," Gable said.

"I know that, honey. You've been very patient with me, and I appreciate it. I know that you'd never do anything to hurt me." She began caressing Gable's stomach with her hand.

It was lulling. Gable's eyes closed.

"And I know I couldn't imagine life without you," she said.

"I'm glad to hear that," Gable replied drowsily.

"Still got that ring?"

Gable was instantly awake again. *Did I hear what I just thought I heard?* "Yes." She held her breath.

"I'm ready to talk about that now. Well not *now*, necessarily. Maybe we should wait until we have a little more privacy and all, and you've had a chance to think about whether you still want to. I mean, if you don't still want to, I'll understand..." She rambled on, uncertain.

"Oh, I want to, love. I want that more than anything," Gable said, her voice breaking as they held tight to one another.

"I love you," Erin said. "And I like saying it."

"Good." Gable kissed her very softly. "Because I want to hear it forever."

About the Author

Kim Baldwin is currently at work on the romance *Whitewater Rendezvous*, which will be released by Bold Strokes Books in May 2006. Her debut novel, *Hunter's Pursuit*, was a finalist for a Golden Crown Literary Society award for Best Lesbian Mystery/Action/Adventure/ Thriller of 2004. She also has a short story in the new Bold Strokes Books anthology *Stolen Moments: Erotic Interludes 2* and *Lessons in Love: Erotic Interludes 3*, scheduled for release in May 2006. Nature, romance, and adventure are key themes in her stories. She lives with her partner in a cabin in the north woods.

Look for information about these works at www.boldstrokesbooks. com.

Books Available From Bold Strokes Books

Force of Nature by Kim Baldwin. Wind. Fire. Ice. Love. Nothing for Gable McCoy and Erin Richards seems to go smoothly. From the tornado that sets its sights on them to the perils they face as volunteer firefighters, the forces of nature conspire to bring them closer to danger—and closer to each other. (1-933110-23-6)

In Too Deep by Ronica Black. When undercover work requires working under the covers, danger is an uninvited bedfellow. Homicide cop Erin McKenzie embarks on the journey of her life…with love and danger hot on her heels. (1-933110-17-1)

Stolen Moments: Erotic Interludes 2, edited by Stacia Seaman and Radclyffe. Love on the run, in the office, in the shadows…women stealing time from ordinary life to make passion a priority, if only for a moment. Fast, furious, and almost too hot to handle. (1-933110-16-3)

Course of Action by Gun Brooke. Actress Carolyn Black desperately wants the starring role in an upcoming film produced by Annelie Peterson, a wealthy publisher with a mysterious past. How far is Carolyn prepared to go for the dream part of a lifetime? And just how far will Annelie bend her principles in the name of desire? (1-933110-22-8)

Justice Served by Radclyffe. The hunt for an informant in the ranks draws Lieutenant Rebecca Frye, her lover Dr. Catherine Rawlings, and Officer Dellon Mitchell into a deadly game of hide-and-seek with an underworld kingpin who traffics in human souls. (1-933110-15-5)

Rangers at Roadsend by Jane Fletcher. After nine years in the Rangers, dealing with thugs and wild predators, Sergeant Chip Coppelli has learned to spot trouble coming, and that is exactly what she sees in her new recruit, Katryn Nagata. But even so, Chip was not expecting murder. The Celaeno series. (1-933110-28-7)

Distant Shores, Silent Thunder by Radclyffe. Ex-lovers, would-be lovers, and old rivals find their paths unwillingly entwined when Drs. KT O'Bannon and Tory King—and the women who love them—are forced to examine the boundaries of love, friendship, and the ties that transcend time. (1-933110-08-2)

Hunter's Pursuit by Kim Baldwin. A raging blizzard, a remote mountain hideaway, and more than one killer for hire set a scene for disaster—or desire—when reluctant assassin Katarzyna Demetrious rescues a stranger and unwittingly exposes her heart. (1-933110-09-0)

The Walls of Westernfort by Jane Fletcher. All Temple Guard Natasha Ionadis wants is to serve the Goddess, and she volunteers eagerly for a dangerous mission to infiltrate a band of rebels. But once she is away from the temple, the issues are no longer so simple, especially in light of her attraction to one of the rebels. Is it too late to work out what she really wants from life? (1-933110-24-4)

Change Of Pace: *Erotic Interludes* by Radclyffe. Twenty-five hot-wired encounters guaranteed to spark more than just your imagination. Erotica as you've always dreamed of it. (1-933110-07-4)

Fated Love by Radclyffe. Amidst the chaos and drama of a busy emergency room, two women must contend not only with the fragile nature of life, but also with the mysteries of the heart and the irresistible forces of fate. (1-933110-05-8)

Justice in the Shadows by Radclyffe. In a shadow world of secrets, lies, and hidden agendas, Detective Sergeant Rebecca Frye and her lover, Dr. Catherine Rawlings, join forces once again in the elusive search for justice. (1-933110-03-1)

shadowland by Radclyffe. In a world on the far edge of desire, two women are drawn together by power, passion, and dark pleasures. An erotic romance. (1-933110-11-2)

Love's Masquerade by Radclyffe. Plunged into the often indistinguishable realms of fiction, fantasy, and hidden desires, Auden Frost discovers a shifting landscape that will force her to question everything she has believed to be true about herself and the nature of love. (1-933110-14-7)

Beyond the Breakwater by Radclyffe. One Provincetown summer three women learn the true meaning of love, friendship, and family. Second in the Provincetown Tales. (1-933110-06-6)

Tomorrow's Promise by Radclyffe. One timeless summer, two very different women discover the power of passion to heal and the promise of hope that only love can bestow. (1-933110-12-0)

Love's Tender Warriors by Radclyffe. Two women who have accepted loneliness as a way of life learn that love is worth fighting for and a battle they cannot afford to lose. (1-933110-02-3)

Love's Melody Lost by Radclyffe. A secretive artist with a haunted past and a young woman escaping a life that proved to be a lie find their destinies entwined. (1-933110-00-7)

Safe Harbor by Radclyffe. A mysterious newcomer, a reclusive doctor, and a troubled gay teenager learn about love, friendship, and trust during one tumultuous summer in Provincetown. First in the Provincetown Tales. (1-933110-13-9)

Above All, Honor by Radclyffe. The first in the Honor series introduces single-minded Secret Service Agent Cameron Roberts and the woman she is sworn to protect—Blair Powell, the daughter of the president of the United States. First in the Honor series. (1-933110-04-X)

Love & Honor by Radclyffe. The president's daughter and her security chief are faced with difficult choices as they battle a tangled web of Washington intrigue for...love and honor. Third in the Honor series. (1-933110-10-4)

Honor Guards by Radclyffe. In a journey that begins on the streets of Paris's Left Bank and culminates in a wild flight for their lives, the president's daughter and those who are sworn to protect her wage a desperate struggle for survival. Fourth in the Honor series. (1-933110-01-5)